ODYSSEY TALE

Odyssey Tale

Cody Schlegel

© 2020 by Cody Schlegel

All rights reserved. This book or any portion thereof may not be reproduced or used in any manner whatsoever without the express written permission of the author except for the use of brief quotations in a book review.

ISBN: 9798666580707

Oh, muse. Sweet muse.

Please sing to me.

Tell me the tale of an odyssey.

Chapter 1

Penelope never wanted children, even as a little girl. When she and her friends played house or castle, her friends would pretend they were mothers to over a dozen kids while Penelope collected lilies and daisies to place in her hair. Once she'd accumulated enough to make a proper crown, both of her friends and all their little children would gather around and watch Penelope wed her imaginary husband. She may not have wanted children, but getting married to the man of her dreams was another story entirely.

Eventually, in real life, her friends would go on to have a dozen children between the two of them, and Penelope would find the man of her dreams. Just like when they were little girls, down to the pairing of fresh-cut daisies and lilies crowning her braided black hair, they all gathered around and watched as Otis and Penelope Seehus were pronounced husband and wife.

Otis was a battle-hardened soldier when they were first wed, and he didn't show much interest in having children either. It was difficult enough for him to leave her behind when he was called off to fight, but he grew ill at the thought of leaving her behind alone and with child.

Odyssey Tale

Otis served in three different wars before his twenty-third birthday, earning a name for himself along the way. He was a brilliant strategist and master tactician. For his efforts in that third war, he was rewarded a much-welcomed early retirement, untold wealth in the form of gold, and a castle on the coast of Ithaca overlooking a blanket of teal water. King Otis and Queen Penelope Seehus. They were as welcomed by their new people as they were happy. Life could not have been any better.

The two spent their days lazing about on the beaches, swimming, eating, making love, and napping—mostly in that order. For some reason or another, Penelope had a tendency to worry the most when things were going their best. So, rather than live in the moment she was in, she began to worry. Mostly, she worried that Otis's royal status would bring pressure. Pressure from the elders. Pressure from the people. Pressure to have kids and ensure that his royal line didn't start and stop with the two of them.

Otis could tell that something was bugging her. He often could. Once she'd told him what had been keeping her so distracted, he laughed it off, relieved that this was her only worry in life. He assured Penelope that he was perfectly happy just being with her. Then one morning, she woke up, and a little baby was growing inside of her. She was frightened, but only at first. All the previous thoughts she'd had of being a mother changed right then and there. Penelope was elated. So was Otis.

There aren't enough words to describe the pride she felt knowing that there was a miniature version of Otis or herself living inside her belly. There was nothing she wanted more

Chapter 1

than to be a mother. It was a positively joyous experience, and it hadn't even begun. She was going to watch the baby learn to crawl, then walk, then talk, and she would teach him or her all kinds of things. Oh, did Penelope have plans for this child. Her body didn't respond well to the pregnancy, however, and they lost the baby. It was painful and challenging, but it didn't dissuade them from trying again. Then again, when they lost another baby.

The physical pain wasn't quite as bad, knowing what to expect when things began to go wrong. Emotionally, however, she was drained. Penelope began to think. Too much so, perhaps. She thought. *Being a mother is not in my destiny.* She thought she was being punished by the gods for all the time she'd spent wishing away children. She thought herself to tears on more nights than she'd care to remember. Nonetheless, they kept trying.

Otis, seeing that she needed to release a swelling collection of maternal instinct, got them a puppy. Grace was the sweetest little black Lab, full of love and kisses, and that unmistakably gentle whiff of puppy breath.

Otis had just finished teaching her how to stay as Penelope approached him in the courtyard with news of another baby. She was cautious with her joy and reluctant with her optimism, but one month gradually turned to nine, and the little miracle baby was still growing strong in her ever-expanding belly. Then it happened. Miraculous. They named him Mac.

Those first few months were so much more rewarding than either of them could have possibly imagined. Penelope was the eldest of four siblings, and helping to raise the younger three had muted any ambition for parenthood. She was often told by her grandmother, "It's different when they're your children." As usual, her grandmother was right.

About three months after his birth, Penelope was rocking Mac to sleep in his nursery when Otis came into the room. He lowered his dull eyes and let out a sigh before telling her that he was being brought out of retirement and called in for duty on the battlefields of Troy. She begged him—pleaded with him—to stay. Every word brought forth its own stream of tears. But he insisted that it was his duty as king and that he'd be back in a month or two.

Two years passed. Penelope waited patiently and tried to stay strong for Mac, but every day was filled with a heavy dread that at any moment, she'd get word of Otis's demise. Then, on a rare gray and rainy June afternoon, it finally happened. Word got back that the war had ended and that Otis was alive and well. Tales of his wit and bravery began to circulate as more information came in. Apparently, Otis had been one of the men responsible for the strategy that would eventually end the war. Over the next several weeks, sporadic fleets of ships filled with hero soldiers returned to Ithaca—but Otis was nowhere in sight.

He had originally been scheduled to arrive on a ship dedicated to the elite unit of soldiers who had served on the front lines and penetrated the Trojan king's walls. According to the ship's route, however, the scheduled portage of Ithaca was one of the last. When an opportunity to leave sooner presented itself, Otis took advantage.

Chapter 1

He and two other men from the elite unit loaded up on a flat iron vessel with limited occupancy. The small boat had been smeared with several aging coats of olive-green paint meant for camouflage. Having been designed for use in a previous war, however, the boat did little to conceal itself, surrounded by lush, lime-green vegetation on either side of the serpentine river.

Mowgli was the youngest of the three. He was also the youngest to have fought in the war, enlisting just after his sixteenth birthday. He was something of a free spirit and the only soldier in the elite unit with long hair. Mowgli had very little to say unless he was correcting someone who had just mispronounced his name. "It's Mowgli," he'd say with an irritated brush of his hair. "Like *cow*. Not Mooooogli."

He was a simple kid, a great navigator, but best known for his hand-to-hand combat skills. He'd spent his childhood in a small village somewhere in the jungle and was part of an indigenous tribe known to outsiders as "berserkers." Their ability to enter a trance during a fight was something that many had heard of, but most needed to witness it firsthand to grasp the concept. On the battlefields, berserkers induced fear into their enemies by growling, screaming, and foaming at the mouth like rabid animals.

Mowgli was no exception to the rule of their behavior and showcased every one of these eccentricities while on the front lines of the Trojan War. In no time, he had a reputation as a "wild man." Hyperbolic tales centered on his youth became something of folklore around battlefield campfires. The most common attribute of these fables was that Mowgli had been raised in the jungle by a pack of wolves.

Curly was the other fellow traveling aboard the dark-green vessel. At twenty-eight, he was just two years younger than Otis, but his sloppy ambiance and wavy, unkempt hair made him appear about twenty years Otis's senior. Curly was in charge of overseeing the provisions. Other than that, very little was known about him. The few who do recall knowing him have all mentioned that he never knew his parents and say that he often spoke of starting a family and settling down on a farm once the Trojan War was over.

As the gentle stream guided them (and a cloud of mosquitoes) toward the peaceful sunset, all three men knew the war was over but still felt its lingering presence nipping at their shoulders. They had little to say, and each one was grateful that the others weren't trying to force conversation. Mowgli gently steered the boat, Curly dozed off on his sweat-stained cot, and Otis indulged in daydreams in which he and Penelope were reuniting after two lonely years apart. He allowed his fantasies to continue on past the sunset and into the night, which made it even more difficult for him to sleep. And sleeping was no easy feat directly after serving time in the battlefield—at least that's how it had been after the others. On this evening, however, Otis laid his heavy head on the softest pillow it had touched in over two years, and he was out.

His eyes blinked open and into focus after what felt like only a few seconds. It was unclear how much time had passed, but the darkness was overpowering. As Otis managed to squint fragments of his surroundings into view, he knew that he was still on the boat, still surrounded by jungle, and docked next to a cavernous opening at the base of a large rock wall. Lured by the flicker of friendly candlelight coming from inside the cave,

Chapter 1

Otis stepped forward, exercising extreme caution. With each step, the light grew brighter, and deep chitchatting voices grew more obnoxious. There was a handful of them, none belonging to Mowgli or Curly.

Otis peeked around the noisy corner, catching a glimpse of roughly two dozen men he didn't recognize except for Curly. Curly was sitting at a weathered dining table next to a man who seemed to be the other men's leader.

"I'll tell ya, boys," the mystery man said. "This. This is good livin'."

"You can say that again, Captain," one of the men replied.

Three roasted turkeys, beers steins, rum and wine bottles, and an assortment of pastries were gobbled and guzzled as if they were all about to turn.

"Why don't you come on out here and join us?" the man said. "Yes. You."

Otis took hesitant steps around the corner, slipping out from the veil of shadows.

"Please, pull up a seat."

Otis pulled up one of several empty chairs and sat across from an apprehensive Curly, who didn't appear as jolly as the company he kept. He took the tiniest bites of a turkey leg and avoided his drink as if someone had spit in it.

Over Otis's left shoulder, Mowgli and several other men lay in a dark corner. Thick clouds of burning opium poured from the damp area, faces only revealing themselves through an occasional flick and flash of a match. Mowgli was in his own little world, ignoring everything that wasn't necessary to acquiring his next flowery pull.

After several minutes of idle prattle from the leader, the man proudly introduced himself as Captain James. After a few steins, he revealed himself to be rather chatty. "But enough about me already. What's your name, stranger?"

Just as Otis was about to answer, he felt someone kick his foot under the table. When he looked up, Curly's wide eyes sent out the warning.

"My name?" Otis asked, still unsure of what to make of Curly's kick, and even less of his look.

"Well, I've already met these two," Captain James said, with a cavalier tone suggesting he'd already bored of them. "Chester and Mowgli. I honestly think I'd throw my own mother down a set of stairs if she'd stuck me with either of those awful names."

"My name's Nobe," Otis said.

"Nobe?"

"Yes, sir. Nobe. Ahhdie."

"So I take it your mom didn't like you either."

"Can we leave the moms out of this, please?" Curly asked.

"What's it to you, *Chester*? You don't even know your mom." Captain James let out a shrieking whistle before three of his men swarmed Curly and dragged him away from the table. They pinned him against a jagged rock wall as two more men stepped in and pressed their swords against Otis's throat. Mowgli paid little mind, as his glossy eyes and dazed demeanor kept him idle.

"What are you doing?" Otis asked.

Curly struggled and squirmed within the men's collective grasp, but his effort was for nothing.

"You didn't think I recognized you, didja?" Captain James either sobered up fast or was faking it as he inched closer to Curly's face. "A lot of you guys probably remember the name.

Chapter 1

Others may be too young. But Chester here, as he calls himself, actually goes by the name Curly...he is a former captain of the Lost Boys." Captain James leaned in closer for a more intimate moment. "Your face has aged quite a bit, but it is you."

Curly reared back and spit at the captain's face, hitting his nose and mouth. Everyone went silent. Captain James, as calm as he'd been all night, pressed a handkerchief against the middle of his face.

"Yeah. It's me," Curly said. "And don't think I forgot about you, Jimmy Seashells."

Captain James's self-satisfied manner shifted to a stern look as hints of red overcame his face. "What did you just say?"

"What?" Curly asked. "Are there guys here who don't know about that?"

"Shut your mouth." Captain James began to tremble with rage as a smirk began to root on Curly's face.

"About ten years ago—"

"I'm warning you."

"Your brilliant captain here traded off every bit of gold his band of dipshits had stole—in exchange for some rare gemstones. The only problem was when they opened the bags, there weren't any gemstones inside. I mean, there were some. A few—on the top. But once they dug through that first layer, nothin' but seashells."

"I gave you fair warning." Captain James shook his head and pinched his nose.

"Your ship had to be sold off. Ended up a stack of firewood, as I recall." Curly chuckled for a moment but stopped when he realized that he was the only one doing so. "What a lubberwort," he said. "I still can't believe none of those guys killed you over that one."

"A few of them tried," the captain said. "The ones I let live call me captain now. In time, you will too."

"Nah. 'Fraid not. You're always gonna be Jimmy Seashells to me."

Captain James licked his lips, gazed off into a random corner of the cave, and let out a regretful sigh as he gently placed his hand on Curly's shoulder. "I really wish you hadn't told that story.

"Nobe. Mowgli. You both seem like a couple of nice fellows. I think in another time, in another place, we could have been dear friends. I mean that. Truly, I do. But you happened to show up here with *him*, so I'm afraid you'll have to—"

Mowgli broke from his pipe-induced trance and into one more fitting of a wild berserker. He let out a screeching war cry as he leaped toward Captain James and wrapped his smoky hands around the captain's throat. With zero hesitation, one of the pirates pulled a bow and fired an arrow into Mowgli's shoulder. Otis reacted in horror as three more arrows zipped into Mowgli's chest, putting him on his back. Captain James sat up, grinned, and ran his fingers over the arrow feathers sticking out of Mowgli's lifeless body as if playing a musical instrument.

"Whoops." Captain James started to cackle. "I don't think Moooooooogli's gonna make it, boys. Ope…excuse me. Mowgli."

Otis sat motionless as the pirate wielding the bow stepped forward and aimed his next arrow at Otis's heart.

"Whatcha say, Nobe?" The captain let out another laugh. "Feelin' brave tonight? Wanna test your luck?"

Chapter 1

Still restrained, and fighting back tears, Curly lowered his head and closed his eyes.

Chapter 2

In the deepest, dampest, and coldest part of an otherwise gorgeous ship, Otis and Curly were stacked in separate cages generally reserved for the transport of animals or slaves. The captain had plenty of room in the brig, but Curly was a "most extra special guest," and by extension, so was Otis.

Otis gazed at the hodgepodge of dirty puddles collecting from the drips, teasing him from above. He would have given almost anything for the satisfaction of just one tiny drop.

"Good morning, my little barnacles," Captain James called down the stairs before stomping down them. "How is the sea treating you on this fine, fine morning?"

Otis and Curly ignored him, as was their routine.

"That's too bad." The captain let loose the tone of a parent teasing a disappointed child. "I suppose this probably isn't going to help any. I've got some rather unpleasant news for you both. It seems that we've entered the waters of an area where people understand the value of their gold. And I may have a buyer willing to part with enough of his gold to make me part with this beautiful, beautiful, telescope and retire this life altogether." Captain James pulled a gaudy golden telescope from his belt and held it on display for a frightened Curly, who was pressed against the back of his cage, shaking like a beaten dog.

"Curly, you and Nobe have been with me for almost a full year now. Could you imagine waking up every morning and not being able to look forward to the delicious breakfasts you get to watch me eat? The buckets of hot and cold water I use to wake you. The scorpions, and snakes, and spiders I put in your cage so you don't get lonely. All gone. Curly, how much do you think this telescope is worth? In terms of gold…not even a guess? How about you, Nobe?"

Silence.

Captain James rubbed his thumb over the telescope and let out a regretful sigh. "I suppose you can't guess its value if you don't know its history. And it's my own fault for not teaching you two about this telescope and where it came from.

"On the surface, it doesn't look like much, I know. There's scratches all over it and a few dents if you look close enough. But this was a very special gift. And like most special gifts, it's not so much about the gift itself, or the thought, as much as it is who the gift is from."

The captain tucked the telescope back on his belt and covered it with his silky jacket. "I never believed in the Sea Witch…I'd always heard that you were more likely to get struck by lightning than to ever see her in real life. I still don't know if that's true or not, but the day I met her, there wasn't a cloud in the sky.

"It started out quiet. There was this thumping at the bottom of the ship. Thump. Thump. Thump. It got louder and quicker. *Thump. Thump. Thump.*" He slammed his massive fist into the cages and paused for a moment, lost within the frightening

Chapter 2

chambers of his memory. "Before any of us knew what was happening, the ship…just…started to crumble like stale bread. I still don't know why she came over to me.

"She could have killed me from fifty feet out, but for some reason or another, she came real close. Face to face. There were at least a hundred other guys, but she swam to me. She was so beautiful. More beautiful than any woman I've ever seen or been with. And trust me, I've been with some of the finest ass in the world. Long, thick locks of blond hair. Great big blue eyes.

"But when she smiled…her teeth—they looked like they'd been covered in seaweed. I didn't know what else to do, so I grabbed a wine bottle that happened to be floating nearby, and I smashed it in her face. The glass cut her to shreds." Captain James put his head down. It was the first time Otis had ever seen fear or respect on the captain's face. There even seemed to be a shred of remorse.

"But she didn't wince or show any signs of pain," the captain continued. "She just ran her hand down her bloody face, smiled, and sank back into the water. I thought for sure she was gonna pull me down—do whatever she does to people. Never happened. She wrecked us about a mile or so off the Calypso Island coastline. Those of us who made it to shore stayed until we could arrange for a new ship. About three months later, we finally left. Our first day out, she tracked us down.

"I was scared. I don't think I've ever been more afraid. All I kept thinking was that I'd have to answer for cutting her face to shreds. But it was like she didn't even remember that it happened. All she wanted from me was more of the 'purple stuff,' as she called it. I wasn't sure if she was serious or not, but I gave her a barrel. In return, she gave me this telescope and a lifetime of gratitude. She's constantly tipping us off on gold shipments, tea, tobacco, silk, slaves…haven't heard much from her lately, but she's still out there. It really is a miracle she picked me that day. And that there was a bottle of wine within reach."

"The real miracle is that you tell that bullshit story, expecting anyone to believe it," Otis said.

"No," the captain said with a serene calmness. "That story is as true as you are here. And that's why this telescope is so valuable. The man who wants to buy it has heard my story, and he knows it's true. Based on the description and unique features, he recognizes this telescope as one from his childhood. You see, he was only a boy when the Sea Witch wrecked the ship he was on. He was also the sole survivor. Everyone and everything else went down—including his father, his grandfather, and a family heirloom that had been passed down for generations.

"Turns out that young man would grow up to accrue quite a fortune. And he wants his family heirloom. Like I said, it's not the gift itself, but who it came from. Now, Nobe. Curly. Knowing what you now know about this telescope, what do you think it's worth?"

"I really don't know," Otis said. "But I'm guessin' it's not a lot if it's all beat to shit."

"What?" Captain James reacted with a puzzled glance before reaching for his belt. The telescope was gone and was somehow within Otis's firm grasp. "Noooo!"

From the back of his cage, Otis choked up on the telescope and swung it repeatedly against the steel bars, smashing it to scrap and sending shards of glass everywhere. Captain James's jaw couldn't have fallen any farther. Devastation filled the moldy air as a lifetime of fortune vanished in the blink of an eye.

Chapter 2

"I don't know how you got your hands on that," he said with a contained rage boiling within. "But you are going to pay—dearly."

Otis smiled, wedging himself further under the captain's skin. "It's probably too late to tell you this, but I don't have any gold on me to pay for that. Whoops."

Seething, Captain James lugged himself back up the stairs.

The following morning, Otis woke up and stretched his arms and legs. "Mornin', Curly. What do you think are the chances of us getting fed today?" Aside from a series of gentle water drops tapping the warped wooden floor, Otis got no answer. "Curly...Curly?" Otis looked down. The cage was still there, but Curly was gone. Otis hung his head low, went to the back of his pen, and closed his eyes.

In the days to come, he got word that Curly had been thrown overboard. His hands and legs had been tied while a cannonball tethered to his restraints weighed him down. Otis didn't sleep for a week. Delirious, he waited and wondered when it would be his turn to pay for that telescope. The minutes turned to hours. The hours turned to days. And just like that, three years passed.

Captain James fancied himself an experimental man. When it came to torture and pushing the physical and mental wills of his prisoners, the captain had had a lot of experience before his encounter with Otis. The captain knew a lot of awful things, most from firsthand experience. He had a good idea as to how long a human body could survive without food or water, or air, or while encapsulated by freezing-cold temperatures.

Odyssey Tale

He also took note that something happens to a person when he's cut off from sunshine for an extended period of time. Something inside him shrivels up and, in the process, dulls the will and edges of even the sharpest minds. The captain determined that survival without the sun was entirely possible, but living was not.

During Otis's time on that ship, he got to see quite a bit from the back of his cage. But not once did he ever get a glimpse of sunshine. Other prisoners would come and go. some individuals, some families. Otis always tried to offer advice when they first arrived. What to say, what not to say, and how to gain the slightest bit of sympathy from the guys the captain would assign to check in on them. "And, whatever you do, never, under any circumstances, ask when you're going to be fed or given water next."

None of the new prisoners lasted for more than a few months at a time before being killed or sold off. For Otis, however, there was no discernible timeline for his death or unlikely conditional release. Just malnourishment paired with droopy eyes and a scraggly beard. His most recent meal had been an unfortunate moth that had flown close to his cage, and his last drink of water had been wrung from a dirty mop.

Throughout childhood, Otis had been instilled with the thought that an untimely death was something he should never accept. "Sure." His mother's voice was as clear as if she had been standing next to him. "It is going to happen someday, but not until you're an old, old man and there's nothing left for you to achieve in this life. But should it try to sneak up and succeed in overwhelming you, give it every shred of fight you have. Never

Chapter 2

give up. And never accept an untimely death as a conclusion to your life story."

Otis was reaching a crossroads in his life story, however, and it was making him question whether or not death would be seen as an antagonist or as a welcome supporting character. An increasing lack of stability within his mind caused hope and optimism to hemorrhage from his cage at an alarming rate.

It was a chilly fall morning. Captain James came down the steps with an elastic water canteen and a ceramic bowl overflowing with spoiled olives.

"Prolly thought I forgot about you down here, huh?" Captain James squeezed the canteen between two steel bars and cringed at the sight of Otis desperately gulping down the water. "Here," the captain said, slowly raising the bowl against the same two bars. "Nobody likes these."

Otis devoured the rotting olives and chugged down what little water he had left. "These from Ithaca?" he asked.

"Yeah," Captain James said, impressed. "Passed through about a month ago. How did you know?"

"Lucky guess…I used to live in Ithaca," Otis said. "Best olives in the world."

"I'll have to take your word for it. I've never acquired a taste. They won't be running out anytime soon, though—in Ithaca. I've never seen so many olive trees in one place. Didn't realize how pretty they were. The whole coast was covered."

"It's heaven on earth in late spring," Otis said, staring at the last olive.

"That's about when we were there."

Otis handed the canteen back before looking disconsolately at the floor and letting a tear escape his eye. "I'm the king there," he said under his breath.

"What's that?"

"I'm the king there. My real name is Otis Seehus, and if you turn back and take me there, I swear on my son's life I'll send you away with more gold than your eyes can see at one time."

Captain James stepped forward and honed his pensive eyes on Otis for the briefest of moments before bursting into laughter. "You about had me there, Nobe," he said, brushing his forearms over his eyes to dry the comical tears.

"I'm serious," Otis said, jolting to the front bars of his cage, closing the distance between the two. "Please. Take me back."

Captain James could recognize the desperation in his captive's tired eyes and perhaps a bit of truth. "Even if you were the king of that tiny little island—you're not anymore. It seems the people have moved on from—what was it you said your real name was?"

"Otis Seehus."

"Why have I never heard of you?"

"Captain, I'm sure there are a lot of kings you haven't heard of."

"What the hell's that supposed to mean?"

"It's not supposed to mean anything," Otis said defensively. "Am I wrong? Are you familiar with every king in the world?"

"No. I suppose not. But I was just in Ithaca, and I didn't hear anyone say anything about their beloved King Otis and how they all missed him so much. No word of search teams or questions of his whereabouts. It seems the people have moved

Chapter 2

on. I suggest you do the same. I don't care what your name is or how much gold you think you still have back there. The only certainties in your life are that you're here, and you're mine." The captain turned his back to Otis and ascended the stairs, still giggling. "King of Ithaca," he mocked while rising out of sight. "I can't wait to tell the guys about this one."

Otis buried his forehead between the steel bars, using pain to ease his anger while fresh tears ran trails down both of his cheeks.

Chapter 3

It was a particularly hot day, even for August. The swift and sweaty movement of the crew was in full force. The men knew they were only several days from Port Royal. More importantly, they were only several days from lakes of rum, flocks of whores, and enough gambling to make a man ill. There seemed to be only one man not performing his assigned duties that day. He stood with purpose just outside the corridor leading down to the ship's lower level and gave the captain a mutinous stare.

"Riley," the captain said. "Something you need?"

"How's your little friend down there?"

Perplexed by Riley's mild hostility, Captain James entertained the unusual question. "He's good. Good as he can be, I suppose."

"Yeah? He like his olives?"

"Yeah. I guess he did. But after a week or two without food, even a leather boot can taste like fresh honeycomb. Why do you ask?"

"It's just that, he's been with us a long time now, and me—and some of the other guys—are just wondering why…sir. You're not selling him. You're not putting him to work. You don't seem to have any intention of killing him. Right now, he's just another mouth to feed."

"I see," the captain said calmly. "And you said some of the other guys feel the same way?"

"They do."

"Well, I'd be lying to myself and all of you if I said you didn't have a point."

Riley squinted curiously as Captain James scratched his head.

"Right now we're about three days from Port Royal," the captain said. "When we get there, we'll take him out of his cage and have him dig a grave. And we'll nip this in the bud before it becomes a real problem. Sound good?"

"Yes, sir," Riley said, happy to secure the captain's approval.

A few days later, Otis lay in his cage reflecting, although distracted by his growling belly. The heavy boots of several pirates stomped down the stairs, followed by the whoosh of a black cloak being thrown over Otis's cage.

Moments later, as the cloak was removed, the harsh sunlight filled Otis's skull with a throbbing headache. His eyelids were so bright that he needed both hands to cover them, and he nearly vomited from the shock of the incoming beams. When he was finally able to see, he found himself surrounded by pirates, Captain James, and a handful of rowdy onlookers enjoying the lawless backstreets of Port Royal. They were just off the beaten path of the small yet rambunctious village at what looked to be the top of a cliff.

"Take your time," the captain said, in regard to Otis's adjusting eyes. "I know it's been a while since you've seen the sun."

Chapter 3

Riley nudged the pirates to his left and right. "See," he said, under his breath. "Best friends, they are. Prolly won't even go through with it."

After allowing what he felt to be a sufficient amount of time, Captain James opened the cage door and tossed a shovel at Otis's feet. "Dig."

Disheartened, Otis picked up the shovel and wondered how many men he could kill with it before the remaining pirates swarmed him. "Where?" he asked.

"Right over there's good. Seems like a nice view." Captain James turned and pointed to a spot that was twenty or so feet away from the cliff's edge.

Otis could barely pick up the shovel but mustered enough strength to dig what was sure to be his grave. He had taken his time, trying to come up with something—anything that would give him the slightest advantage to escape. He thought of diving over the cliffside but knew that it didn't lead to water. Again, he toyed with the notion of using the shovel to fend off his would-be attackers, but it didn't play out in his head any better the second time around.

As his hole began to take its unmistakable shape, he slowed his pace, thinking and continuously coming up short. Every escape plan was sure to lead to a quick death. But maybe that wasn't such a bad thing. *What if they bury me alive?* A rush of panic washed over his chest as he paused to wipe the sweat from his forehead.

Captain James nodded at a beefy pirate who was standing closest to the growing hole. Before Otis had realized that someone else had hopped into the hole with him, the man's hulky fist flew into Otis's cheek, rendering him unconscious.

"Get him up outta there," the captain said, scanning the crowd. "Riley. Do you have a knife?"

"Sure do," Riley answered, giddy and eager to please.

"Is it sharp? Really, really sharp?"

"Yes, sir, Captain. Sharpened it this morning."

"Good," Captain James said with a devious grin. "I sharpened mine this morning too. Now you and I are going to get into that hole, and one of these knives is going to kill one of us. And whoever lives will get to be captain of the *Jolly Roger*. Whoever dies won't waste the other's time by needing to be dragged to a grave site."

"Captain, I'm sorry. I never meant for you to—"

"Save it, Riley," the captain said, lowering his lanky legs into the hole. "Now get in here. Let's see how sharp that knife is."

With nerves of cotton, Riley stepped over to the opposite side of the hole and lowered himself inside. His reluctant hand reached for the knife on his belt and began to tremble as he raised it toward his captain.

"Ready?" the captain asked.

"Captain, we don't have to. We can discuss this."

In one swift motion, Captain James reached for his dagger and tossed it at Riley, impaling him just above the heart.

Riley immediately fell to his back and howled out in pain. He could taste the dust that would soon fill his nose and mouth and began to cry. "Please, Captain."

Captain James wrapped both hands around the dagger handle stuck to Riley's chest. Before the captain could drive it farther in and pierce Riley's pounding heart, the neighing of a nearby horse made him pause.

"Johnny," he said. "Go get me that horse."

Chapter 3

"I don't know whose horse that is, Captain."

The captain rolled Riley on his side, tied his hands behind his back with a small length of twine, and threw him up out of the grave. "What did you say?"

"Nothing," Johnny replied, hurrying away.

Captain James emerged from the grave, looked around at his crew, and rested his shiny boot on a whimpering Riley.

Johnny quickly returned with the first horse he could snag. The captain grabbed the back of Riley's neck and firmly tied wrists and threw him over the horse like a saddlebag. The captain went back into the grave to retrieve the knife Riley had dropped. "It really is sharp," he said, rubbing the blade and guiding the horse toward the cliff's edge. "Any last words, Riley?"

"I—"

Captain James drove the knife into the horse's hind leg. It screamed before leaping off the cliff, causing Riley to scream as well.

Captain James turned to face his silent crew. "You see that guy over there?" he asked, pointing to an unconscious Otis. "That is my prisoner. Just like the *Jolly Roger* is my ship, and you are my crew. Riley seemed to have forgotten that when it comes to handling business on the ship, it's my goddamn business," he exclaimed, driving both thumbs into his chest.

"And Riley, may he rest in peace"—the captain struggled to hold back a chuckle—"told me that he wasn't alone in his dissatisfaction. I don't know if that's true or not. I don't want to point any fingers because he didn't name a single name. But I'm thinking we need a fresh start. From this point forward, you can either be loyal and do your job and let me do mine—and trust that I know what I'm doing and that every decision I make is for the good of the ship—or you can join me down there in that hole with your knife. You just better hope it's faster and sharper than Riley's. No one?" he asked, scanning the crowd. "OK, then. Get Nobe back in his cage, and put him where he belongs. Let's put all this mess behind us. And let's enjoy all the debauchery that Port Royal has to offer," he concluded to a chorus of cheers.

When Otis awoke and found himself back in his cage and stowed in the bottom of the ship, his emotion boiled over into the physical realm. He balled up both fists and began to pound the lock of his cage until every one of his knuckles had split open and was leaking blood.

"Why couldn't you have just killed me?" he asked, sobbing.

"You can pound all you like," the captain said, emerging from a dark corner. "But you'll never get out like that."

"What the hell do I gotta do to get outta here?"

"Tell me something," the captain said, strolling into the light. "What keeps you going? How is it that I haven't broken you yet? It's never taken this long. Hell, one time, I had this little savage girl on board. Tiger Lily. I bought her over in the Americas—was told I got a great deal and she was a good worker. Turns out neither of those things were true. So we decided to lock her up until we could figure out what to do with her. She got loose from her cage the first day we had her in it. Stabbed two guys and jumped overboard. Drowned. She preferred death over one more day alive in this very cage. But not you. You refuse to die. You refuse to kill yourself. You've spent over ten times as many days in this cage than anyone else before you. Why is that?"

Chapter 3

Otis pondered for a moment. "I guess I'm willing to sit in a cage forever, as long as I can hope for one more second of freedom."

"Seriously?" the captain asked, unimpressed. "That block of cheese is all you got?"

Otis shrugged his shoulders.

"Tell me something, Nobe. Do you think you could ever find it in your heart to call me Captain?"

"I already do."

"No. I mean for real. Like you mean it."

Otis let the words hang in the musty air.

"Do you think you could be a loyal member of this crew?" the captain asked. "You'd have freedom in the sense that you wouldn't have to sit and rot in this cage. But I would expect you to do what I say, when I say, as long as I see fit. Do you think we could make that work?"

Otis thought long and hard. He thought back to the times in which he and Curly hadn't eaten in days and were forced to watch a team of rats and flies devour a half-eaten steak dinner that was just out of reach. He remembered the cold months in which there were consecutive weeks without a wink of sleep until his body shut down.

"Yeah, if it means getting out of here. I'm willing to do whatever it takes, Captain."

"It's not going to be easy."

"What about this so far has been easy?" Otis asked.

"That's the spirit, Nobe." Captain James let out a cackle and stomped up the stairs.

Otis didn't see him again for another month.

Odyssey Tale

In a remote part of the ocean, the magnificent *Jolly Roger* basked in the sun's rays as the crew took some leisure time to indulge in the Caribbean climate. Through the delicate waters that cradled the ship, Captain James noticed the approaching remnants of some wreckage fifteen to twenty feet down.

"I think this is it," he said. "Drop anchor, boys."

Despite Otis's strength being too depleted to fight even one pirate, the captain sent down four to escort him up to the deck.

"Nobe. Today is a big day for you."

Otis watched as ten or so pirates carried a massive glass plate and used a series of ropes and pulleys to lower it flat onto the water. Once on the surface, it created a viewing window down to the eerie shipwreck resting on the ocean floor.

"Down there, in one of the rooms, there are six or seven chests filled to the brim with gold doubloons. I need you to go down and find them. And when you do, you'll have to net them so we can drag them up here."

"How do you expect me to do that?" Otis asked. "I'm a good swimmer, but I can't hold my breath that long."

"You won't have to." Captain James stood up and unveiled a large coil of leather tubing. "You won't be able to see or hear anything. But you'll be able to breathe just fine. Just put one end of this in your mouth, grab a cannonball, and hop on in. We'll keep you tethered to the top, and make sure you have plenty of slack…and fresh air."

Chapter 4

Words cannot describe the fear that one experiences when all senses are submerged in fifteen to twenty feet of water. Otis had thick bits of wool stuffed into his nostrils and ears, but the sting of salt water still crept in. The darkness pressed against his eyelids while the taste of moist, salty sea air coming from the top of his tether was nearly enough to make him gag. He could barely hear his own thoughts over an overworked heart, and he couldn't feel the water through the trepidation wrapping his skin.

Weighed down by a cannonball, Otis unwound his coil as he slowly stepped through the decades-old shipwreck and explored, using his left hand as a guide for vision while his right handled the loop. He went from room to room, experiencing chills more related to the locale than the water keeping him cocooned. He wondered how many ghosts were down there with him, watching.

Upon entry of a new room, he would start along the outside walls and work his way in. Then he'd follow the coil back to where he'd entered the ship's massive wound and move on to the next room. At first, he didn't entirely trust the coil or the mask wrapped around his mouth. But after the first hour or so, both were distant concerns.

Up on deck, Captain James and those who could get a view watched through the glass they had placed on the surface. No one could see Otis, but they all knew he was still down there, somewhere inside the ship.

The captain glanced at his pocket watch and then over his shoulder in the direction of the coiled tether resting on the deck. He began to walk toward it with a sad pace, drawing the attention of his comrades.

"What's the matter, Captain?" one of the men asked.

The men slowly and collectively turned their attention toward Captain James and gathered around him. None of them had ever seen him look so somber.

"What is it, Captain?" another man asked.

Captain James looked down at the coil and made eye contact with each and every member of the crew before letting out a sigh. "Right before Riley died, he asked me what my intentions were with Nobe. And he asked why I hadn't killed him yet. But the way he asked, the attitude…it made me question his loyalty.

"Now, since then, I have heard that some of you aren't very happy with the way I handled that situation. Some of you—and I know who you are—some of you think that I chose Nobe over Riley. But the fact of the matter is this: Riley chose himself over this crew. He wasn't loyal. And if you must know, I have killed Nobe. I've killed him several times. No human I've ever met has been able to withstand what I've thrown at him. He should have starved to death, froze to death, and died from dehydration dozens of times by now. But he won't. Nobe is a specimen.

Chapter 4

"And, not that it's any of your concern, he also took something from me a long time ago that I never told any of you about. So don't jump to conclusions before the story's even started."

Captain James let the words rest on his men for a moment to let them catch up. "Does anyone know how long he's been down there?"

No one answered. Too many times in the past, they had suffered the humiliation that followed a verbal response to one of the captain's rhetorical questions.

"He's been down there for five hours now," the captain said. "Five. Hours. This is a man that I've had in a cage for almost four years of his life. And he's down there right now, looking for something that he's not going to find."

Puzzled glances sliced through the air so fast the captain could almost hear them.

"What I told him was down there—it isn't really down there. And he's looked for it—for five hours—without coming up and complaining, or asking for anything, or telling me that he can't find it. How many men here would have done that for their captain? Even just one hour?"

He ran his frustrated palms over his face and let out another sigh. "And yet I keep hearing this groveling. *When we get to port, I'm gonna find another crew. When we get to port, I'm gonna find another captain. I'm just gonna put in my time and do my job until we get to port, and I'm done*...bunch of bawl babies.

"Any of you can be replaced at the drop of a hat. None of you are necessary. The hardest worker I have on this ship is at the bottom of the ocean right now...but I'll never have his loyalty. Without that—he's useless."

In a move that would shock the crew for years to come, Captain James picked up the sizable coiled tether, walked it to the side of the ship, and tossed it overboard. He turned back to face his crew and lowered his eyebrows. "I don't care how good of a worker you are. If I have to question your loyalty, you're no more good to me than Nobe was. Now let's get going."

The *Jolly Roger* sailed off toward the setting sun, leaving Otis behind in the belly of the wreckage. By some miracle, on the water's surface, the coil remained wrapped in such a way that it kept afloat. Despite the opening's vulnerability to the surrounding water eagerly waiting to fill it up, Otis was given a stay of execution.

Down in the frigid confines of a room he had searched twice before, Otis was growing frustrated. Hungry, thirsty, and tired, he sent a scream from his mask to the surface. He hadn't found anything even remotely resembling a chest filled with doubloons. He'd stumbled across plenty of tables, chairs, and bottles. He also thought he'd found a wooden serving bowl until his thumb slithered through the opening of an eye cavity, revealing the bowl to be a human skull.

Otis knew he couldn't go up empty handed, as his potential freedom hung in the balance. But he also knew that his potential freedom was precisely that—potential. What if it was all a trick and Captain James had no intention of living up to his end of the deal? Otis thought and wondered as to whether or not he would be better off just to take the mask off right there. At the

Chapter 4

very least, he could take satisfaction knowing that he controlled his own fate.

He raised both palms to either side of the mask and let them rest on it. But no matter how appealing the quick breath of water sounded versus another four years—or more—stuffed in that cage, a stern voice echoed in his mind. "You can't do it. You can't take that mask off down here."

Otis gathered what was left of the day's mental strength and carried his coil back toward the ship's opening. He used the mossy walls to guide him back. They were the same walls he'd been using all day, but somehow, on this rotation, his coil got snagged beneath the blade of an ill-placed sword. He could feel the resistance and began to pull the tether, causing the blade to apply more pressure to his lifeline.

Through the continued guidance of the coil, he inched his way closer to the snag. By the time he realized the obstruction was a sword, however, his right hand had been gashed, and a painful jerk caused the sword to lift upward. As his left hand instinctively covered his right palm and he felt the hot sting of salt water, the sword sank back down to the floor and sliced his tether.

Water instantly filled his mouth and throat, causing him to cough and remove any air he had stowed away. Having no idea where he was in the ship or how much farther it was to the opening, Otis dropped the cannonball and began to swim with what little might he had left.

Nearly a minute went by as he scanned his palms over the ship, looking for any way out. His lungs had almost reached their breaking point, and he could feel himself beginning to go unconscious. Then, out of nowhere, three beautiful mermaids swarmed him. Otis thought he had died, but the crushing pressure of water trying to extract what little breath he had left told him he wasn't gone just yet.

Two of the mermaids began to swim around him, creating a wormhole that increased in size with the speed of their circling. The third mermaid whispered into his ear, "Take my hand."

Otis reached out. She grabbed his hand and whipped him into the cyclone before joining the other two mermaids, who were sustaining its shape and size. Guided by the intense stream, Otis went along for the ride. The spiraling mermaids escorted him out of the ship and up toward the water's surface. He was going to make it.

Suddenly, the cyclone stopped, and Otis lost momentum. The mermaids vanished just as quickly as they'd arrived, and the shadow of a large fishing net began to swallow Otis whole. It was at this point that he finally went unconscious.

Several hundred feet away, the three mermaids rose to the surface and watched the fishing boat reel in its net. The alpha mermaid glared at the boat. She combed her fingers through thick brunette locks, wringing out the water they had collected. "Dammit."

"We had him too," the second mermaid said, shaking the water out of her hair.

"Do either of you know who that was?" the alpha asked, before receiving an empty response. "That was Otis Seehus. King of Ithaca."

"How do you know?" the second mermaid asked.

Chapter 4

"He's on the Sea Witch's list. She's got a painting of him. He looks like shit now, but that was him. I'm going to follow that boat. You two go home, and don't say anything about this to anyone. She'll kill us if she finds out we let him get away."

"It wasn't our fault," the youngest mermaid said.

"She won't feel that way. But it doesn't matter. Because he's not getting away."

The alpha's words struck confidence in the youngest before the mermaids went their separate ways.

Having no memory of the mermaids or fishnet, Otis felt his eyes jolt open as water burst from his throat. He coughed himself back to life and was soon happy to discover that this boat was most certainly too small, too shabby, and much too filthy to be the *Jolly Roger*. His joy was short lived, however, as one of the three men staring down from a silhouette smiled and smacked him in the face with an oar, rendering him unconscious once again. He woke up with the same violent jolt that had accompanied his near drowning. The only difference now was that he had been gagged, had his hands tied behind his back, and been stuffed in a wooden crate. He was being moved smoothly, as if on wheels. He could hear many different sounds: the muffled banter of negotiators, the clucking of market chickens, and a variety of other click-clacking metropolitan noises. But only tiny slivers of sunlight were able to sneak through the crevices of the crate boards, and they were far too bright for him to see through.

Odyssey Tale

"We snagged him in one of the nets. Thought we saw some dolphins, but he's all we pulled up." The man speaking had a deep, rugged, raspy voice, and had no concern about anyone overhearing him. "We thought he was dead, but he started spitting up water. Charlie knocked him out before he could say or see anything. Now. You're sure she'll buy him?"

"Oh yeah," a second voice answered. This voice was much more high pitched, with a dishonest, weasel-like quality. Otis couldn't hear well enough to know if it was coming from a man or a woman. Nor could he decipher the words being exchanged. "She'll buy him all right. I've got a great relationship with the lady who handles these kinds of transactions for the queen."

"Good to know."

"Let me know if you get any more about his size." The joyful weasel man was about to burst with villainous laughter as if he'd made the deal of a lifetime.

"I thought she paid per pound," the rough voice replied.

"She does pay per pound. But she prefers 'em lean. Like the one you got in there." The crate shook with the light tap of the man's foot. "So if you get any more about his size, you know where to find me."

Chapter 5

Within the bustling town square of a cozy village, street merchants spilled out from cramped storefronts to pedal services, food, tonics, and other random knickknacks to any passersby. The vendors specifically targeted those who made eye contact.

Clumsily slicing through the crowd was a squeaky cart whose wheels kept taking turns getting stuck in the muddy street. The wagon carried a coffin-shaped crate, and a particularly unclean and weasel-looking merchant pushed it toward an ominous block-shaped building. The vine-covered domicile was shrouded by more shadows than it rightfully should have had, but thick yellow letters were bright as day on the charcoal plaque hanging above the front entrance: Ogygia Village Hotel. Despite the friendly and welcoming moniker, this was no hotel.

Inside, a savvy woman with sassy wit and an excess of attitude sat behind a tall desk, filing her fingernails and waiting for the next annoying guest to arrive. The squeaky sounds of an old cart being wheeled through the hallway broke the sweet silence, and she knew it meant only one thing.

"You again?" she asked. "How many times do I have to tell you? We don't allow bums in here."

"As many times as I gotta tell you that I ain't no damn bum," he said. "I work for a livin'. Look at them hands."

She craned her long neck and cracked a condescending smile. "Soft."

"Yeah. OK," he said, rolling his eyes.

"You look like a bum. You smell like a bum. You have no money—like a bum. But every time you come in here trying to peddle your rabble, you insist you're not a bum. And then I tell you to hit the road. And you walk away from here pouting like a *widdle* baby. I don't see today being any different. The queen doesn't want your scrap."

"She'll want what I got today," he said.

"Yeah? And what do you got today?"

The merchant slid the lid off the crate to reveal Otis, still tied and gagged.

"Hmmm," she said, intrigued, looking Otis up and down. "He looks a little scrawny. And he's filthy. Look at that beard. Where did you get him?"

"Does that mean you're not interested?"

"Wait a minute. I never said that. How much does he weigh?"

"Ten stone."

"Come on," she said.

"What?"

"There's no way you can seriously expect me to believe he weighs ten stone."

"I don't give a damn what you believe," he said. "Ten stone is what the man weighs. You want him or not? Make up your mind. I got stuff to do."

"Calm down. I'll take him. The last thing I want to do is cut into your day. I know you've got a lot of coins to beg for, and

Chapter 5

they're not going to collect themselves. You want gold or a line of credit in town? It's good for anywhere but the whorehouse."

"Where else am I gonna wanna spend it?"

"Anywhere else you please. Might I suggest the bathhouse?"

"How long has this whorehouse credit policy been in effect?"

"It's not policy," she said with a smirk. "It's just that I have a good relationship with them over there, and I'm not going to send you in there with a line of credit."

"Why the hell not?"

"For starters, you're disgusting. Your hair looks like someone sewed three or four squirrel pelts together. You seem to be in some sort of contest with that man in the crate to see which one of you can go the longest without having a bath. Your teeth—your teeth kind of look like corn, but corn isn't typically that yellow. Or crooked. And you smell like shit."

"Well," he said, with a defeated and agreeable nod. "Gold, I guess."

"Very good," she said, plopping a preweighed sack of gold and a skeleton key on the counter. "Don't spend it all in one place. Put him in room 13. Last one on the left. Do not—I repeat, *do not*—cut him loose."

"Yeah, yeah. I know how it works."

The merchant pushed the cart down a narrow hallway and into the dim confines of room 13. After a brief struggle with the lid, the merchant harshly tipped the crate and emptied Otis onto the floor.

"Enjoy your stay," the merchant said, sliding the heavy door shut.

Otis looked around the room, trying to make use of what little candlelight he had coming from adjacent walls. Sliding around the floor like a frightened caterpillar, he inched his way around the room in search of a possible way out or weakness in the calloused stone walls surrounding him. As he reached the darkest corner of the room, a mysterious breeze enlarged the flicker of the nearest candle. In doing so, it revealed a still, thick yellow coil. After another breeze and subsequent flicker, the coil started to unravel, and glowing snake eyes eased open.

"Oh, shit," Otis said.

The giant python's eyes absorbed and amplified the candlelight as it wagged its hungry tongue and ripped forward, stopping just short of Otis's wincing face. It pulled this maneuver two more times but appeared to be growing impatient to the point of being disinterested. Eventually, it slithered back into the room's darkest corner, recoiled, and rested its once-glowing eyes.

Sometime later that day, in a room directly next to room 13, the elegant and beautiful Calypso Queen watched Otis through a one-way mirror. His rugged and masculine looks were something she quickly took note of. She saw through his dingy beard and grimy appearance; this handsome stranger was a rather captivating sight.

The innkeeper entered the room, joining the queen, who was preoccupied with the calmness of this enticing man.

"Did I miss anything?" the innkeeper asked.

"No," the queen replied. "It's fascinating, really. It's been so long since Kaa's done this, I almost thought he'd grown out of it. It's like this guy isn't even in the room."

"You think that's what it is? Or do you think Kaa's sick?"

Chapter 5

"No. I've seen what he looks like when he's sick. This is something else. There's something special about our guest here."

"What do you want me to do?" the innkeeper asked.

"Wait an hour. If Kaa doesn't eat him, replace him with someone else. If he eats the next guest, get our new friend here situated in the guest quarters. We'll see if I can find out what's so special about him."

A little more than an hour later, Otis was moved to a different location, a much different location. When his blindfold was taken off and his hands were untied, he found himself in the luxurious suite of a strange castle. The vivid colors of blueberries, strawberries, honey, tea, and a variety of apples were made brighter by the black-stone walls, furniture, and hardwood floors that made up the large room. Upon second glance, Otis spotted pitchers of water and milk. Then he noticed the bed, complete with fluffy blankets and thick pillows.

"Wow," Otis said. "Why did you bring me here?"

The armored guards who had escorted him up had been vetted and trained to never speak—even when spoken to by guests. But one of the two stepped forward and pointed at an envelope Otis had overlooked when he spotted the berries. As he picked it up, the guards left, closing the door behind them.

"To my honored guest," Otis read, ripping the envelope open. "Please enjoy the assortment of beverages and berries and a hot bath. In the cupboard closest to the balcony, you'll find a chew stick and a copper razor. My guards will escort you to dinner at seven this evening. Until then make yourself at home."

To say that Otis's new accommodations were lavish would be an understatement of epic proportions. He was so overwhelmed at first that it began to feel like a dream. At any moment, he was prepared to close his eyes and open them again, only to find himself back in his cage on the *Jolly Roger*. Or worse, tethered to the shipwreck.

Otis's first priority was the water. He ignored several glasses that had been put out and chugged it straight from the pitcher, dousing himself and the shredded rags clinging to his chest. After dumping just over half of the pitcher down his throat, he moved on to the pitcher of fresh milk and repeated the process. Once he had guzzled the milk, he moved on to the berries, smashing them in his mouth and inadvertently all around his cheeks. Moments later, he was on the balcony throwing up.

Once his stomach settled, it was time to enter the hot bath that had been drawn moments before his arrival. Using the most beautiful soaps made from olive oil and a razor-sharp copper blade, Otis washed and trimmed the last three years from his body and face. "Thank you," he said, to anyone—or any entity—who may have been listening. "Thank you so much." A tear slid down his smiling cheek as he cupped two satisfying handfuls of warm water over his face. It was not a dream.

At ten minutes until seven o'clock, the same armored guards who'd escorted Otis up to his room came to take him to dinner. As they approached the dining hall, Otis wasn't sure who or what to expect. Nonetheless, he was surprised to spot a candlelit feast for two, laid out on a massive black dining table. The guards pointed Otis to his seat at one end of the table and left the room. The spread was magnificent. An aromatic collage of

Chapter 5

chicken, duck, and shrimp was accentuated by butter-drenched breads and colorful custard pies.

As Otis began to hope that his host didn't keep him waiting, the Calypso Queen emerged seductively from the darkest corner of the room. "Good evening," she said, her suggestive doe eyes refusing to look away from Otis's. "Thank you for joining me."

"My pleasure. I suppose I have you to thank for the accommodations."

"Please," she said, waving him off. "No need. You're him, aren't you?"

"Excuse me?"

"Otis. Seehus. You're him. Aren't you?"

Otis raised his eyebrows.

"I recognize you from paintings," she said. "Especially now that you've trimmed your beard. You're a hero."

"I don't know about all that, milady. But I am Otis Seehus."

"Please accept my apologies for your initial treatment. The man who turned you in had you mixed up with a local thief. As did we. I just thank the gods the mistake was corrected in time. Where have you been these past few years? According to everyone out there, you're dead."

"It's a long story," Otis said.

"It's not every day I get to break bread with a war hero."

The queen stepped farther into the light and took a seat at the opposite end of the table. She was beautiful. Her dark hair and chestnut eyes exuded a mesmerizing sheen while the form-fitting cut of her elegant black dress highlighted the voluptuous curves of her hips and cleavage. Regular baths in buttermilk kept her skin soft as a lamb. With youthful freckles covering her cherub cheeks, she looked to be about twenty-five years of age, despite the fact that she was over forty.

"I trust that you have everything you need in your room."

"Yes. More than enough, in fact," Otis replied, gratefully tipping his wineglass in her direction. "You'll have to forgive me, though. I have no idea where I am or how I should address you."

"You're on the east coast of Calypso Island. For now, you can just call me Your Majesty. I am the queen here."

"Your Majesty, I can't even begin to tell you how grateful I am. These past few years—they've been rough. Since the war ended, all I've wanted was to get back home. But I keep getting pushed further and further away."

"Where is home?" she asked, gently placing a small piece of bread onto her tongue.

"Ithaca."

"My word. If you left from Troy, how on earth did you end up all the way out here?"

"As I said before, Your Majesty, it's a long story."

Although it pained him to do so, Otis went into great detail about his time on the *Jolly Roger*.

"My goodness." She wiped a tear and a trail of eyeliner away from her cheek. "That is, without a doubt, the saddest story I've ever heard. I can't even fathom how much it must hurt, having never really met your son. Having never watched him walk, or heard his voice."

"That's the thing," he said. "I've been so focused on surviving these past several years. Now that I have, all I can think about is the likelihood that they believe I'm dead. I can't help but wonder, has Penelope remarried? If so, will my son ever see me as his true father? If not, what will he see me as?"

Chapter 5

"I can't answer any of that," the queen said. "But I can make certain he gets to meet his true father. There's a passenger freight that comes to the island every six months. It takes a while to get there, but it does pass through Ithaca. It's scheduled to be back in two weeks or so. I'll make sure there's a cabin onboard reserved for you."

"Thank you so much. Truly. But I'd really like to see if I can figure out something sooner than that."

"I'd hate to be the bearer of bad news, but there isn't anything sooner than that."

Otis looked down at his lap.

"Please don't be upset," she said. "I promise that when it does arrive, you'll be the first to know. And the first onboard. If you prefer, of course."

Hesitant, Otis nodded and put on the most genuine smile he could. "That would be wonderful. But I'm afraid I don't have any way to pay you—or anywhere to stay during that time."

"I will gladly cover the cost of your passage, and there are plenty of hotels around willing to exchange work for room and board. But as long as you're on the island, I insist you remain in my guest quarters."

"You're too kind," Otis said humbly. "Are you sure it's no bother?"

"Of course not," she said, growing somber. "It's actually quite nice to have some company at dinner. You see, my husband passed away recently," she said, staring at a bowl of nearby apples.

"Oh, no. I'm so sorry," Otis said. "When?"

"A few months back."

"How did it happen?"

"Still unsure. He seemed just fine one moment. Then the next moment, he wasn't."

"How awful."

"Yes," she said, staring off into blank space before snapping out of it. "Do you have everything you need? Enough berries? Water? Are the bed and goose-feathered pillows comfortable enough?"

"Everything's perfect," Otis said with another grin. "A thousand times, thank you."

Chapter 6

As per the queen's wishes, Otis spent the next several days making himself at home in the guest quarters. The subtle attention to detail and luxury was head and shoulders above anywhere he'd ever been, including his own castle. Fresh fruits, flowers, milk, drinking water, and bathwater were brought in every morning. Every evening, a local woodcutter would bring in a stack of firewood, cut and split from his own apple and cherry orchards.

The massive walkout balcony extended forward and in both directions. Its considerable size and weight made it a structural marvel and one of the most impressive appendages on any castle at the time. Its latticed ledge overlooked a three-hundred-foot drop and endless ocean views of the eastern sky. There were several hand-carved chairs, a hammock, and an oval bronze tub that had been propped on stilts in the southwest corner. Beneath the tub sat a small mobile fire pit.

"Just use three logs at a time to heat the tub," the queen had said at their most recent dinner. "Any more than that, and the water is just a bit too hot, in my opinion."

Otis slept a lot those first days. Most of the daylight and much of the night were spent in a cloudlike bed that embraced him the way an expecting mother's womb does her baby. Despite the many thoughts raging in his mind, he was tired and hadn't gotten a decent night's sleep since before having left for the war. It was only during the predawn hours that Otis found himself wide awake, percolating with depressing and disorderly thoughts, most of which were about Mac and Penelope. How were they doing? What were they up to? What were they thinking about at that very moment? These were just a few of his concerns.

His thoughts didn't so much come in the form of words or questions but in images. His troubled imagination projected visuals within his mind that showed him that they were happy—very happy. He pictured Penelope waking in their bed next to another man while Mac scampered into the room to wake them. Otis imagined the three of them going into town, mingling with friends and merchants. Perhaps they had their own favorite places to visit, where they would smile, laugh, and make the type of memories that would wash Otis away forever. Eventually, the three of them would go home and tuck Mac into bed. Then Penelope and her new husband would retire to the master suite, where he would build a fire, and the two of them would make love savagely, with a type of connection that she and Otis never shared.

Otis didn't know any of this to be accurate, of course. And it wasn't. But the influx of increasingly troubling images had an equally devastating impact on his predawn emotions. While the hot water encasing him was enough to relieve the ache of physical injuries accumulated in years past, there weren't enough logs to burn off his mental soreness.

Chapter 6

As Otis lay in bed, staring through the intricate etching scribbled about the room's black ceiling, someone knocked on the door. It took a moment for Otis to gather enough strength to speak. "Come in."

The queen, escorted by her two most trusted guards, entered so gracefully one might assume she was walking on air. "Good morning," she said, with a pearly smile. "Care to join me for a walk on the beach?"

"Oh, stop," she said, stomping her bare foot in the damp white sand. "You do not."

"I sure do," Otis said, cracking a mischievous smile. "He was even at my wedding. We go way back."

"Well, I don't believe you," she replied, growing flirtatious in her tone.

"Why is it so difficult to believe? He's just a normal guy like the rest of us who were there."

"I've heard stories. And I've seen paintings. Robin Hood was not just a normal guy."

"He did always have a way with the women. I will say that. And he would have liked you. Contrary to all the stories, he always had a thing for the dark-haired girls."

"Well, I'd ask you to put in a good word for me when you see him next, but unfortunately, these days, I'm just a dark-haired old lady."

"Oh, stop it," Otis said. "You're lovely, and you know it."

"Used to be," she said, slowing pace over the crinkled tides coming into shore. "Nowadays, when I meet a suitor, he seems to be more interested in my castle than in me. When I was a girl, so many men proposed. And all of them were so romantic in their presentation. Feels like centuries ago now."

"Well, you're beautiful and charming. And wonderful company," Otis said. "Any eligible man would be out of his mind to want your castle more than you. I'm certain your days of romantic proposals are far from over."

"We'll see," she said, grinning and raising her eyebrows with newfound confidence. "How did you propose to your wife?"

Pleasant images finally claimed some space in Otis's mind as he recalled that beautiful day. "Well, I knew I wanted it to be a surprise," he said. "Some of her friends and family had been expecting it for a while, so I knew it wouldn't be easy to catch her, or them, off guard. So I planned a little romantic getaway. We stayed in a cozy inn just south of Ithaca, right on the beach—much like this. We, uh…" Otis wiped his eye before it was able to birth a tear. "We spent the days being lazy. We ate—too much, got a little bit frisky. A lot frisky, actually. And we slept. It was the best vacation ever, actually," he said with a short laugh.

"So. When did you ask her?" she asked, giggling along.

"I didn't. Not right then, at least. The vacation ended, and we went back home. All her friends stopped by over the next few days—'Did he ask? Did he ask?' They were all shocked when she told them no. Some were even upset."

"Well, yeah. How are you going to get a girl's hopes up like that?"

Otis grinned. "About a week later, we were going for a walk. And we stopped at the oldest olive tree on the path. I said, 'Penelope, I have a surprise for you. Just a little gift. No

Chapter 6

big deal. But I think you'll like it.' Then, I reached into my pocket and pulled out a silk handkerchief and handed it to her. She'd always wanted one, and silk wasn't all that easy to come by in Ithaca, so she was ecstatic. She looked at it and rubbed it against her soft face and thanked me several times before she noticed the ring in my other hand. After the initial shock wore off, she said yes—and proceeded to soak the handkerchief with happy tears."

"My goodness," the queen said with delight. "I do believe you're going to have to stop talking now. One more word, and I just might fall in love with you right here and now."

The two shared a laugh and finished their walk along the dark water's edge. It was the first time since leaving home that Otis could genuinely remember what it felt like to be happy, and he was grateful for the visit from that memory.

As the ocean's twinkling ripples swallowed that day's sun, Otis stepped out of the warm bronze tub, closed his eyes, and let out a happy sigh. For one reason or another, he couldn't shake the warm embrace of optimism. He wrapped himself in a cozy robe before stepping over the threshold that divided the balcony from the guest quarters.

A gentle series of knocks coming from the door made him think the queen was stopping by for an evening visit, but when he told her to enter, it was the woodcutter who walked in. Otis greeted the young man, who responded with silence as he carried a mixed stack of apple- and cherrywood.

The woodcutter headed for the balcony, keeping one eye over his shoulder, fixated on the door he'd just entered. Otis sat on the edge of the bed and dug his bare toes into the floor.

Much like the guards roaming about, the woodcutter had been given specific instructions not to speak to any guests. Otis didn't know this, but since the woodcutter had practically ignored him up to this point, Otis was caught off guard when the strange man sneaked back in and began to whisper into Otis's ear.

"Shhhh," the woodcutter warned. "We haven't got much time."

Puzzled, Otis reared back and quickly noticed the grave concern radiating from the woodcutter's eyes.

"You're in terrible danger."

"What are you tal—"

The woodcutter placed a finger over his own mouth and shushed Otis.

"Before you came here, were you locked in a cell with a giant snake?"

Otis nodded, equal parts concern and curiosity.

"And it left you alone, for the most part?"

Otis nodded again.

"Where do I start?" the woodcutter asked, keeping his voice hushed. "For years she's fed that snake more men than I can count. But every once in a while, it'll ignore one. When that happens, the queen gets it into her head that she's meant to spend eternity with that man, and she moves him into this room to see if he's worthy of being her husband."

"She said her husband died just a few months ago."

"What? No," the woodcutter replied. "He died fifteen years ago. She poisoned him."

The searing weight of fear began to push down on Otis's shoulders and chest. "Whenever a new man comes in, she puts

Chapter 6

him in this room. At first, they seem grateful—even thrilled by the accommodations. But eventually, they ask for something they don't have. They always want more. So she says. One man insisted that fresh fruit and milk be delivered to his room every morning. Another asked for that bronze tub out there. No one's made it more than a month before she labels them as greedy. This room and all its amenities were designed and handpicked by the ghosts of previous guests. And the reason it's been painted black is because that's the only color that will hide the bloodstains.

"She's not right—in her mind," the woodcutter said. "She's got this mirror in her room that she talks to. And she thinks it talks back to her. But the voices are just inside her head. I know you're expecting to leave here soon. But you need to know that she will never let that happen. She's going to keep you here and groom you to be her husband unless she decides to kill you first."

"She told me there was a passenger freight coming, and that I'd be on it when it left," Otis said.

"She's lying."

Otis stood up and ran his fingers over his forehead and through his thick hair. "I have to go. I have to leave—right now."

"Out of the question. You leave now, and she will have you followed and killed. She controls every mode of transportation on and off the island. The only way you're getting out of here alive is if you have outside help come get you. Even then, it's likely a death sentence. She has eyes and ears everywhere."

Otis sat silent for a lingering moment. "What can I do?"

"Bide your time. Don't ask for anything. I—I've hidden some ink and a small book filled with blank paper under your

Odyssey Tale

firewood on the balcony. Once a week, someone will come by to collect your milk bottles. As long as you don't do it every week, they won't notice when you keep one. Write for help, stuff the paper in a bottle, and toss it as far as you can off that balcony."

"Then what?"

"Pray that it lands on another island."

"Can I write one up now and send it with you?" Otis asked.

"Oh, no," the woodcutter said. "They don't do it often, but every once in a while they search me on the way out. I've helped all I can. I wish I could do more, but I've got my kids to think about. As I said before, she's got eyes and ears everywhere."

"Why are you helping me at all, then?" Otis asked.

"My father served in the Trojan War. He was too old to fight and had no business being there. But what's right is right, he always used to say. Anyway, he suffered a large cut to his leg and probably would've bled to death if you hadn't been there to wrap it in a tourniquet."

"Oh," Otis said, surprised.

"My family and I have and always will be grateful for what you did. And I wish I could do more to help you now. But I can't. Good luck, Otis. May the gods be with you.

Chapter 7

It was a rather dreary and crisp morning. Chilly winds and the pitter-patter of raindrops plagued the windows all throughout the castle. As the Calypso Queen dipped her breakfast bread into a small plate of wine to soften it, she looked across the table at Otis and noticed his lack of cheerfulness as compared to previous mornings. "Something the matter?" she asked.

"What? No," Otis replied. "Just not that hungry today for some reason." His pasty complexion and tired eyes made him look as though he was coming down with some sort of illness. A fake smile soon followed as he inquired about the passenger freight.

"It should be here any day. Any moment, actually," the queen said. "How's your meal?"

"Good. Very good," Otis said.

The words left behind by the woodcutter were starting to dig further into Otis's core; with his weak appetite, he struggled to force down the tiniest bite of bacon. "I can't tell you enough how grateful I am for all your help and hospitality."

"And I can't tell you enough that you need to stop thanking me. It's truly no bother at all."

"Still. I feel I'm beginning to overstay my welcome," he said.

"Nonsense."

"Are you sure you don't prefer I find a room in town? It's really no bother. I won't be offended. You've done so much for me since I've been here. I'd hate for it to reach a point where either of us feels as though I've taken advantage of your kindness."

"Otis," she said, locking her eyes with his and cracking a small smile. "Don't make me beg you to stay. I can't in good conscience let you leave here just to end up in one of those rat-infested hostels while your room here just collects dust."

It was the first time she'd referred to the guest quarters as his, and he felt the back of his neck grow warm.

"As long as you say so."

"And you're quite sure you have everything you need? Fresh linens, food, water? Firewood?"

"Yes, Your Majesty. I can't think of a single thing I've wanted for since my arrival—with the exception of a visit from my wife and son, of course."

For an instant within an instant, Otis caught a glimpse of raging jealousy beaming across the table.

"She really is the luckiest woman in the world. True love is hard to come by these days. It's only more difficult to maintain when you love someone who has monetary incentive to love you back."

"That's a sad way to look at it," Otis said, struggling to chew and swallow another bite of bacon.

"It sure is," she said. "But it's true, unfortunately." She lowered her eyes to an empty spot on the table and stared into the past for several moments. The clanging rhythm of armored footsteps broke her from her trance as she turned her attention

Chapter 7

to a guard who had just entered. He approached her from the left and leaned down to whisper, staring at Otis with a look suggesting that he close his ears and mind his own business.

"Oh, my," the queen said, with false surprise. "Well, that's awful. Send out as many men as we can spare, and keep me informed. In the meantime, see if we can get someone to fill in for him temporarily."

The guard stomped out of the room, closing the heavy door behind him.

"What's wrong?" Otis asked.

She let out a phony sigh of concern. "I'm afraid the man who delivers our firewood has gone missing, along with his children."

Otis carefully swallowed a nervous lump. "That is awful," he said, raising his eyebrows.

"It's just so uncharacteristic. He's always been dependable, barely leaves his property. I'm already starting to fear the worst."

"How old are they?" Otis asked.

"Who?"

"His children."

"Oh. I'm not sure. Young. Maybe four to six. Somewhere in there."

"Maybe I can go out and help some of your men look for them," Otis said, his insides swelling with petrified guilt. "They've got to be on the island somewhere, no?"

"They do. But my men are the very best. They'll find them. I just pray nothing bad has happened to any of them. My late husband and I tried our best to make this island a safe place to live. But, sometimes, bad things happen here. "Hopefully, they find them soon, though," the queen said. "We're going to need more firewood before long."

That night, Otis lay in the bronze tub. Despite the warm water encasing him from the neck down, the frosty air chilling his damp hair and face made his entire body feel as though it was covered with ice. He didn't want to believe that the queen knew about his conversation with the woodcutter. Even more, he didn't want to believe that she had anything to do with the disappearance of him and his children. However, it was difficult for him to shake the intuitional suggestion that she had known and that she was involved. *Such timing.*

He rose from the tub and drip-dried on the balcony before walking to the ledge, staring at the pitch-black sky as it rested on an even darker ocean. In the distance, he spotted the incoming flicker of candlelight. It twinkled through a series of estate room windows, lining a slow-moving passenger freight.

"Heh," he said, feeling a bit relieved.

Otis slipped further into the night and into the soft cotton sheets pinning him to the plush mattress. He closed his eyes, keeping them shut through the entirety of the night, but he never fell asleep. As the red sun carried the new morning into view, he pried his body out of bed and listened to a series of cracks and pops work their way from his toes and ankles and then up to his neck. After a thorough stretch and a lukewarm bath, he left the guest quarters and joined the queen for breakfast.

"Good morning," he said, stepping into the dining hall.

Chapter 7

For the first time since his arrival, Otis felt the dominating presence of the queen's mood. She had a supernatural ability to control the ambiance of the entire room, as a thick and somber humidity radiated from her chair. With light and curious footsteps, Otis approached his usual seat and sat down.

"Good morning," she said, finally acknowledging his presence.

"Everything OK?" he asked.

"No...no, I'm afraid not. Still no word on the woodcutter or his children." She stared out the window as if looking for answers. "Did he say anything to you? At all?"

"The woodcutter?" Otis asked.

"Any of the times he came into your room?"

Otis felt his heart begin to race. "No. Not a word, in fact. Why?"

"It's just—some of the people we talked to said he was acting very peculiar the day after his last delivery here."

"Hmmm," Otis mumbled. "I didn't notice anything out of the ordinary. But I don't know what he's usually like. What do you think?"

"Honestly," she said, scraping her thumb across her chin, "I have no idea. There is some good news, though. The passenger freight has arrived. You should be leaving here in a few days."

"That is good news," Otis said. "Although, given the circumstances, it feels bittersweet. Is there anything I can do to help—with the search efforts?"

"My men are on top of it," she said. "And they'll get to the bottom of it."

After breakfast, with an armored guard on either side, the queen took gentle and graceful steps down to the castle's lower level. Once she'd reached a certain depth, the smell of death and moldy, iron-rich air plugged her nostrils.

"Let's make this quick," she said, glaring at one of her guards.

She nodded her eyes at a warped wooden door, prompting him to open it and reveal a dim, musty dungeon. Inside, strapped to a rack with ropes around his wrists and ankles, lay the woodcutter. His face had been beaten and was swelling as though it had pockets of water amassing beneath his skin.

"Please, no," he cried. "No more."

The queen stood in front of him with a stoic and unapologetic stare. "Are you ready to start telling me the truth?" she asked.

"I have told you the truth," he said, sobbing through each syllable. "I didn't say a word, and I don't know how you got it into your mind that I did." The panic surging through his heart almost made him forget about the excruciating pain stabbing his back, hips, shins, and ankles.

"It's never taken you more than half a minute per room to deliver firewood, yet you were in there with Otis for over three. What—did you tell him?"

"I don't know what you want me to say," he cried. "I swear. I didn't tell him anything."

"Then what were you doing in there for all that time?"

"I already told you; I tipped my cart on the balcony and had to pick it all up. Then I had to broom up the dust."

Chapter 7

"OK," she said. "I've heard enough. My patience is wearing thin." She ran her polished black fingertips over the bruises where his thumbs had been clamped.

"I'm going to go see Otis and ask him what happened while you were in there. You better pray that he tells me the same thing you just did. Because if he doesn't, I'm going to kill your kids."

As she and the guards turned to leave the room, the woodcutter finally began to cooperate. "Stop," he said. "Don't. I'll tell you everything. Just don't hurt my children."

She turned back to face the broken woodcutter with a satisfied grin.

Up on the guest quarters' balcony, Otis took advantage of another soak in the bronze tub and began to envision getting his own for his balcony back in Ithaca. Now that he'd actually seen the passenger freight with his own eyes, dragon-sized butterflies swirled in his belly as a whole new battle of nerves began to rage inside him. An ambush of harsh realities consumed his afternoon. While he'd only been gone for roughly four years, they were difficult years and had taken a tremendous toll on his mind and body.

What if she's forgotten about the love we shared? What if I don't look how she expects me to? Little did Otis know that he and Penelope were tied together with these thoughts, as she had the same fears regarding his return. She couldn't fathom a life in which he didn't love her with as much passion and vigor as he did when he left. And her biggest fear, outside of him being dead, was that Otis would return a different man. She worried that the man he'd become would have no use for her anymore. She even feared that he might return to Ithaca with a new true love.

And perhaps this new mystery woman was the reason he'd been gone for so long.

Down in the dungeon, still strapped to the rack, the woodcutter felt his heart weigh heavy with anticipation of the queen's next words.

"Thank you," she said, gently. "It's just unfortunate that you couldn't have told me this sooner. Otherwise, your children might still be alive."

"What? No," he cried. "You said you wouldn't hurt them."

"And I didn't. I don't think I can, the way they are now."

"No," he said, losing control. "You didn't."

"No. *I* didn't," she said, with fictitious sympathy. "It seems that one of your neighbors found out they were alone. He dressed up like an old woman and lured them over to his house with promises of candy and other sweets. Once he got them there—and this is so awful; I'm so sorry you have to hear this from me—once he got them there, he burned them alive in his oven."

Tears streamed down the woodcutter's bloody face as several piercing howls echoed through the dungeon chambers. His entire body went limp, and he privately prayed for death.

"Where does one learn such violent behavior?" she asked. "Is it something they're taught? Or maybe something inside them? I mean, whoever heard of such a thing? I just wish you would have confessed sooner. Maybe you would have been there to stop it. Pity. I guess we'll never know."

The queen walked out of the dungeon, invigorated. Once out, and with the door shut behind her, she turned to her loyal

Chapter 7

guards. "Kill him," she said, assigning the one to her left with the task. "As for you," she said to the other, "go pay the warlock his fee, and once his guard is down, kill him. I'm thinking the official story will be that the woodcutter died trying to save them, but several trusted members of the queen's guard arrived and killed the witch, just in the nick of time, saving the children. People love a good close-call story."

"Will it be a problem that the kids are, uh—"

"No," she exclaimed with buoyancy. "No one needs to know they're not alive. We'll say that between the trauma and the fact that they have no family on this island, it was in their best interest to leave here. Just make sure there's a written record to show they were on the passenger freight, in case any of the gossips start to pick apart the official story. Once it's on paper, spread the word. The queen's men are heroes."

"What do you want me to do with Otis?"

"Mmmm, yes. Otis," she said. "Let me sleep on it. I still haven't decided what I want to do with him just yet."

Otis rubbed his pruning fingertips together under the surface of the hot bathwater. With a wet washcloth resting over his face, he continued to fantasize about his return home. At first, his thoughts were pleasant and jubilant. As the steam escaped his washcloth, however, more harsh realities began to arrive. *What if they're no longer living in Ithaca? What if they're no longer living? No. I can't—I won't—believe that.*

"I've missed you so much," he said, using his imagination to look into Penelope's eyes. "More than you know."

"Well," the queen answered, "I've missed you too."

Otis ripped the washcloth off his face and sat up in the bronze tub. "Your Majesty, I was just—"

Before he knew what was happening, two armored guards placed a sheet of wood on top of the tub, holding one of the edges against Otis's throat.

"What the hell are you doing?" he asked.

"Why don't you tell me?" She sashayed to a nearby stack of firewood and retrieved a few logs before bringing them back and placing them on a tiny fire beneath the tub.

"What are you doing?" he asked, beginning to feel the heat of the rising flame.

"The woodcutter told me everything that he told you," she said.

"So?" Otis replied. "I didn't believe any of it."

"Then you're a poor judge of character," she said. "I'm afraid that he was telling you the truth."

"Please let me out of here. I'll do anything you ask." He raised his body off the tub's floor as the surface tried to sear his skin.

"I'm afraid it won't be that easy," she said, taking a seat and running the back of her fingertips down his cheek. "I love you, Otis. I've loved you since the first time I looked in your eyes. I saw the hurt. It's the same hurt that I've felt most of my life, and I never thought for one second that I'd meet someone who shared it with me. Yet here you are. And I thought I had you all to myself. But then you mentioned her. Again. Now, I don't know what she could possibly have that I can't give you. But I do know that you and I are meant to be together. Someday, hopefully sooner than later, you'll know it too."

Chapter 7

Otis's forehead poured sweat as the excruciating heat began to coat his insides with nausea. The queen stood up, prompting the guards to remove the dense barrier. Otis burst from the tub. His red and blistering body crashed on the balcony, trying to soak up any relief it could from the cold concrete.

"Your only son has no idea who you are," she said. "And surely, Penelope has moved on. Even if they haven't, they'll never be able to love you like I do, Otis." She nodded one of the guards toward the woodpile.

He promptly walked to it before kicking it over and revealing a book of blank paper and a small bottle of ink.

As bits of Otis's skin peeled off and cooled to that of the air's temperature, the queen smashed the bottle, making the ink disappear on the concrete. "From now on," she said, "there will be no more secrets between us." She reached down for the book of paper and tossed it over the balcony ledge.

Otis turned his burning body sideways and into the fetal position as uncontrollable whimpers caused tremors to run over his entire body.

"Now get some rest and heal, my darling," she whispered into his ear. "It's been a very long day for everyone."

She and her guards left the room as Otis gathered enough strength to stand. He considered throwing himself off the balcony. He stared for hours at the raging waters, crashing into the jagged rocks below. But he couldn't do it. There was still a sliver of hope.

It may have been hubris or just a lack of attention to detail, but the queen failed to notice that one sheet of paper had been ripped out of that book. And one milk bottle was unaccounted for. Indeed, there was a sliver of hope. While the value and

Odyssey Tale

shelf life of that sliver were both in question, Otis was willing to wait it out, as another ten years slogged ahead, and she kept him locked away.

Chapter 8

Several thousand treacherous ocean miles southwest of Calypso Island sat a small yet rambunctious port known as Junction. Its year-round tropical climate made it a pleasant place to visit in terms of views and comfort, but its reputation for corruption, indecency, and sinfulness attracted only the harshest kinds of people. While the distant docks of Port Royal prided themselves on offering any and all vices to those willing to pay, the bustling little metropolis of Port Junction was where these vices had been birthed.

Hidden by shadows just outside the town's main drag was a shoddy two-story log cabin known by locals and visitors as the Point. Inside, thick clouds of smoke and the upbeat tune of a saloon piano drenched the sticky air, as a handful of women took part in the oldest profession known to mankind. The place was always loud and crowded and only became more so as the night burrowed into the early-morning hours.

Upstairs, behind one of many locked doors, a young man in his early twenties sat on the edge of a squeaky bed and combed his rough fingers through his wild hair.

"There were probably fifty orphans on that ship," he said to the young woman lying beside him. "Maybe even a hundred."

Odyssey Tale

"My goodness," she said.

"Yeah." His boastful manner filled the room, silencing the crowd and piano downstairs. "And the fire was so big. I honestly didn't think I was gonna make it out of there."

"You're so brave," she said, sitting up and wrapping her arms around his slender frame.

"If I've learned one thing in this life, it's that a man's got to be brave if he wants to do the right thing. Anyway, I didn't notice till just now, but it seems that the fire got ahold of my britches and burned a hole through my left pocket. And that's where I usually keep my, uh—my coins. So I'm little light on funds at the moment. But I'll be back in a month or so, and I swear I'll pay you what I owe you, plus some for the trouble. Is that all right?"

Normally, the young woman would roll her eyes at such an excuse and the dirty vermin who'd come up with it. All she had to do was yell out to security, and they'd throw him out on the street, face first. But there was something intoxicating about this dreamy young man, and something comforting in his honest emerald eyes.

"I suppose that would be OK," she said.

"Thank you. So much. I can't believe I didn't notice sooner. I feel like such an asshole."

Downstairs, two rugged members of the young man's crew, who also appeared to be in their early twenties, sat opposite each other at a wobbly, ring-stained wooden table. The red-haired ruffians took turns nipping sips from a dwindling bottle of whiskey as a young maiden approached and helped herself to a seat.

She looked them both up and down and noticed they were identical twins—something she'd heard of before but had never

Chapter 8

seen. "Well, I'll be," she said. "In all my years, I've never seen such a handsome devil. And lucky me, there's two of you. What do you say the three of us go upstairs, and you show me if you're—exactly the same?"

Neither answered the charming young woman, but that didn't hinder her persistence. "What are your names?" she asked, running her soft fingers over one of their beards.

"I'm One," One said. "He's Two. And both of us have zero interest in anything you have to offer, sweetheart. Beat it." One nodded her away from the table, and she sulked away. As she disappeared into the smoky crowd, One and Two were bombarded by another visitor. This time, it was a portly young man named Tootles, who was also part of their crew.

"Oh, man, this place is incredible," Tootles said, taking a seat. "You guys are missing out."

"That was quick," Two said.

"Shiiiit," Tootles replied in a mocking tone. "That girl's gonna need at least two days of rest after what just happened up there. I had her hotter than a two-shekel dagger."

"Looks like she's cooled off," One said.

"And she don't look all that tired," Two added.

All three glanced toward the crowded bar and noticed the girl Tootles had just been with upstairs. She was quite awake and was acquiring her next customer.

Several stools away, the young woman who had just been told that ridiculous orphan and fire story was in the process of handing over a percentage of her nightly earnings to the manager working behind the bar. The manager was a rather gruff and homely woman. Her sharp, no-nonsense attitude and even sharper temper were hard to take seriously, as they were often paired with a tight, bobbing bun of frizzy gray hair that resembled a bird's nest clinging to the top of her head.

"Where the hell's the rest of it?" the manager asked.

"My last customer. He said he lost all his coins on his previous job—saving some orphan children. Isn't that sweet?"

"What?" the manager asked, tilting her head.

"He said he'd pay me back in a month or so when he returns. Plus some."

"You stupid dunce. That's the dumbest thing I've ever heard."

"Normally, I'd agree. But this one seems different."

"Where is he?" the manager asked, almost in disbelief.

The young woman glanced around the room until she spotted the handsome rascal. "Over there. Coming down the stairs."

"Him?"

"Yeah."

"His last job wasn't saving orphan children, you dumb cow. It was retrieving a load of rum that some pirates highjacked several weeks ago. And I know the little bastard has coins because I just gave him a whole sack of 'em. Hey Pan. Paaan!" the manager hollered across the room.

Back at the wobbly wooden table, One, Two, and Tootles watched as several beefy security guards headed for the stairs.

"Looks like Pete's gettin' us thrown out of another whorehouse," Two said. He then took one last pull from the whiskey bottle.

Several moments later, Pete Pan—or Peter, as he was more commonly known—was thrown face first out the front door and down several steps into the muddy street. The rest of the group was asked politely yet firmly to leave.

Chapter 8

Once all were outside, the manager planted her feet in the threshold. "And stay the hell out," she screamed. "You're a disgrace to Lost Boys everywhere."

A fifth member of the crew, Nibs, had been outside on a rocking chair, smoking and staring up at the stars. "Another one? Really?" he asked.

The manager stomped back inside and approached her lead security guard. "I think there's one more in here somewhere," she said.

"No. I think he was outside all night."

"Not that one," the manager exclaimed, scanning the crowd. "There's another one—an older one. You and Roscoe check upstairs. That'll be the last time I ever hire a Lost Boy crew to do anything. Dirty sons of bitches."

Upstairs, the last remaining member of the crew watched from a bedroom window as Peter dragged his tongue over his teeth to scrape off the grainy clumps of mud. "I'll be eating sand for the next six months."

"Oh, not again," the man muttered. He turned away from the window toward a sink and mirror on the other side of the room and cupped some water in his hands before gently patting it over his middle-aged face.

The young woman with whom he'd just been intimate still lay in bed, her blushed face and giggly manner still overwhelmed. "What did you just do to me?" she asked, tapping the tips of her fingers over her numbing cheeks. "That was amazing. I mean, I say that to every slob who walks through that door, but I can't recall a time—ever—where it was true. Not to say you're a slob. Quite the opposite, actually."

Odyssey Tale

The man's initial response of silence made her a bit self-conscious, but a few moments later, he relieved her worries. "You don't have to make up stories just to boost my ego," he said, smirking.

"Do you know when you're going to be passing back this way?" she asked, sitting up and concealing herself with a thin bedsheet.

"Not yet. But I will be back." He cupped another puddle of water in his hands and splashed it over his face.

"What's your name?" she asked, despite knowing that particular question was against house rules.

He knew she wasn't just boosting his ego. And he knew there was something special about him. In fact, those who knew him well didn't think of him as a man at all. Over the years, his Greek-god physique, luminescent presence, and ability to perform what could only be explained as magic set him apart from everyone he encountered. He had answered to many different names over the years, but now, as a free man who'd spent most of his life enslaved, he only responded to one.

"Jinni."

"Jinni. I've never heard that before." She continued speaking. It was something or other about unique names she'd encountered over the years. "Not on the job, of course, but you know—just out in the world." She went on and trailed off as everything in Jinni's world went silent.

Sitting on the ledge of her sink was a milk bottle with a rolled-up sheet of paper inside. Jinni gave the bottle a pensive look and wrapped his fingers around the top.

"Where did you get this?" he asked, privately growing terrified.

Chapter 8

"What?"

He brought the bottle close to his face and took note of several large stingers piercing through it. They resembled what could only be described as overgrown pine needles that had been doused in turquoise ink.

"Oh, that," she said, laughing. "Had a guy try to pay me with it one time."

Jinni pulled the cork from the bottle and carefully slid the paper out before unrolling it over the nightstand.

"You wouldn't believe what some guys try to pass off as payment these days."

Jinni ignored her every word as he studied the document with meticulous focus.

"One guy even tried to pay me with some old soybeans," she said. "Soybeans. Can you believe that? Tried telling me they were magic. Whoever heard of such nonsense?"

"Have you read this?" Jinni asked, never taking his eyes off the note.

"Yeah. A whole bunch of times. Still don't know if it's actually from him, though. I heard he was dead."

"Yeah. That's what I heard too," he said.

"And it was like that when it came here," she added. "Those little blue things sticking out. And that one passage where the ink's faded. I could never quite make it out. Can you?"

"No." The very sight of those little stingers made him petrified, but he couldn't put the bottle down. "Is it OK if I keep this?"

"What's it worth to ya?" she asked, raising flirtatious eyebrows.

It was around this time that security guards kicked in the door.

"You. Time to go," the manager said. "And tell your scumbag captain that if he ever shows his face in here again, he's gonna die an extremely young man. Got it?"

Jinni didn't have much of a reaction. His fears were still reserved for that bottle. "I got it," he said.

The manager and guards stayed to watch as Jinni finished getting dressed. While they didn't place their hands on him, the guards were invasive with their presence as they escorted him down the stairs and to the front door. Just as Jinni was about to step on the porch and make a successful, incident-free exit, the young woman he'd been with shouted out in horror.

"He stole my Otis bottle! He stole my Otis bottle! Stop him."

Jinni locked eyes with the security guards, who had already started walking back to their posts, and the chase was on. Jinni ran out the front door, leaped off the porch and into the muddy street. The two guards followed in close pursuit.

He could hear them starting to breathe heavily and smiled, knowing that he was just getting warmed up. He sprinted so hard and so fast through the crowd that both he and the guards blasted right past Peter, Nibs, Tootles, One, and Two without noticing any of them.

Peter and Tootles were in line for some street meat, as a grouchy old woman with a heavy smoker's cough slow-cooked lush piles of red meat on a cast-iron skillet.

"Why is it that every time we stop for food at the end of the night, it's only the skinniest and fattest ones eating?"

"Shut up, Two," Tootles said, turning around and stepping forward.

Chapter 8

"Why don't you make me, Tittles?" Two said, reaching up and pinching Tootles's nipple and surrounding flesh.

"Why don't both of you shut up?" Peter said, turning away from his place in line. As Peter turned back around, the unpleasant woman taking orders was already staring through him as if he had just wasted the last thirty years of her life.

"Ahem," she said.

"Yeah. Sorry. I'll take the, uh—"

She turned her head away from the counter and began coughing uncontrollably in every direction, and very close to the meat she was about to serve.

"Ribeye," Peter said deflated.

"Me too," Tootles said.

She responded with a wet cough, causing both to recoil.

"Hold the gravy," Tootles said. "Actually, you can just hold mine altogether," he added, before stepping away.

Peter handed over a few shekels in exchange for the steaming plate. "You know you can skip one every once in a while," he said, raising his fingers to his mouth to make a smoking gesture.

"Just take your plate and get out of here, wiseass."

The group walked away, laughing all the way back to their vessel, the *Elvira*. As they stepped on board, Tootles began to hassle Peter for his last remaining bits of fat and gristle.

"No," Peter said, shielding his plate from Tootles's pudgy fingers. "You was standing right behind me, and you didn't get any, so you ain't getting any of this. You're always pullin' this shit too."

Peter, One, Two, and Tootles stomped belowdecks to find the last remaining member of their crew, Slightly. Slightly lay awake in bed, groggy from the laudanum sitting on his nightstand.

"Back so soon?" he asked, his eyes half shut.

"Pete got us thrown out of another whorehouse," One said.

"Nuh-uh." Slightly gently placed his forearm over his eyes.

"Be careful with this stuff," Peter said, picking up the laudanum bottle.

Slightly nodded. "I will. I am. Just wanted to get a good night's sleep while we were docked."

As Tootles disappointedly watched Peter throw the final bite of rich steak fat to Cecil the cat, Jinni rushed down from above deck and closed the hatch behind him. He was covered in mud, out of breath, and wearing clothes that he hadn't been wearing when he left the Point.

"What the hell happened to you?" Peter asked.

"Those guys were faster than I thought," Jinni said, struggling to catch his breath.

"Why were they chasing ya?" Nibs asked.

"I found something." Jinni raised a rolled and tattered piece of paper to eye level and grinned. "You guys need to see this.

Chapter 9

The *Elvira* wasn't the most massive mode of transport in her day, but what she lacked in size, she made up for in the spirit carried by her youthful passengers. The seasoned and splintery craft was hued in several tones, as a patchwork of different woods and stains had been used to conceal her scars over the years. Great white sails fluttered like bedsheets drying out in a summer breeze and complemented the skulls that had been crudely stenciled on both sides of her bow. From a distance, they looked like classic pirate skulls, but up close, a pair of lifeless red tongues dangling from jagged teeth and dagger handles protruding from all four eye sockets were quite noticeable. These were the marks of the Lost Boys.

As the *Elvira* sailed off into the night winds and away from the jubilant Port Junction coast, Peter, Slightly, and Jinni were the only ones still above deck. The group hovered around the sturdy flicker of an oil lamp as Slightly unrolled a tattered map.

"Look," Jinni said, prodding his finger on the musty, yellowing paper. "Right there. Ithaca's not more than two days off our path."

"Slow down," Peter said. "We don't even know if we can stretch our provisions out another two days."

"I talked to Tootles about it already," Slightly said. "Shouldn't be a problem."

"Thanks, Slightly." Peter said. "Way to keep your mouth shut."

"Come on, Pete," Jinni pleaded. "Let's at least go to Ithaca. If Otis hasn't made it back, and there's still no word on what happened to him, maybe we can find a clue as to where we can start looking."

"This whole thing sounds like a lot of fun," Peter sneered. "But I'm looking to get paid."

"Pete—"

"Shut up and let me finish, Jinni. I don't know where Otis Seehus is—any more than you or anybody in Ithaca does. But I'll tell you what I do know. I know that he's dead. He died in the war. That's common knowledge and has been for a while now."

"But it's not true," Jinni said.

"Git the hell outta here—not true," Peter scoffed.

"The war was over. Otis and two other guys left on a small cargo carrier, and no one ever saw any of 'em again."

"Yeah," Peter said, pinching the bridge of his nose. "That's what happens when people die. You don't ever see them again."

Jinni stood up. "Whatever you say."

"I'm telling you, this is a wild goose chase. That note is probably a fake. You said yourself, some guy tried to use it to pay the whore you stole it from. Trust me, I've done a lot weirder to get out of payin' a whore."

"That's the part that worries me, Jinni," Slightly said. "How can we possibly commit to this thing without knowing for sure the note is real?"

Chapter 9

"We can't," Peter said. "Even if it is real, the part where he tells us where we can actually find him—it ain't in there. It's smudged. That's convenient."

"No, no. You can make out some of the letters—if you look close enough. I was going to have Nibs take a look tomorrow when we can get some daylight on it. See if he can come up with some town or island names based on the placement of the letters."

"Gimme that," Peter said with a hostile reach.

As Jinni handed over the Otis letter, a gust of wind ripped it from their fingertips, out of sight and into the ocean.

"Nice," Peter said, casting blaming eyes on Jinni. "At least we still have the bottle."

"What if it's not a fake?" Jinni asked. "Do you guys have any idea what kind of fame and fortune would come if we saved Otis Seehus? We'll all be able to retire fifty times over. We'll never have to buy another drink, or whore, as long as we live."

"I don't want to retire," Peter said, on the fringes of feeling insulted.

"The whore and money part sounds OK, though," Slightly added.

"Shut up," Peter said.

"You guys are missing the point," Jinni said with a blunt sigh. "I don't want to retire either. But if we do this, and we succeed, not only will this job come with an unbelievable amount of wealth, but we'll be able to get any rate we want going forward—on any job. Ever. Worst-case scenario, we'll snag a delivery job for a shipment headed to Nestor Island. Come on, Pete. It's barely out of the way. Easy money."

Peter thoughtfully rubbed the peach fuzz on his chin. "I don't know."

"First round's on me." Jinni had to stop himself from smiling, knowing he had delivered the final blow.

"What the hell," Peter said. "Why not?"

"That's first round of drinks," Jinni said. "Not whores. Just so we're clear on that."

Over a groggy high-noon breakfast, everyone else on board was informed of the new changes to the schedule and navigational patterns. The rhythmic pitter-patter of raindrops plopping on deck was nonstop throughout the day as the *Elvira* sliced through fog that refused to dissipate.

The heavy, battling breaths of One and Two manipulated the airborne moisture as their swords collided during intense fencing practice. They were extremely competitive when it came to any contest in which they went head to head—always trying to gain the upper hand as to which *version* of the pair was superior. Each proudly laid claim to the title, but it often changed hands depending on what kind of competition they had just endured. The results of their footraces and fencing often leaned in favor of One, while speed swimming and archery were more Two's forte.

Should there have been any controversy as to which of them actually won, a fistfight was sure to follow, the winner of which would be anyone's guess, as they were quite evenly matched in their pugilistic talents. During the rare times they weren't arguing or physically fighting about some trivial nonsense, they were the best of friends, and each would've gladly given up his own life if it meant saving the other.

Chapter 9

Slightly was the *Elvira*'s navigator. He was a quiet fellow, but it wasn't from a lack of confidence. He just wasn't much of a conversationalist and often thought that if his voice annoyed others as much as their voices annoyed him, he'd do everyone a favor and just keep quiet. Still, he had plenty of personality and was a dashing and debonair young man. When he did speak, he could do so as a proper gentleman, or he could string together the types of words that would make even the most daring of brothel managers turn red in the cheek. It really just depended on whom he was with and what he was after at that particular moment.

Not counting Jinni, Nibs was the eldest Lost Boy of this respective charter. Nibs was also a notorious ladies' man. He had the looks, charm, and silver tongue necessary to live up to the Lost Boy reputation. He wasn't a jerk or a chauvinist, but he did project the blind confidence and flirtatious manner of one. And despite his being the sharpest person and most profound thinker in most of the rooms he entered, Nibs often had the most fun playing the role of a deaf-mute or airheaded fool.

Almost every night, he gazed up at the stars with his paintbrush and recreated the night sky that surrounded them, all the while wondering what it would be like to sail through the heavens. Nibs and people like him were often referred to as sky sailors. They were born at the wrong time, maybe in the wrong universe. Their vibrant imaginations were hindered only by the limitations of reality. As often as Nibs fantasized about one day navigating the bright celestial planes, he couldn't help but conclude that it just wasn't meant to be. Perhaps his mortal eyes simply weren't equipped to handle such splendor and beauty.

Then, there was Tootles. There's not much to say about Tootles that his name didn't say on its own. He was a dirty, clumsy slob and by far the laziest person onboard. But he was loyal, handy with a bow and arrow, and second to none when it came to calculating the proper number of provisions needed for a given journey.

Two often joked that the only reason Tootles was so good at his job was because he couldn't stand the thought of missing a single meal.

Wherever they were, whatever they were doing, one thing was always evident: Peter was their fierce and trusted captain. He may have despised the title, but he was undoubtedly the sole authority on and off the *Elvira*. He didn't have anyone to answer to, and he didn't give a damn if anyone liked him or his decisions.

To his men, this was part of the appeal. While all captains wanted to be liked, Peter's calm assuredness worked effortlessly to maintain love, loyalty, and respect from his crew. His deeds and decisions were always pending his own final approval, but one thing that set him apart from other captains was that he was always willing to accept counsel—even though most of the time, the only counsel he actually took to heart came from Jinni.

They all wanted to be more like Peter. They all wanted Peter's approval. And they all wanted this team to last forever, with him as their captain, even though they knew it could not.

While Jinni was a relatively new acquaintance and had been hired only two years earlier, the rest of the guys had grown up together in a home for children whose parents had either died or left them. It was a large plantation, somewhere in the Americas, in a place they affectionately referred to as Cherokee

Chapter 9

Country. Some time while in their early teens, they escaped the harsh conditions of forced farm labor and found freedom by living off the land.

They hunted, gathered, and moved from one desolate mountain camp to another before finally hitching a steamboat ride to the eastern seaboard. While in transit, they successfully fended off multiple attacks from hostile Indians and river pirates. By the time the steamboat arrived at its final port, their reputation had preceded them. They were recruited by the Lost Boys and given their very own charter and vessel.

There was a time when Lost Boys could be found in almost any corner of the world. It was the most demanding, deadly work one could ask for. They did the dirty jobs that no one else was willing to do—always in the name of good, but never for free.

An endless number of adventures awaited with the right employer, whether it was a shipment of rum that had been highjacked by pirates, a tobacco delivery in need of armed security, or a personal escort through waters that no one else was willing to travel. Lost Boys were widely believed to be the biggest thrill-seekers of their time, a stereotype that was well earned and proudly hyped.

They had since become a dying breed, however, as a noticeable pattern began to emerge during their peak years. Most Lost Boys were somewhere between the ages of sixteen and twenty-one when they signed on. And many, once they'd reached the age of twenty-one, began to realize that they weren't immortal and that some scars do not heal.

Another reason for the regression in prevalence was that the vast majority of Lost Boys who didn't die before their twenty-first birthdays would eventually get greedy or lazy—or both—and retire into piracy. Old-timers like Jinni were an anomaly within the Lost Boy community. Jobs that were once readily available were no longer being offered, as previous employers became wary that they were contributing capital to a group of impending pirates.

Jinni understood this all too well. Blessed with a unique ability to recognize patterns and use them advantageously, he knew there would soon come a day when Lost Boys were no longer credible or wanted. And when that day should come, individual crews with strong résumés would reign supreme. Jinni had been around long enough to see the writing on the wall. Perhaps this is why he took such an interest in Otis's writing.

At first, Jinni just wanted that note to be real. Then, it grew into something more significant. He *needed* that note to be real. Finally, with help from a little spark deep within his consciousness, his bias was confirmed. He was always receiving signals like this one. They were little moments of clarity that seemed to beam in from somewhere else—somewhere far away. More often than not, these fateful hunches would prove to be correct, but rarely did they ever feel this powerful.

Rarely did they ever feel this important.

Jinni sat in silence on the bow, with his legs crossed, his palms up, and only his mind's eye open to the universe ahead. He could feel the olive-rich beaches of Ithaca pulling him closer and closer as he grew more confident. The note was real. *It was, and always has been, meant for us to find.*

Peter was more of a meat-and-potatoes kind of guy when it came to the religious experience. He was pragmatic, with a hint of Indian culture unique to the Americas. For him, it was more about connecting with nature and the peaceful harmony

Chapter 9

that followed. He could never get used to Jinni's strange spiritual antics. *But to each his own, I s'pose.* Whenever Jinni dove that deep into his personal space, Peter would simply sit back, watch quietly, and wonder. This was one of those times: *What's that crazy bastard gettin' us into now?*

Peter removed his dingy shirt and began to walk around the vessel, letting the cool, breezy mist overtake his scrawny yet chiseled chest. He kept to himself but quickly noticed that everyone around him was working to get better. While there weren't many rules on the *Elvira*, the most essential rule stated that if you ain't gettin' better every day, you better be gettin' off this boat.

While he was proud to see his guys getting better, he knew that they were doing so out of fear. They, too, were starting to see the writing on the wall. And they all knew that when Jinni began to act like this, things were bound to get strange.

One and Two worked their arms ragged amid a heated pull-up contest. Nibs and Tootles were further mastering their archery skills on some unfortunate paper targets and wooden barrels. Slightly studied and redrew some maps that he'd been planning to consolidate for some time. Even Cecil the cat was showcasing a dead rat he had just killed earlier that day.

Peter soon realized that he was the only one on board who wasn't gettin' better. Not one to be outdone by his crew, or cat, Peter walked to the stern and wrapped a length of rope around his ankles and legs. "I'm going for a swim," he said, knotting the rope tight. "Can someone pull me up in about an hour?"

Nibs looked at Peter with a nervous admiration. "Yeah. I gotcha."

Odyssey Tale

Peter dove headfirst off the stern. Instantly, the slack of the rope snapped straight and dragged him through the wake like a wounded whale. He gained control of his posture and rotated his arms as if swimming away from the vessel. It was a rigorous routine, both physically and psychologically, as it brought forth the combined dread of his two greatest fears. The first was drowning. The second was mutiny. Only by chipping away at these fears did Peter believe he would *get better*.

The demanding exercise should have kept his mind focused and occupied, but all he could think about was Jinni, sitting still and silent up ahead on the bow. It felt as though Jinni's already-radiant personality was being amplified into the atmosphere and around the vessel. The powers that manipulated the tiniest wrinkles of the universe wanted him, and those closest to him, to know that he had been correct to trust the note's authenticity.

"There it is." Jinni closed the eye in his mind and opened the eyes on his face to release several tears. It was the feeling and moment he had been waiting for. Otis was still alive, waiting for them to find him.

What's that crazy bastard gettin' us into now?

Chapter 10

Ithaca, at this time, was a rather dark place for some. While she would later regret her lack of gratitude for the roof over her head and clothes on her back, all Penelope could think about was what she didn't have. And that was Otis. As difficult as it had been for her to watch him leave for the war, something in her heart told her that he would make it through just fine. That first year was by far the worst. Every day, her heart would swell with a hurt that only his presence and touch could relieve.

Every pity-filled beat, however, told her that he was alive and well, somewhere. She stood on their balcony every morning, day, and night, patiently waiting for that mystery ship to peek over the horizon. But the more she waited, the less her heart could take. Before long, Penelope's mind took over and convinced her that the best antidote to her heartache was waiting at the bottom of a laudanum bottle. At first, it was.

Never had anything so bitter been so sweet. It wiped away her worries, her pains, and her inability to get a good night's sleep. She'd never felt safer. Not even the warm embrace of Otis's arms could have brought forth the ecstasy contained inside that deceiving little bottle—or pulled her away. Before she knew it, her cares and ambitions had been eroded, and the only task that received her full attention was making sure she procured another bottle before her current one dried out.

Eventually, the glittery glow that came with each pleasant drop became more difficult to achieve. Her feeble attempts to chase and revisit that initial burst of chemical happiness gave Penelope no more relief than before she had started taking it. At first, she blamed it on weak batches, so she took more. But as the daily doses increased, so did her tolerance. The help she sought from that bottle was no longer there, nor was it in any of the bottles that followed.

This would forever be one of the great regrets of her life. She looked back at this time and wished she could visit her younger self. She wished she could have gone back and slapped that first nip right out of her hand and smash the bottle against the wall for good measure. But she could not. She just had to live with her current self as best she could and accept the frustrating fact that she wasn't there. She wasn't there for herself. She wasn't there for her people. Most importantly, she wasn't there for her son, Mac, at a time when he really needed his mother.

He was nearing his sixteenth birthday. It should have been a marvelous time for him, as it was for most young men that age. But the political landscape that came with being a king's sole heir had him on edge. Since Otis was no longer around to claim his throne and was widely presumed dead, Penelope was the sole heir to the throne of Ithaca. However, due to bureaucracy and ancient rules beyond anyone's understanding, her time was limited and running low. If she didn't choose a husband soon, a council of elders would see to it that her son would be named king.

Chapter 10

While this may have seemed like a good thing and the most logical outcome, had it happened, Mac would have been trounced in the struggle that was certain to follow. There existed traditions and terms of honor that prevented anyone who sought the crown from hurting or killing a queen. A king, on the other hand, was always just a shallow breath away from having a knife stuck in his back. If the elders were to make it official, Mac would have been challenged nonstop by battle-hardened soldiers unwilling to bend their knee to a teenager. Mac knew this. Penelope knew this. And dozens of self-proclaimed "suitors" knew it too. They invaded the castle and made themselves at home, waiting for the sand in their proverbial hourglass.

It was a morning like most others that summer in Ithaca. Powerful ocean waves crashed into the base of a large cliff whose peak cradled Otis and Penelope's massive stone castle. The gray, moss-covered structure was as strong as it was old and held several balconies that overlooked an endless blanket of teal sea. On one of those balconies was Mac. He was a slender yet rugged teen, and even though he wasn't much of a morning person, every sunrise found him burrowing through a rigorous routine of push-ups. Once he'd reached the point of exhaustion, he would perform a series of pull-ups on the stocky branch of an olive tree growing near the ledge of his balcony.

To make it in this world, one has to be tough. He'd tell himself these words every morning. It was something that Penelope's mother taught her, that mother taught her, and it was a core value Penelope had instilled in Mac since he was old enough to listen. He would go on to hold these words in exceptionally high regard, having grown up without the guidance or protection most commonly offered by a father.

Odyssey Tale

On most mornings after his exercise, Mac would bathe, get dressed, and peel two navel oranges for breakfast. In recent mornings, however, slight wrinkles were added to his routine. He called them baby steps. Each one alone didn't add up to much, but when put together, and in the proper order, these steps would potentially lead to Mac taking his own life.

It started with feelings, thoughts. *What would it be like—to kill myself? Would I know? Would I regret it? Would it matter?* That was the first step. The next was deciding how. *Which way would be best? Which way would cause the least amount of mess, and the least amount of heartache for my mother?* Soon after answering that question, he found himself in possession of a length of rope. Sitting at the foot of his bed, he'd run his fingers over the harsh twine and place it against the back of his neck, just to see what it felt like on his skin.

Some would have called Mac selfish, but the entire reason he prepared himself to die was not because he feared what the suitors might do to him. He did it so he could ease Penelope's burden. Mac knew that she didn't want to be with anyone but his father, and he figured that if he took his own life, the council would allow her as much time as she saw fit to choose a husband.

Mac soon found his feet clenching the narrow handrail of his balcony. After several jitter-steeped minutes of balancing, Mac stepped down onto the balcony and back into his room. It took longer than it had the previous mornings, but the rushing wave of panic that overtook his midsection finally began to recede. This day was not going to be the day.

He removed the noose from his neck and coiled it neatly under his bed before getting up and walking to the door. He gave the knob a nervous, hesitant glance, wondering what kind

Chapter 10

of torment and ridicule the suitors had in store. He was caught off guard, however, when someone on the other side began to knock.

"Who is it?" Mac asked.

The person answered with another knock.

"Who is it?" Mac asked, raising his voice.

"I'm an old friend of your father's. I was hoping we could talk."

Mac retrieved a dagger from his nightstand and tucked it into his right boot before opening the door and sizing up the mysterious visitor. "What can I do for you?"

"Name's Jinni. Pleasure to meet you," Jinni said, extending his brawny arm for a handshake. "You must be Mac."

"Yeah," Mac said. His squinting eyes and heavy jaw gave his curiosity away. "I'm sorry, but we don't have any rooms available here. Not sure we're going to any time soon."

Jinni couldn't help but notice a striking resemblance between the young man in front of him and paintings he'd seen of a young Otis Seehus. "I'm, uh—I'm not lookin' for a room, kid. I'm lookin' for your dad. I asked around downstairs. They said to either talk to you or your mom. But your mom didn't answer her door."

"Yeah. She's in one of her moods again. My dad's not around. Hasn't been for a while now. How do you know him again?"

"I'm an old friend of his."

"Really?"

"Yeah," Jinni said. "You say that like you don't believe me."

"No. It's just—he hasn't been here for over fifteen years. Most of his friends know that. Even the old ones."

"I suppose that does seem a bit strange," Jinni said. "But I am a friend. I was just passing through on my way to Nestor Island and wanted to say hello—meet you and your mom."

Mac opened the door and stepped aside, easing the harsh front he'd been putting on up to this point. "I see…in that case, come on in. Can I offer you something to drink?"

"Yeah. Sounds great. Got any ale? Or whiskey?"

Mac tilted his head. "I have coffee. Or tea."

"Coffee's perfect."

Mac slid a steaming porcelain cup across the glass top of a table crafted from the messy knot of an olive tree's root ball.

"This castle and everything in it used to belong to my father," Mac said. "Three years after the war ended, he still hadn't returned. That's when some of the guys you met downstairs started moving in. One by one, they took over each room."

Jinni could see a frightened sadness in Mac's young eyes. "Whose room is this?"

"Mine," Mac said. "I got to keep my room. And Mom got to keep hers. It's still technically her castle."

"If it's her castle, why doesn't she just tell them to get the hell outta here?"

"It's not that easy. They don't listen to her unless they feel like it that day. And they sure don't listen to me. The council of elders tries to oversee certain aspects of the castle. Finances. Food. Things like that. But their authority is…really more of an illusion. Aside from tradition and a few ancient rules, there's really nothing stopping anyone from taking over the place—if they really wanted to. So how did you know my dad? From the war?"

Chapter 10

"What? No. I fought in a different part of Troy than where your dad was." Jinni trod carefully over his next words, knowing the best lies were vague but carried the perfect amount of detail. "I knew him before the war. Some years back, he saved my life—and the lives of some people that mean an awful lot to me. If I knew where he was right now, I'd gladly return the favor. I heard that he ran into trouble getting home after the war ended." Jinni took a sip and gently placed the empty cup on the table. "I didn't realize he never made it back. A lot of guys went missing right after the war, but most of 'em turned up eventually."

"Most, but not all," Mac said.

"I'm sorry if my being here brings up bad memories for you. I didn't come to pick old wounds. You just say the word, and I'll get out of your hair."

"Not at all," Mac said. "You're fine. We used to get visitors all the time—when I was a little kid. Old friends like you or guys that knew him from the war. They don't stop by as much as they used to, though. Is this your first time here?"

"Yeah, actually. I was somewhat…detained…for a while. I've been trying to make up for lost time by traveling and seeing old friends."

"Detained? Like prison?"

"Something like that," Jinni said, with hesitation. "So where do you think he is?"

"I'm not sure. Everyone around here thinks he's dead."

"Do you?"

Mac paused. "I really don't know anymore. I've been told so many different things by so many different people. I don't know what to believe.

"What about your mom? What does she think?"

This time of year was always the worst for Penelope. The image that Mac most commonly visualized in association with his mother was a closed bedroom door. When Penelope wasn't in bed with the aging black Lab Grace, she was out on their balcony, only willing to spend time with two mature olive trees and a variety of pink-and-purple flowering pots and hanging baskets. Encumbered by rose-colored spectacles, courtesy of the laudanum, she'd look out to sea and imagine that it was Otis's gentle fingers, and not the wind, brushing her dense hair. Soon after, she would snap out of it and shed a few tears. *Otis. Where are you?*

"I'm not sure what she thinks these days," Mac said. "If at all. But she always speaks of him as if he's still alive. When I was about six, the council started to put a little pressure on her about remarrying—getting a proper king back in the castle. She told them that she would be willing to remarry, but first she wished to knit a shroud for my father—in his honor. And upon its completion, she'd seriously consider choosing another husband.

"I don't know what's become of that shroud, or if she still works on it. But if she doesn't finish it soon and remarry, one of two possible outcomes will unfold. Either the council will name me king and the suitors will try to kill me—and likely succeed—or the council gives my mom all the time she wants, and the suitors lose patience. In which case they'll either kill us or kick us out on the street."

"Damn," Jinni said, embellishing his empathy. "That is a tough spot."

Chapter 10

"But if by some miracle my father shows up—everything changes."

"So nobody has any idea what happened to him or where he ended up?" Jinni asked, rubbing his forehead.

"Nope. Just about everything after the Trojan Horse incident is a complete mystery. All I heard was that he skipped a ceremony so he could get back here sooner. He left with two other guys. I can't remember their names offhand, but no one knows what happened to them either."

"Hmmm. Well. I wish I had more information to share with you, Mac. But it sounds like you already know everything I know. I'm sorry."

"Me too," Mac said. "But don't sweat it. I'm not any worse off than I was before you got here. And forget what I said about not having any rooms available. Any friend of my father is always welcome here."

Jinni took one last sip from the coffee cup before looking out the window. "That's kind of you, and normally I'd take you up. But I have to get going."

"Are you sure?"

"Yeah. My ride will be leaving, with or without me, come sundown. Thank you for your hospitality, Mac. Take care of yourself."

"Will do. Thanks for the visit. Don't be a stranger."

As Jinni wandered down the stairs and into the commons area, he took a closer look around and grew disheartened at the lack of respect shown by virtually everyone in sight. Drinks and food were spilled and carelessly trampled into a slippery mush. The crashing sounds of breaking glasses from different parts of the room were constant and usually met with laughter.

Odyssey Tale

Once Jinni reached the front door, he turned around for one last look and let out a sigh. "Godless heathens," he said under his breath. "Good luck, kid."

Upstairs, Mac had just finished drying the coffee cups and was about to stow them away when another knock interrupted his peace. As it was an unusual occurrence for someone to knock on his bedroom door, Mac assumed it was Jinni again.

"You forget something?" Mac asked, opening the door with a grin.

"Who was your little friend?"

Mac was both surprised and terror-stricken when he found out Jinni was not the one who knocked. Casting a shadow over Mac with his tall stature and V-shaped frame was a man named Eury.

Eury considered himself the premier alpha male among all suitors and likely to be the next king. He was a dashing man with handsome, masculine features. But he was as mean as a young rattlesnake—and less predictable. He was the only suitor who wasn't originally from the area and one of the few who was independently wealthy. Still, that didn't stop him from enjoying a free room, meals, ale, and anything else he could get his grubby hands on. And tormenting Mac was his favorite sport. It gave him a strange relief, like scratching a mosquito bite or releasing a deep sneeze.

"Sorry, Eury," Mac said, shuddering. "I didn't know it was you."

"So who was it?"

"Who?"

"Don't get cute with me, boy." Eury glared, causing Mac to look away. "Who was it?"

Chapter 10

"Nobody. Just some old friend of my father's. Came here for a visit."

Eury stepped forward and grabbed Mac by the front of his shirt. "Don't give me that bullshit. I know that he wasn't some old friend of your father's. He's a Lost Boy."

"What?" Mac asked, lowering his eyebrows. "No way. He looks like he's in his forties."

"That doesn't change the fact that he came here on a Lost Boy boat. He's been all over town asking about your dad. So I'm gonna ask you one more time. And this time you're going to tell me the truth. Who was he?"

"I told you already," Mac said, trembling. "He's nobody. Just some old friend of my father's. From before the war."

"If you think, for one second, that getting rid of me or any of those guys downstairs is going to be as easy as hiring a Lost Boy crew, you're sadly mistaken, Mac."

"I swear. On my mother. I didn't invite him here, and I didn't hire any Lost Boys for anything."

Mac felt Eury's grip loosen, and Eury took a few subtle steps backward.

"That's good," Eury said. "Good boy."

Mac's heart was nearly bursting from his chest.

"I know I've told you in the past what will happen if you ever try anything like that. But while I'm up here, maybe I should show you." Eury stepped forward and jabbed Mac twice on the cheek with his right fist. Mac hit the floor, sliding. Eury shut the door behind him. Mac's still-pounding heart began to sink as he heard the lock latch shut.

Eury picked him up and slugged him two more times. The only thing keeping Mac upright was Eury's grip on his shirt.

"Please, Eury. I know. I won't. I won't do anything."

Slug. Slug. Slug. Mac took another hard spill onto the floor. He was beginning to lose consciousness but happened to glance to his left and see the noose still neatly coiled under his bed. For a moment, he wished that today had been the day.

Simultaneous drops of blood and tears rolled off the curves of his smooth cheeks and onto the floor.

"Please don't, Eury."

Eury bent over to pick Mac up, but he, too, caught a glimpse of the noose. "Well, well, well. What do we have here?" Eury asked, reaching under the bed and pulling out the coil. "Coward's way out. Big shocker."

Mac's vision became blurred while the rest of his senses were scrambling to run or hide. Suddenly, he felt a familiar feeling. The rope was around his neck. "It's brilliant, actually," Eury said, dragging Mac like a dog toward the balcony's handrail. Using his free hand, Eury wrapped the other end of the rope around the balcony handrail and gave it a firm tug. "I've been thinking of ways I can kill you without getting on your mother's bad side, and here you were about to do it for me."

Mac's fight, strength, and will were depleted. Through two swelling eyes and a mouthful of blood, he begged one last time. "Don't. Please."

"Nice knowing ya, Mac." Eury grabbed Mac by the shoulders and threw him off the balcony.

Chapter 11

While the rest of the Lost Boys were planning an evening of whoremongering and drunken debauchery, Tootles walked alone over a narrow strip of beach. Its dead end led him to the bottom of the cliff that held Otis and Penelope's castle in the sky, and he admired it for a moment before something peculiar struck his attention.

"What the hell?" He leaned forward and squinted, barely able to make out the scene unfolding on Mac's balcony. "Oh. Shit." Tootles said. While the distance kept the details a bit murky, Tootles was sure that he was witnessing someone attempting to hang himself.

With both hands clenching the rope above his neck, Mac dangled, desperately trying to free himself from the noose. His hands had been ripped open, having squeezed the rope during the fall. What remained of both palms was shredded, and they would have felt as though they were on fire had it not been for the surge of adrenaline rushing through his veins. He'd willed himself to climb up enough to create enough slack to remove the noose, but the stubborn knot wouldn't loosen enough to slip over his chin.

He reached into his boot for the dagger he had tucked away earlier when Jinni knocked on his door and desperately cut at the rope that kept him suspended to the balcony. Mac stopped cutting to reposition the dagger between his bloody fingers and watched in horror as it slipped from his grip and into the water below. He tugged the rope violently but lacked the weight and strength necessary to finish what the dagger had started.

Mac let out a sigh of disappointment, then one of determination, and began to pull himself upward. He was only five or six more pulls from being able to kick his leg over the side of the balcony, but with each pull, his strength wavered, and the fiery pain in his hands that was once going unnoticed was becoming unimaginable.

With his final destination just out of reach, Mac ran out of momentum and clenched the rope. Despite knowing what fate awaited him when he let go, he couldn't gather the strength to climb any further.

Blood continued to pour from his hands, making his once-secure grip more slippery. Several hefty gobs slipped down his wrist as he closed his eyes and let out a tear. He let go of the rope and felt his stomach jump to where his heart should have been. As the rope's harsh grip applied pressure to the top of his throat, Mac could feel his insides tighten from bottom to top. In that very instant, the rope snapped. His eyes jolted open, and his young blood boiled with shock as he fell into the water below.

Mac never saw what happened or how, but on the beach in the distance, Tootles just shook his head, threw his bow over his shoulder, and walked away, satisfied. *There's only handful of people in the world who could have made that shot.* "You're welcome," Tootles muttered.

Chapter 11

Mac's fall took him just short of the ocean floor before the hopeful air in his lungs resurrected him, causing him to launch through the surface. He tilted his head back, grinned, and soaked in the sweetest ocean air he'd ever known before yanking the noose off his neck and tossing it aside like a week-old apple core.

"Thank you," Mac said, unaware of how he'd struck such great fortune. "Thank you." He let out a celebratory yell before the pain in his hands came back, only to be amplified by the saltwater in which they were submerged. His jubilant love affair with life was short-lived, however, as the realities of how he'd ended up there began to set in. What now?

Mac concluded that his best course of action was to stay quiet and lay low. As far as Eury was concerned, Mac was a corpse. And he figured that if Eury was willing to kill him once, it was unlikely that Eury would have any reservations about repeating the process. Mac also knew that his disappearance wouldn't go unnoticed for long and was curious as to what the rumors would entail.

Mac swam around the long end of the cliff and in the direction of the town docks. It was a high-traffic area filled with tourists and avoided by most locals. Here he could blend in and likely go unrecognized by most he encountered. While the swim was no easy feat, his energy levels were in high supply, with him having just escaped the hungry fangs of death.

Once he'd made it to the other side, Mac took notice of the hustle and bustle and the docks filled with vessels of all shapes and sizes. Just as he'd hoped, no one had noticed him. He swam to the nearest boat, using it to conceal himself as he climbed up on the dock and merged seamlessly with the area's heavy foot traffic. He walked down the line and admired the craftsmanship and vibrant colors of most of the vessels on display, but as he reached the end of the line, one stood out more than the rest. The ship wasn't particularly nice or even well kept, but the insignia that it brandished held one of the most recognizable symbols of its time.

"Lost Boys," Mac said, under his breath. As if on cue, Jinni entered his peripheral vision and stepped aboard the idle *Elvira*. "So he *is* a Lost Boy." In awe, Mac gazed over the boat. Having heard countless bedtime stories involving the Lost Boys' heroics, a nostalgic pride expanded within his chest and out to his shoulders. It quickly began to erode, however, as he felt the cold stare of strange eyes burrowing into his face. At first, he thought everyone was starting to realize who he was, and that any moment someone would shout, "Look, it's Mac Seehus! Look! Look! The prince is out."

Finally, someone approached him, looked deep into his eyes, and asked with genuine concern, "Are you OK?" Mac was relieved the stranger's inquiry was more related to his appearance than his identity, but after a quick glance at his hands and his reflection in a nearby shop window, Mac became aware that he was drawing too much public attention and was in dire need of the medical sort.

"Yeah," Mac said, awkwardly turning away. "I'm good." He nearly tripped over his feet to get out of the public eye and sneaked down a back alley to claim a moment of privacy to contemplate his next move.

Chapter 11

Onboard the *Elvira*, the Lost Boys were scattered about in patches as the crimson sun began to take its nightly swim. While at port, the only time they could all be found on the ship this early in the evening was when they were set to leave the following morning.

One and Two were in the process of rolling a barrel of wine into the cargo area. Its brute size and weight dwarfed those of the twins, so getting it to take off was a chore in and of itself. Once they had it moving and close to its intended spot, they propped it up, nearly losing their grip twice. After getting it upright, Two hugged the full barrel and attempted to scoot it backward, along with himself, rotating the bottom in half circles.

"Reeeeeeeeeeeer." Cecil shot up on all four legs and scratched Two's ankles before dashing out of sight.

"Ah. Dammit!" Two yelled, stopping to fire a glance over his right shoulder. "Well, don't lay there then. Goddamn cat."

Toward the front of the ship, Tootles, Slightly, and Nibs passed around a bottle of whiskey.

"You are so full of shit," Slightly said.

"Am not." Tootles sat up, wide-eyed. "Ya know. Sometimes you just know, when you let an arrow go, that it's gonna be a good shot. That's not how this one went. I thought it was gonna whiff. But it hit clean. Guy dropped into the water like a stone."

"The only whiff I'm getting around here is of your horse shit."

Downstairs, in the dusty and dusky confines of the ship's sleeping quarters, Jinni and Peter huddled around the flickering sanctuary of a small lamp running low on oil and resting on a map that both had practically memorized. They kept their conversation to a gentle hush, occasionally catching snippets of banter from Nibs, Slightly, and Tootles, as the three were getting noticeably louder by the sip.

Jinni kept his mysterious aura cloaked in the shadows of the darkest part of the room, his head and back pressed firmly against the wall. "I asked around, and no one knows anything."

"Well, that's disappointing," Peter said with a contradictory tone.

"But," Jinni continued, "I spoke with a farrier in town. He told me Otis's last visitor was the carpenter who designed and built the Trojan Horse. Apparently, Otis and this carpenter got to be pretty good friends during the war."

"So what does that mean?"

"Maybe nothing. But he's one of the last guys to see Otis alive, so he may know something."

"If he came here to visit Otis, he don't know anything."

"Maybe not. But guess where he lives," Jinni said, leaning forward.

"Nestor Island." Peter let out a half smile and leaned away.

"You got it," Jinni said. "Nestor Island."

"So I suppose you think that's some sort of coincidence."

"What are the odds of that? The last guy to come here to visit Otis happens to live on the island of our next scheduled stop."

"Which part of the island?" Peter asked, crossing his lean, rugged forearms.

Jinni answered softly, knowing he was delivering unwelcome news. "The south end."

"Are you serious?" Peter uncrossed his arms and leaned back out of the light.

Chapter 11

"I know it's a pain in the ass, but—"

"Is this really gonna be worth it? I mean, what do you think this guy's gonna be able to tell you?"

"I really don't know," Jinni said. "But as long as we have a lead, we might as well follow it."

"What about our cargo? You do realize it's set to be delivered in the north?"

"It'll add a day," Jinni pleaded. "Maybe two."

Peter replied with a roll of his eyes.

"Don't do that," Jinni said. "If you got something to say, say it."

"I don't. I just worry that this guy is gonna lead us to another guy, then another, then another…at what point do we cut our losses chasing this thing and get back to work? Believe me, of all people, I know how much fun it can be looking for gold at the end of a rainbow. But it just ain't practical.

"And I did a little asking around on my end. Even if Otis is alive, and we get him back here, it's hard to say how much he'll be able to pay us. From what I heard, he comes back to claim this castle and fortune, he's gonna have a hell of a fight on his hands. Getting paid might not be as easy as just bringing him back here."

"Trust me when I tell you that he is alive," Jinni said. "I can feel him. And since when are you afraid of a little fight?"

"I ain't." Peter smirked. "You know that. But I'm not getting anyone killed for what could turn out to be a so-so payday. If this feeling of yours is right, and he is out there, and he does need us to get him out of whatever hole he's trapped in, we're gonna need to talk turkey first."

"I can live with that," Jinni said. "I'm looking to get paid too."

It was at this juncture that Mac crawled out from under a bunk, revealing his beaten and swollen face. "I knew you were full of shit," he said, rising to his feet to square off with Jinni. "You didn't know my dad at all. Did you? You were just here in search of a payday."

After the initial surprise had worn off, Peter and Jinni examined the bruises and cuts covering most of Mac's visible flesh.

"What are you doing here?" Jinni asked.

"And what the hell happened to ya?" Peter added.

"It seems your visit to the castle caused quite a stir," Mac said. "Why didn't you tell me you were a Lost Boy?"

"Didn't think it mattered," Jinni said.

"Well, it did. One of the guys at the castle thought I hired you to help me get rid of him and the other suitors, so I ended up getting my ass pummeled."

Peter stepped forward, tilting his head to get a closer look at Mac's cheeks and forehead. "Looks like he got your face pretty good there too."

"Ha-ha-ha," Mac said. "Hilarious." His elevated voice roused the attention and curiosity of the Lost Boys, who were starting to come down the stairs.

"Holy shit. That's him," Tootles said.

"Who?" Slightly asked.

"Who do you think, hedge-creeper? It's the guy who tried to hang himself."

Jinni stepped forward, puzzled. "What?"

Chapter 11

"I wasn't trying to hang myself," Mac exclaimed. "Eury wrapped a noose around my neck and threw me over the balcony."

"Pretty impressive to see you're still alive," Peter said. "One. Two. Please escort Mr. Seehus off the *Elvira* and make sure he gets back to his castle."

One and Two took one step toward Mac, and he replied by retreating two.

"No. I'm coming with you," Mac said.

"I don't think so," Peter said.

"Why?"

"Because we're not in the business of giving free rides to strangers. Especially spoiled princes looking to escape their ivory towers."

Mac turned toward Jinni to plead his case. "I'm not looking to escape anything. And if you're going out to look for my dad, I'm coming with you."

"Sorry, kid," Jinni said regrettably. "He's right. This is no place for you—no life for you."

"I'll work. I can clean. I can cook. I'm good with a bow and arrow. I'm OK with a sword, but I'm a fast learner. At least take me as far as Nestor Island. If we don't learn anything more from this carpenter guy, we can part ways, and you'll be rid of me forever. Please. I can't go back home. Not now. And I've got nowhere else to go."

While the other Lost Boys were sympathetic toward Mac's cause, Peter didn't sound sincere when he finally agreed. "Fine. But you're gonna earn your keep."

Not even the purple surrounding Mac's eyes could hide his delight. "Absolutely. Anything."

Peter pointed Mac toward a vacant bunk and informed him that his chores were still to be determined. "And as for you," Peter said, shifting his focus to Jinni, "ya better be right."

"What about?"

"This feeling you keep talking about."

"I'm certain," Jinni said. "Whatever powers that run the universe are clear on that. I can't describe it, but I can feel him. As if he were in this room."

"Let's hope you feel Otis better than you did him," Peter said, tilting his head toward Mac. "'Cuz he *was* in this room. And the universe didn't tell you shit about that."

Chapter 12

An increasingly impatient line of ships and smaller craft ranging in size, cargo, and intentions extended from the southern port of Nestor Island. While the island was quite large, there were only two legal ports of entry. Nestor Island's emperor was a rightfully paranoid fellow, and his "watchmen" kept a close eye on the coasts. Lethal penalties lay in wait for anyone attempting to gain access to the island outside the sanctioned ports. As a result, traffic could get a little backed up—especially on the south end, where more goods were traded. Peter knew this better than most, and despite Jinni's insistence that the traffic "wouldn't be too bad this time of year," Peter's concerns were eventually confirmed.

"Good call, Jinni," Peter said. The skin over his knuckles grew as tight as leather as he squeezed the bow's railing in frustration.

"It's not that bad," Jinni said, knowing full well that no one in his or her right mind would agree.

"It won't be here in a minute," Peter said, walking toward the vessel's wheel. "At least there's one thing you can always count on when it comes to South Nestor's traffic." Peter grabbed hold of the wheel and turned it with ferocity. "Someone's not paying attention."

The *Elvira* whipped around the nearest vessel and swirled ahead like a turkey buzzard about to land. Most who had been waiting in line noticed and were well aware of Peter's intentions. Some yelled out, expressing their displeasure.

Just as Peter had predicted, someone wasn't paying attention. When the watchmen guarding the entry port raised the water gate, allowing the first ship through, the *Elvira* slipped into a perfectly sized spot toward the front of the line.

"Heeeeyyy, what the hell do you think you're doing?" a gruff, muscular middle-aged man hollered out. "Get your ass to the back of the line."

"Thought this was the back," Peter yelled.

"Awww, bullocks."

"You weren't moving, so I didn't th—"

"Typical Lost Boys, acting like they own the island." The man extended his middle finger.

"Sorry." Peter grinned and turned his back to the man, satisfied.

"It ain't funny," the man yelled out.

With a continuous grin, Peter turned back toward Mac and the Lost Boys. "Which one of you sons of bitches was laughin'?"

No one had been laughing before, but they all were now.

"Smart-ass, huh? Just try to stay afloat long enough to cross the gates in that glorified chunk of firewood." He concluded his angry tirade by spitting off his vessel and in the direction of the *Elvira*.

"Nicer than that chunk of shit you're weighing down, you fat fuck," Peter yelled.

Chapter 12

"You want to come over here and say that to my face?"

"You go practice spitting out teeth and find me when you get to port."

"Ah, blow it out your ass."

"Have a good one, sir." Peter turned around once more, and the man lost his energy and interest in the situation.

An hour or so later, the *Elvira* made it to the front of the line, and several watchmen boarded to investigate the contents of the Lost Boys' provisions and cargo.

"What are these?" one of them asked.

"What do they look like?" Peter asked.

"Shoes," he said. "Glass shoes." The watchman pulled a glimmering high heel from its box. "Doesn't seem very practical, does it?"

"You wouldn't think," Peter said. "Certainly not with some of the walruses you've got here on Nestor Island."

If any of the watchmen had a sense of humor, they weren't sharing it.

"But apparently, they're trendy," Peter continued, straight faced. "Or so I'm told."

"The delivery log says these are headed to Tellico," another watchman said, glancing over some paperwork. "That's on the north port. Why you stopping here?"

Peter hesitated. "Just stocking up on more provisions."

"Looks like you've got more than enough to get you to the north docks. So I'm going to ask again. Why you stopping here?"

Peter was growing red in the face and beginning to feel heat settle on his forehead and neck.

"Because I instructed them to," Mac said.

"And who are you?"

"My name's Mac. My father runs a kiln back in Ithaca, and he's the one who designed these shoes and put me in charge of their delivery. He also hired these guys to see to it that I made it there unscathed. As impractical as they are, the shoes are custom fit, quite expensive, and rather time consuming to make. Along the way, I had a difficult time finding my sea legs, and I'm in dire need of a good night's sleep that doesn't involve puking off the side of the ship every fifteen minutes."

The watchmen all gave Mac a brief, stern look that percolated with uncomfortable silence. "Well, hell," one finally said, breaking the tension. "I can't keep my lunch down out there either. Welcome to Nestor Island, fellas. Behave yourselves. We are everywhere."

The *Elvira* proceeded through a narrow canal surrounded by roving hillsides covered with bare treetops and glided to a graceful stop at the first available dock. As diverse as the Lost Boys could be in personality, one thing they all had in common was their need to unwind after an overseas journey, regardless of the length.

Joined by their typical self-assuredness and strut, Peter, Jinni, and the remaining Lost Boys guided Mac over the cobblestone streets that lined the hectic area. Houses and storefronts were jam-packed throughout the grid, but neither Peter nor the Lost Boys could remember the location of their favorite local establishment.

"There it is," Tootles said, pointing to a crude wooden sign with chipped lettering. "I told you guys it was called Candlewick's."

"Nobody gives a shit, Tootles," Two said.

Chapter 12

As the group approached the entrance, Peter pulled Mac aside.

"Listen," Peter said. "I wasn't too sure about bringing you along for this, but you've gone above and beyond when it comes to cleaning and the meals you made. And feeding Cecil. Lucky cat's as fat as he's ever been. Anyway, you've earned more than just a ride, so here's a few shekels. Have some fun tonight." Peter handed Mac a small sack filled with coins, and the two stepped into the smoky sanctuary known as Candlewick's.

They approached what looked to be the only open table and glanced around the room and its occupants.

"Where'd everybody go?" Mac asked, surprised.

"They're around here somewhere." Peter scanned the room. "There's Nibs," he said, pointing.

Nibs was in the process of invading a table occupied by the four most attractive and elegant women in the saloon. All were in their midtwenties, dressed to impress, and began to recoil in horror as Nibs dipped his filthy finger in one of their drinks and placed it in his mouth. "Mmmm," he said.

"Gross," one of them uttered.

"You are disgusting," said another.

"I don't suppose any of you gals happen to be watchmen," he said.

"Do we look like watchmen?"

"Not really, but if you want to get out of here, I'll let you strip search me anyway."

"Get lost, piglet."

"Last chance," he said, grinning.

The only woman who hadn't spoken finally had heard enough. She stepped forward and smacked him in the face with a robust open palm.

"Nibs," Peter yelled from across the room. "Get your ass over here."

At this point, One, Two, Tootles, and Slightly had joined Peter and Mac at their table. "All right, fellas. First round's on me," Jinni said.

Nibs approached the table, rubbing the palm-shaped discomfort from his face.

"How'd it go over there?" Slightly asked, smirking.

"She might be the one."

"Ales all around?" Peter asked. "Mac, ale good with you?"

"Make it a whiskey," Mac said, prompting a few looks from his new bar buddies.

"All right." Peter's lips curled into a mischievous grin. "Whiskey it is."

With the help of One, Peter brought back the table's ale and Mac's whiskey. In no time, their first drink was a distant memory, and Nibs and Slightly were retrieving the table's sixth round. Everyone expected Mac to switch to ale at some point, but he'd only had minimal experience with ale and had yet to acquire a taste. While whiskey wasn't his preferred flavor, either, he found it easier to hold his breath, slug it back, and endure the burn that followed.

"Next round's on me," Mac slurred, turning toward the bar.

"Two. Go help him," Peter said.

"This'll be his seventh shot," Slightly said. "He's gonna be shit housed."

Chapter 12

"I don't know," Two said. "Doesn't look like his first go-around with whiskey."

"Where'd Jinni end up?" Tootles asked.

Peter took the final swig and set his mug on the table. "He's out looking for some carpenter that knows Mac's dad. Told us to keep an eye on him, and he'd find us later."

"How much later?" Slightly asked. "One or two more shots and he's gonna be blastin' mutton all over this place."

"No way. Kid's a natural," Two said.

"You care to place a friendly wager on that, Two?" Slightly asked, taking advantage of Two's love of gambling.

"What's the bet?"

"He yaks in the next twenty minutes, you buy my drinks for the rest of the night. He doesn't—I'll buy yours."

"Oh, you're on." Two reached out and shook Slightly's hand.

Less than ten minutes later, Mac was out back, bent over, and letting loose a foul stream of warm whiskey and bile. As if losing the bet wasn't punishment enough, Peter ordered Two to keep Mac company. And because One was Two's brother, Peter ordered him outside as well.

"That's it," One said, patting Mac's back as if burping a baby. "Get it all out." He turned to Two and glared. "I oughta beat your ass for this."

"What? I'm not the one who made you come out here."

"Yet somehow, once again, I'm on the ass end of one of your stupid bets. It was so obvious he was going to puke. Now I'm stuck out here, playing nursemaid. With you."

"Shut up," Two said. "This place is boring tonight anyway."

As if on cue, a massive burst of flame shot out the nearest window, followed by roaring applause and a random voice.

"Hey! You girls need to get your clothes back on if you're going to be downstairs."

One refreshed his glare. "I hate you," he said, before looking away and patting Mac's back.

Jinni turned the corner of the alley and joined them. Two was the first to spot him. "Hey, Jinni. You find him?"

"Yeah. Guy's shop is closed right now, though. We're going to see him first thing tomorrow morning."

Mac let out one last burst of vomit, followed by a miserable groan.

"What the hell happened to him?" Jinni asked.

The following morning, Mac was the last one to wake and only did so in response to a water-filled ladle, courtesy of Jinni.

"What's this about?" Jinni asked.

Mac dug the backs of his fingers into his eyelids. "What's what about?"

"This. Are you here to find your dad? Or are you here to join the party?" Jinni knew as well as anyone that young men want nothing more than to impress their fathers. But when that young man has grown up without the guidance of his father, he wants to impress everyone. Sometimes—oftentimes—it'll lead him down the wrong path.

"Sorry," Mac said, sitting up with a handful of his forehead. "I've heard stories about the Lost Boys. I just wanted to keep up. Maybe earn a little respect."

"Well. You didn't do either last night," Jinni said. "Get up. Get dressed. The day's wastin'."

Chapter 12

Once Mac had shaken off the brown-bottle cobwebs and gotten dressed, he and Jinni wandered outside of town to an area where the tight cobblestone grid stopped and a vast plain of desert began. As they approached the modest cottage, they were only looking to speak with one man, but when they reached the front door, two voices were coming from inside.

"Are you calling me a liar?" one of the voices yelled.

"You bet your ass I'm calling you a liar," said the other. "I gotta a few other names I can think of, too, if you prefer."

The conversation reached a sudden halt and was followed by a heavy thud that shook the outside walls. The front door swung open with fury, and a slender man was tossed end over end with just as much. As he landed in the sunburst sand, a portly freckle-faced man with angry, rosy cheeks filled the doorframe. "If I ever walk in on you running your scam on my father—or anyone else around here again—I'm gonna kill ya."

At this point, the larger man disregarded the smaller man as no more of a threat than a nearby cricket that happened to be watching from an open spot on the wraparound porch. The hefty fellow looked away from the man he'd just tossed, and up at the surprise surrounding Mac and Jinni.

"What the hell do you want?"

"Good morning, sir." If Mac had a hat, it would have been in his hands.

"Save it. What do you want?"

"We're looking for a man named Carlo Geppetto."

The man was taken aback that someone as young as Mac was asking for Carlo. "He doesn't want to see anyone."

"Please, sir. My father. He's been missing for years. One of his last visitors was Mr. Geppetto. If he's heard anything about him, or he can point me in another direction, it'd be a tremendous help."

"Your father?"

"Yes, sir."

The man took a hesitant breath and nodded Mac and Jinni inside. "Come on in," he said, extending his hand for a greeting. "Name's Pinocchio."

"Mac."

"Jinni."

"Carlo is my father, and I'm happy to let you talk to him if you think he'll be able to help you. But I must warn you, his memory is far from where it used to be."

Pinocchio led Mac and Jinni inside the home. The initial light was made brighter by the vibrant colors bouncing off the painted models, toys, and puppets on various shelves lining the walls. The hallway ran from front to back, choking the daylight as its dead end opened to the darkest room in the house. It was lit by dust and smoke-filled beams of natural light sneaking in through three small windows.

"He just sits there most of the time smoking his pipe," Pinocchio said, regretfully watching as his father's mind withered further away.

Mr. Geppetto sat in a wheeled chair, mumbling to himself with varying voices and inflections.

"One day, he and I were having a conversation, and he couldn't remember my name. A couple of weeks later, he tried to set the house on fire. I watched him do it like it was no big thing—like he was putting together a birdhouse. It wasn't until a few weeks ago, he stopped walking." Pinocchio paused and

Chapter 12

stopped himself from shedding a tear. "I put him in here and pulled out everything that could catch flame."

"I'm so sorry," Mac said.

Pinocchio failed to hide the years of pent-up emotion as he knelt beside his father's wheelchair. "Dad...Dad. There are a couple of gentlemen here to see you." Pinocchio waved Mac over.

Mr. Geppetto's eyes lit up, and he began to smile from ear to ear when Mac stepped into the hazy light. "Otis. What the hell are you doing here?"

"Not sure," Mac said, puzzled, but only at first. "Where should I be?" Mac took a step back. "He thinks I'm my dad."

"Have you seen the horse yet?" Mr. Geppetto leaned forward and lowered his voice while his eyes scanned the room for potential spies. "They're only halfway finished with her, but she looks magnificent. You guys are gonna give 'em a hell of a fright when you burst from her belly. What I wouldn't give to be a fly on the wall."

"Who?" Mac asked. "Who are we going to scare?"

"The Trojans." Mr. Geppetto squinted suspiciously. "Who the hell you think?" He leaned back into his seat.

"Wait. Who's your dad?" Pinocchio asked.

"Otis Seehus."

"Your dad is Otis Seehus?"

"No. No," Mr. Geppetto said. "Otis only has one son. And he's just a baby."

"Mr. Geppetto, do you know where I can find Otis?" Mac asked.

Odyssey Tale

"You feeling OK?" Mr. Geppetto asked, looking at Mac and feeling as though this was just another one of Otis's pranks, albeit stranger than the others.

Mac stood in front of Mr. Geppetto's chair and lowered to a knee.

Mr. Geppetto's body was overcome with frightened chills as Mac pulled Otis's milk bottle from a satchel and held it up. The old man slapped the bottle from Mac's hand, sending it sliding across the stone floor, eventually coming to a stop when it shattered against the wall. The unscathed cork rolled to a halt over a pile of broken glass and the strange turquoise pine needles. The frightened old man cowered and shook in his chair as he covered his ears with his hands and began to rock back and forth. "Get those away from me. Get them away."

As his fit grew more frantic, Mac and Pinocchio moved in closer to console him while Jinni stepped over to the shattered remains of the bottle. He reached down, snagged four or five of the needles, and wrapped them in a cloth. Jinni stuffed them in his pocket before anyone else could notice.

Pinocchio stood up, concerned and displeased. "I think you'd best be on your way now, fellas."

"Of course," Mac said.

Back at Candlewick's Saloon, a disheartened Mac sipped on a glass of water and grimaced as he watched Jinni slug down a gulp of whiskey.

"Sorry, kid," Jinni said, swirling the caramel liquid. "That's all I got. I had a really good feeling about this too. Call it a hunch. Or positive energy. I really thought we were going to learn something from that guy."

Chapter 12

A bolt of lightning and volcanic vibration snapped out. The torrential downpour that followed dripped in through the saloon door's threshold and open windows. Jinni drank down what was left in his glass and signaled the bartender for another. "Looks like we'll be here for a while."

Back at his cottage, Pinocchio carried a dustpan full of broken glass and scattered turquoise pine needles out of Mr. Geppetto's room. Once Pinocchio had left, Mr. Geppetto did something he hadn't done since senility had robbed him of his ability to walk. He wheeled his chair across the room.

He stopped to examine the area in which the bottle had broken and observed several stingers that Pinocchio had missed. Mr. Geppetto reached down and picked one up, as another crack of lightning filled the room with an ivory hue and shook the entire town. He held the mysterious object to his eye and studied it, pinching and rolling it between his fingertips. Mr. Geppetto then took a deep breath and closed his eyes before jamming the sharp end into his right thigh.

His eyes began to glow with youth, and his lungs took in a deeper breath than any other they had in the past twenty years. Suddenly, a mirage of flashing images and voices ran wild through his mind, and a tapestry of memories came rushing back. As if reborn, he wasn't some crazy old man in a wheelchair who needed help using the outhouse. He was *the* Carlo Geppetto. The most exceptional carpenter to ever live—architect of the great Trojan Horse. And the only person who could guide Mac Seehus to the next clue.

Odyssey Tale

"Pinocchio," Carlo yelled, regaining his senses. As once-charred bridges within his mind began to reconnect, he was overcome with joy and shed tears of raw emotion. "Pinocchio. Hurry up and get in here. I've got some things I need to tell you." His tears of joy soon shifted to tears of remorse. "Pinocchio. Hurry. I'm not sure how long this is going to last. We may not have much time."

Chapter 18

As the predawn hours approached, the herd of patrons at Candlewick's Saloon had thinned substantially. The piano player was still going strong, the bartender was counting her tips, but the only customers aside from Jinni and Mac were a table of four that kept quiet and to themselves.

Mac burped and looked away as Jinni took another sip of whiskey.

Jinni, not typically one to concern himself with the emotions of others, began to feel somewhat guilty for raising Mac's hopes. "There's probably a handful of passenger ships that can take you back to Ithaca," Jinni said. "You think you're going to be OK?"

"I don't know," Mac said, staring holes into the bar top.

"Because—if you want—I could probably talk Peter and the guys into hiring you full time. Pretty much keep doing what you did on the way here."

"I appreciate it, but I can't just leave my mom back there by herself."

"Listen, Mac. For what it's wor—"

From behind, Pinocchio interrupted the conversation, stepping between the two and startling both. "Follow me," he said.

Odyssey Tale

Pinocchio led them to a quiet corner table and requested the server leave them three glasses and a bottle of whiskey and be on her way. His paranoia directed his eyes around the room as he pulled a small wooden case from his breast pocket and dumped its contents on the table. It was the remaining needle-like objects he'd found while cleaning his father's room. "What the hell are these things? And don't play stupid and pretend you don't know. They were in that jar that nearly gave my dad a fit."

Mac turned his palms toward the ceiling. "I wish I could tell you. But I have no idea what they are."

"Me neither," Jinni added.

"One moment, he was more afraid of that jar than anything else in the world. I leave the room for a moment, and he jams one of those things into his leg. Then he started talking to me—like he was normal. Asked how I was. Asked how my daughters were doing. He seemed to know everything that's going on in my life currently. But at the same time, it was like he'd been away for a few years and was just stopping by for a visit. Then he started talking about you." Pinocchio nodded toward Mac.

"Me, or my dad?"

"You. Kept calling you Otis's boy. And he wanted me to tell you to go see the emperor and the empress. He said the information you seek is only known by a handful of people. Elite people. It's a rather small circle, but if your father is alive, they might be able to help you locate him."

"Did he say anything else?" Mac asked.

"He did." Pinocchio turned toward Jinni with a confident delay. "He said to speak to the one who didn't talk and ask him where to get more of these blue things. 'He'll know where to find them.'"

Chapter 13

"I'm guessing he wants more," Jinni said.

"You'd be guessing correctly. That was all he said. Then he fell asleep. What are they?"

"They're something you don't want to be messing with. I promise. Whatever good came from them isn't going to be worth it long term."

"My dad is eighty-seven years old," Pinocchio said. "There is no long term."

"So what's in it for me if I do tell you where to find them?" Jinni asked.

"Simple. I'll tell you how to get to the emperor and empress."

"That's not something we can do on our own?" Mac asked.

"Most people around here don't even know how to get in touch with the emperor—much less how to find him."

"I'm sure if we ask around enough—"

"You really are from Ithaca, aren't you?" Pinocchio smiled.

"What do you mean?"

"The emperor's home is not an easy place to find. And it's not a subject you want to be asking strangers about. People around here aren't as hospitable as they are where you're from. You go around asking where you can find the emperor, people are either going to think you're a watchman trying to sniff out traitors—or worse, you'll accidentally ask a watchman. Some of these young guys don't ask a lot of questions before they draw their swords. The emperor takes his security and his wife's security very seriously."

Jinni rubbed his chin and pointed to the cloth. "So if I tell you how to find more of these, you'll tell him how to get to the emperor and empress unhindered?"

"Yes. I've only got three more of these things back at the house. I'm not sure how long each one will subdue my father's… symptoms."

"Tell you what," Jinni said. "You take Mac to see the emperor and empress, instead of just telling us how to get there, and I'll go get you more of those things personally. More than you'll ever need."

"Just that easy?" Pinocchio asked.

"For you," Jinni said. "Not for me."

Bright and early the following morning, with the remaining shekels that Peter had given him, Mac bought a fresh change of clothes and the provisions necessary for two weeks in the raw desert. While Mac sought out the best deals from different storefronts, Jinni sat on the edge of his bed, seemingly alone, until Peter stepped out of the shadows.

"Wondered when you were going to say hello," Jinni said. "What are you doing?"

"Tootles told me you were leaving."

"Yeah. And?"

"I'm thinking back to when you said this little excursion would add two, maybe three days. According to my estimation, you and your little buddy's journey to see the emperor is gonna take at least a month."

"I'm not going with him," Jinni said. "I have to go somewhere else."

"Where?" Peter asked.

"Somewhere I thought I'd never have to go again."

Chapter 13

"I don't suppose it has something to do with those blue things from the bottle. The ones you've been carrying around in your pocket."

Jinni reached into his pocket and pulled the cloth. With steady thumbs, he unrolled it, revealing the contents within. "Do you know what these are?"

"No."

"Well, they're valuable. Rare. So much so that people make fake ones and try to sell them to tourists. People make tea with them. They smoke them. I've even heard of some who smashed them to dust and snorted them up their nose. They make you feel a certain way. In some instances, they make you see things. Things that either aren't there—or part of this universe."

"What about those? Those fake?" Peter asked.

"Afraid not. I wish they were, but they're the real deal."

"So you have me interested, and I'm not trying to be an asshole when I say this, but when do we get to the part where we sell 'em and get this shipment delivered on time?"

Jinni ran his palms over his forehead and dragged his fingers down his face. "Will you shut up for two seconds about the goddamn shipment? Where I'm going, what I'm getting—it'll pay for this shipment six times over."

"Let's hope so." Peter wasn't accustomed to losing arguments, but he was quick to acknowledge when he had lost and even quicker when it came to moving on. "So Mac'll be gone for a month. How long you gonna be gone?"

"Two weeks," Jinni said, holding up corresponding fingers. "I'll make you a deal. If I come back empty handed, we won't have to wait for Mac."

"Really?" Peter asked. "And what if you're not back in two weeks?"

Jinni had the words but was hesitant to say them aloud. "It means I won't be coming back. Because I'm dead. In which case you don't have to wait for Mac. And you'll only be two weeks behind instead of a full month."

Armed with one of six remaining stingers, Pinocchio entered Mr. Geppetto's room and opened its only curtain.

"Time to get up, Pop." Pinocchio sat on the edge of the bed and squeezed the lower part of his father's leg. "Dad. Dad... Dad?"

Mac and Jinni attended Mr. Geppetto's funeral, a gesture much appreciated by Pinocchio and his family. "Thank you both for coming," he said.

"If there's anything we can do, you know where to find us," Mac said.

"I appreciate that. Listen, I, uh. I'll still take you to see the emperor and empress." Pinocchio turned to Jinni. "And you don't have to worry about those things. You were right. No good came of 'em."

"If you're not up for it, I understand," Mac said. "Even if you just wanted to tell me how to get there, I'm sure we'll be able to figure it out."

Chapter 13

"Kid, I gotta wife and five daughters, and my dad just died. A four-week round trip through the desert sounds like a pleasant dream right now. Just give me three days to get some things sorted out and arrange for some mules, and we'll leave at dawn."

And so they did.

Around the time Pinocchio and Mac were running short of daylight and seeking out a suitable campsite, Nibs was the only Lost Boy present on the *Elvira*. The rest were out and about, stirring up mischief. Nibs took a drag from his hand-rolled cigarette and pressed a charcoal briquette against a large sheet of paper, confident that this drawing was going to be special. Before he could get settled and delve into what he referred to as his artistic zone, he was startled by Jinni's emergence from the lower deck.

"Didn't know you were here," Nibs said. "Scared the shit out of me." The surprisingly bright light of the crescent moon accentuated the thick breath of smoke pouring from his mouth and nose.

Jinni looked determined, angry, and terrified, all at once. Shirtless, and with a small burlap satchel slung over his shoulder, he walked with the attitude of a man about to leave town.

"Where you goin'?"

"Nowhere you want to know about, Nibs."

"Don't do anything I wouldn't do."

Jinni lowered the *Elvira*'s only lifeboat into the warm water, where he and it were swallowed by the fog.

Over the next three days, Jinni covered more nautical distance than any human rightfully should have in such a short time and without a sail. Eventually, he brought the lifeboat to a stop over open waters that were all too familiar. Jinni reached into his burlap sack, pulled out a bottle of wine, and guzzled it down, only breaking three or four times before it was empty. He placed the bottle back in the sack and exchanged it for a dagger. With his eyes closed, Jinni took two long breaths and ran the dagger over his left palm, cutting it deep in the process. He balled his gushing fist, allowing a steady stream of black blood to drip and dissipate into the water. Then he jumped in.

The graceful flow of his swim bordered on ornamental. The poetic presentation and pure beauty of his movements were reminiscent of a dancing jellyfish. He stopped for a moment to admire the stars and catch his breath. Just as he was about to dive back under, a curious dolphin joined him and smiled. Jinni nodded and returned the creature's grin before its friendly demeanor turned skittish, and it fled with the type of speed that could only be inspired by a predator.

Jinni, knowing what was coming next, closed his eyes and took several deep breaths, timing the last one perfectly before someone—or something—plucked him under the water.

Chapter 14

In a place beyond the tapestry of coastal coral and the vibrant ecosystem it cradled, Jinni awoke to pitch-black conditions. He had been chained to the wall in some sort of cave or grotto and was slowly regaining his remaining senses. He pulled the shackles around his wrists and faced his palms together. He began to transfer some sort of energy from one palm to another, creating an orb that put off enough light to fill the grim cavern. The light continued to scout the jagged rock room, revealing a large pool that served as the grotto's entryway. The light also revealed a substantial collection of milk bottles, most of which contained a paper message. Finally, and much to Jinni's surprise, the light revealed someone else in the room with him. It was a man, frightened beyond belief and chained to an adjacent wall.

"Who are you?" the man asked, clear waves of panic in his fear-cracked voice. "*What* are you?"

Jinni acted as if he hadn't even heard the man's inquiry. "Do you remember how you got here?"

"What—no. I know I went out to go fishing. Next thing I remember, I was here. Only it was dark. How did you do that thing? With the light in your hands?"

"Have you seen her?" Jinni asked. "Have you talked to her?"

"Who?"

"The—thing that brought you down here."

"No. You're the first one I've seen since I woke up."

Jinni took a long, panicked breath as his light went dark, and the cavern's watery entry began to glow with a neon turquoise.

"Shit," Jinni said. "Pretend you're asleep. Don't talk."

Lurking beneath the surface was a creature that was often mistaken for the most beautiful mermaid to ever grace the seas. Thick locks of shiny blond hair rested over bare breasts as her bright eyes matched that of the glow in the water from which she emerged. Extending from her lean navel were forty to fifty stringy tentacles. They were similar to that of a sea wasp, and they emitted a turquoise hue that was only visible to anything unfortunate enough to be within the range of her grasp. She could extend them anywhere from three to one hundred times the length of her torso, while years of trial and error had allowed her full control over the millions of regenerative pine-needle-size stingers and the searing venom they discharged. She leaned toward Jinni. Her radiant glow dominated the room.

"Well, well, well," she said, smiling to reveal a dark-green sap coating her teeth. It had the consistency and coloration of fresh seaweed, a fact she seemed to be proud of, often turning the final word of her sentences into a lingering smile. "It's been a long time."

"Yes, ma'am. It has," Jinni said.

"How have you been, Jinni?"

"How do I look?"

"Tired," she said with another smile. "I gotta be honest. I never thought, in a thousand years, I'd ever see you again.

Chapter 14

Where did you get these?" She tossed the cloth Jinni had been using to carry the stingers.

"Those were in a bottle, along with a letter from Otis Seehus—asking for help. Not sure if the stingers were supposed to be some sort of payment, or if you got ahold of this bottle and lost it."

"The letter was probably a fake. Like these," she said, pointing at the cloth and stingers at Jinni's feet.

"It wasn't fake. Neither are they."

"And I suppose you jabbed yourself with one—to test it."

"Didn't have to." Jinni glanced at the nearby pile of milk bottles. "Quite a collection you've got there. Those all from Otis Seehus?"

"No. Not all of them. But a good many. Particularly the ones with napkins. Creative fellow. It seems he didn't have access to ink or paper most of the time. Some of them are written in berry juice, ashes, even blood."

"So what's your deal with Otis?"

"No deal," she said, mildly amused.

"Well, why are you stopping these bottles from getting out?"

She lowered her eyebrows as if the answer should have been obvious. "Because I want him, Jinni. You know as well as I do. There are only a handful of humans out there who are impressive—a small handful at that. I'm talking truly impressive. And you know what I mean."

"I don't know," Jinni said. "I never really thought much of any of the ones they call heroes, if I'm being honest. But I don't hate them, like you."

"I don't hate them. I miss them. There aren't near as many as there used to be, and they're much harder to come by. This new generation is weak. Soft. Why do you think that is?"

"How the hell should I know?"

"Come on, Jinni," she said. "Humor an old friend. You're up there, and I'm down here. What do you think? I just don't remember it being this bad."

"What does this have to do with Otis Seehus?" Jinni asked.

"It seems, since you and I last saw one another, I've acquired a taste for these so-called heroes. There's something about their blood—their flesh. It's tastier than the ones they call normal."

"Horseshit," Jinni said. "All those years, going up and down the coast—hunting. You're just now figuring this out? Who do you think you're talking to? The bravest man in the room. Biggest coward in the world. They both taste the same. And you know that. So what is it, really?"

"Believe what you wish, Jinni," she said with a chuckle. "But you're in no position to demand anything from me—least of all, information.

"I can't get to him, if it makes you feel any better," she added, turning her back to Jinni and giving life to the dark parts of the cavern with the shift of her glow. "He's been the Calypso Queen's pet for some time now. She's got him all to herself in that dungeon she calls a castle."

"And what? You're just out here on the coast waiting for her to finish with him? A buzzard waitin' for the eagle's scraps."

"I'm sure whatever she leaves will be worth the wait," she said, flashing another sinister green smile. "And the queen is almost due for a new man. Or so I hear from the mermaids. Until then, I'll just have to snack on sailors and fishermen." She

Chapter 14

nodded toward the other prisoner, who pretended to remain asleep as a frightened lump filled his throat.

A neon tentacle whipped out from under the water. Like a vine extending toward Jinni's face, it stopped just short of his cheek before reaching to caress it. "Oh, Jinni. It really is good to see you again. You should stick around this time," she continued, now wrapping the tentacle around Jinni's throat. "We'll have some fun. Like the old days."

"No thanks," he said with a grave expression. "Not sure I remember 'em quite like you. *Fun* doesn't strike my memory."

"Oh, don't be like that. Aside from that tiny little incident with your little mermaid, you know we were magical together."

Jinni scowled. "You know damn well there was no 'we,' you crazy bitch. It was her. It was always her."

"I really do mean it when I say it's good to see you." Her tentacle became inflamed and pierced his throat with several glistening turquoise stingers.

In the fringes of town on the south of Nestor Island, the Lost Boys entered a whorehouse unlike any they had frequented before. The rich chestnut floors outlining the room were covered by thick carpet shaded with various grays that worked its way up the walls in the form of floor-to-ceiling drapes. The exotic fabric wrapped around each piece of furniture looked tight and bouncy to the touch, and so clean it looked as though it had been upholstered earlier that evening.

Led by Peter, the Lost Boys entered with quiet, casual steps. As their eyes roamed around the room, they all thought the same thing.

"This is the fanciest whorehouse I've ever seen," Tootles said quietly.

"There's not even any sawdust on the floor," Nibs said.

"Hi there, sugar." An elegant young woman grabbed Nibs by the arm. "How you plan on spending your night?"

"But I didn't come here for sawdust," he said, disappearing.

One by one, all of them were taken by the arm and escorted away. All but Peter, that is. Having waved off each attempt to subdue him, he found himself in the presence only of women he'd already rejected. The madam looked down from her balcony. Despite her smile and pleasant demeanor, he knew she was judging him. *Another stinky lot of Lost Boys.*

"Not seeing anything you like, dear? Or maybe it's not a woman you seek?"

Peter smirked. "No. Just a little tired right now. I'm afraid if I were to take one of these lovely ladies upstairs, it would be noticeable. And I can't stand the thought of being remembered like that. Not at a lovely establishment such as this."

"I'd offer you a room, but the rate's the same with or without a girl in there. Are you sure you're tired?"

Another hand reached out and gently grabbed Peter's right arm. Then another, on his left. Neither were used to being turned away. And although Peter was quite hesitant when a third arm joined, he left the brothel and ended up at a saloon closer to town.

Peter felt much more at home here. The saloon looked like it could have been a room in the *Elvira*. Wooden ceilings creaked

Chapter 14

under the heavy footsteps of hotel guests above as dim candles dripping with white wax told the time of night. It was the type of place that one could go drinking—after a night of drinking.

Peter grabbed a stool and made himself comfortable at a corner of the bar with a line of sight that covered the entire room.

"Whiskey, please," he said.

Also at the bar were two gentlemen having a pleasant conversation with a young lady—or so it seemed. With each passing moment and the words they brought forth, it was becoming quite clear that this young woman was not enjoying the aggressive courtship.

"I told you once already," she said. "Stop touching me."

The pleas were met with hearty laughs from the imposing figures sitting on either side of her.

Peter slammed his second glass of whiskey and swirled the empty glass to signal for another.

"Oh, don't be like that. Plenty of women would kill to get a chance at this touch."

"Themselves, probably," the young woman quipped back. "I said, stop touching me."

"OK, OK. We can take things slow," the other man said, sounding as though he was genuinely trying to ease the tension. "Do you swallow?"

She leaned back, deflated.

Peter fired back his third glass of whiskey, seemingly minding his own business as the man with curious hands and a big mouth lit a cigar. It was short and not too big around, but it shrouded the entire bar with a thick blanket of smoke.

"Aw, that's just great," Peter said, locking eyes with the man.

"Excuse me?" the man replied.

"That's just what I want to do when I'm tryin' to enjoy a nice glass of whiskey—is smell your stinkin'-ass cigar."

"In case you hadn't noticed, this is a saloon. If you don't like it—there's the door."

Peter stood up and kicked his bar stool like a mule, sending it halfway across the room. "If you don't put it out by the time I count to three, I'm gonna put it out, and then I'm gonna beat your ass in front of your girlfriend."

"I'm not his girlfriend," she said pronouncedly.

"I wasn't talkin' about you, sweetheart," Peter said, winking. He turned his attention back to the man. "Now, do you want to put that out, or do you want to go outside and talk about it?"

"Neither."

"Then you can go," Peter said.

"Excuse me?"

"Leave." Peter moved a different stool to his spot at the bar and sat down. The man sat, stunned, and embarrassed. He had only been challenged a few times in his life, relying on his bark to get him through most of it. He thought of looking over to his friend for help, but that would have been more embarrassing. Plus, his friend had no interest in getting anywhere near this wild-eyed ruffian. "All right," the man said calmly. "You can come with us, sweetheart." He snatched the young woman's forearm, yanking her out of her stool.

"I don't think so," Peter said. "She stays."

Distracted by Peter's demand, the man failed to notice his lovely young captive had just put a large dagger against his throat. That was the only thing his friend needed to see before leaving in a hurry.

Chapter 14

"That is—if she wants to stay," Peter said, his eyes affixed to the young woman's dagger.

With a constant exchange of banter and smiles, she and Peter kept the man at bay with both their blades until an on-duty watchman stopped by the saloon. After hearing what had happened and verifying the pertinent information with several witnesses, the watchman escorted the man to the area's closest dungeon.

The young woman and Peter remained at the bar until the sun came up, sipping on whiskey and chatting as if they had been acquainted for years.

"That's quite a piece of steel you carry around," Peter said.

She pulled it from her boot and placed it on the bar. "I'm never out without it."

"You shouldn't be. A girl like you."

"What is that supposed to mean?" she asked.

"You know what it means." He tilted his head forward and lowered flirtatious eyes.

"I used to be part of a traveling theater. One night I was attacked. He didn't do—everything he set out to do. Thank the gods. But the very next day, I went out and got my first dagger. I trained. I practiced. In case it ever happened again."

"I'm sorry," Peter said. "Some guys need some more manners smacked into 'em."

"I try not to think about it often. And I have so many fond memories. Traveling. Meeting new people. I try to focus on those things whenever I think about that moment in my life. It's funny how you could spend months…years…with someone, and when they're out of your life, you forget them. Just like that. But at the same time, you could only have met someone and known them for a single day—and spend the rest of your life thinking about them—wondering what they're doing. How they're doing. If they think about you every once in a while like you think about them."

"What do you say we get outta here? While the night is still young."

"It's dawn."

"So what," he said, with some strange new burst of energy. "Let's go. Let's get outta here."

"You are trouble incarnate, aren't you, Peter Pan?" She cast a wicked grin that made him blush.

"The very worst kind," he replied, reaching out for her willing hand.

Chapter 15

Jinni woke up groaning and took a few seething breaths while trying to constrain and compartmentalize the pain overtaking his senses. With a dose of venom flowing through the skin surrounding his throat and back, Jinni dangled lifelessly from the shackles holding his wrists. Beyond the pain originating from Jinni's rash, his neck and arms had become sore from their positioning during confinement.

"You finally awake over there?" It was the same man as before. Jinni recognized the distinct sound of his calm defeat.

"Yeah," Jinni said. He was depleted of energy, but with every blink, he healed just a bit more.

"That thing you did with the light. You think there's any way you could do that again?"

Jinni could hear the man's tears rolling over the dried trails of others that had come and gone. Jinni closed his eyes and took several deep breaths, and his arms began to vibrate. The girthy chunks of iron around his wrists began to turn cherry red with the heat.

The glow filled the room and the other prisoner watched in disbelief as each shackle split in two and plopped onto the damp cave floor. Once again, the entire room went dark. In silence,

Jinni approached the other prisoner. Just as the other shackles had done, these turned red with heat and split before falling to the rock floor, returning the room to darkness.

"How did you do that?"

The long wick of a white wax candle gave birth to a flame. As it filled the ominous cavern with a dim glimmer, Jinni was revealed to be the candle's holder.

The man leaned in and gazed at the rash developing on Jinni's throat. "What are you going to do now?"

Jinni waved his arm over the dark, watery entrance. "I'm going to dive into this pool, find my way out, and go home."

"You've been here before, haven't you?"

Jinni stared at the water, his mind swirling with memories and regret. "A long time ago."

"Take me with you," the man pleaded. "I don't know what she's going to do to me, but if I had it my way, I'd rather not find out."

"I can't take you with me," Jinni said. "Once you get to the bottom of this pool, there's a long water tunnel. It stretches roughly three miles before it opens to the ocean. And once it does, you're two miles below surface."

"What?" New surges of panic began to rush over the man's cheeks. "How'd she get me down here?"

"She has her ways."

"I have to try," the man said, beginning to tear up. "There's nothing you can do?"

"If there was, I'd be happy to help you out of here, but I'm afraid there's not."

"How is it that you can survive it?"

Chapter 15

Jinni nodded. "I don't know." It was true. Jinni had no idea how or why he was able to do some of the things he was able to do.

"Oh, please, no." The man lost control and began to sob.

"I'm sorry," Jinni said. "I really am sorry. And I don't know the best way to tell you this, so I'll just give it to you straight. Your best course of action is gonna be to follow me into that pool, take a big deep breath, and…let yourself go.

"I know that's not what you want to hear right now. But it's the truth. If you don't, and she comes back here and has her way with you…I'm tellin' ya right now. It's going to hurt. Her stingers. Her poison. It's like feeling a red-hot iron being pressed against your skin. Only worse. Eventually, an iron will burn your skin off, and you won't have to feel it anymore. What she does—it doesn't go away. It takes over your blood, makes your whole body spasm with the most awful pain. And if that isn't enough, it makes you see things. Things that aren't there. Your most terrifying nightmares become reality. By the time it's done running its course, you've been dead for several hours."

"What if drowning is my most terrifying nightmare?"

"Then you haven't got much of an imagination." Jinni hopped into the unwelcoming waters and adjusted to the chill and saltiness saturating his wounds.

"Wait," the man cried out. "Thank you for letting me loose."

"Don't mention it," Jinni said.

"I always thought she was a myth, ya know? Is it really her? Is she really the one they talk of, when they talk of the Sea Witch?"

Jinni nodded. "Just don't let her hear you say that." He dove under the water and disappeared. Whether the man decided to drown himself, or wait for the Sea Witch's return, was anyone's guess.

When one thinks of a desert, images of the relentless sun, cacti, and sand so hot that its temperature is visible are usually the first thoughts. It's often underappreciated how cold the desert can get. Luckily for Mac, Pinocchio had packed an extra coat and more than enough blankets from a buck he'd killed a year earlier. Even so, it was a bitter night. The two of them sat at the open end of their tent, keeping warm by the robust fire.

"It's colder than a well digger's ass out here," Pinocchio said. Like a small child sneaking sweets, Pinocchio slowly pulled out a sizable portion of cake he had stashed on his mule. "Want some of this?" he asked.

"No. Thanks," Mac replied, gazing curiously at the contents of Pinocchio's plate.

"Suit yourself." Pinocchio scooped his first bite. "I never have dessert at home, so this is going to be a real treat," he said with a mushy mouthful.

"Can I ask you a question?"

"Go for it." Pinocchio wasted no time digging in for another bite.

"Do you think the emperor and empress will be able to help me?" Mac asked.

"Hard to say. But when it comes to the topic of heroes, your dad's a fan favorite around here. And to them."

"Yeah?"

Chapter 15

"You bet. There are all kinds of stories about him. Even the ones I've heard over and over again don't get old."

"I've heard a handful over the years from visitors," Mac said, with a somber gaze into the fire. "They don't show up like they used to, though. You have a favorite?"

"Hmmm. As I'm sure you know, the king of Troy started the war, and he had a bunch of innocent people locked up in his castle."

Mac nodded.

"His castle had these tremendous barriers and steel gates thicker than any others in the world at that time. For two whole years, our guys tried to break through, and climb over, and dig under. But every attempt was a bust. And every attempt resulted in a lot of lives lost. So one day, your dad gathered everybody together and told them that the war was costing more lives than it was worth, so they should just give up. Pack it all up and go home."

Mac looked away from the flames, sending an inquisitive look toward Pinocchio.

"He said they should withdraw forces from around the castle and build the king a gift. Something really nice that he'd love." As Pinocchio's narrative furthered, so did a youthful enthusiasm. "The king really liked horses, so your dad came up with the idea to build this huge wooden horse and put it outside his gates. Your dad knew that when the king saw it, he'd assume the war was over, and that he'd won...at least that's what your dad wanted him to assume.

"My dad designed the plans for the horse and did most of the framework. In fact, there's a little model replica on a shelf back home. When we go back, you'll have to take a look at it.

But your dad, my dad, and a bunch of guys helped build it. Late one night, they put it outside the gates. The king's guys brought it in, and just like your dad predicted, the Trojan king thought he'd won the war. So he told his men to celebrate. But your dad, Robin Hood, King Charming—back when he was still a prince—and a few other guys in this special elite unit were hidden inside the horse. They came out of a trap door and were able to open the castle gates from the inside. Soldiers poured in by the hundreds. And the rest is history. Within hours, the war was over, and they managed to save everyone the Trojan king was holding prisoner."

"Whoa," Mac said, mesmerized.

"You had to have heard that one," Pinocchio said.

"A long time ago. And certainly not the way you told it. Why's that one your favorite?"

"Are you kidding?" Pinocchio asked. "My dad working side by side with the great Otis Seehus to end the Trojan War—how could it not be my favorite? My dad might not have known who he was toward the end, but no one will ever be able to take that away from him. No one." Pinocchio smiled and winked while finishing the last of his cake. "Mmm. That was quite good."

Without notice, their tent was whisked off its props and thrown to the ground. What they first thought to be a gust of wind turned out to be two grungy thieves roaming desolate portions of the desert, fully aware and taking advantage of the fact that the emperor's watchmen were concentrated primarily on the coastal regions of Nestor Island.

Both men had lanky, unsure postures. Within the shadows and flickers of the fire, one of the men looked like a fox, complete with beady black eyes gently placed over a cluster of gruff

Chapter 15

whiskers. The other man's face was more like a cat—somehow made darker by the flame while his red eyes popped out from the night sky surrounding them.

Both men wielded sharp, heavy swords and the upper hand.

"You've got to be shitting me," Pinocchio said, more agitated than afraid.

"Take whatever you want. Just don't hurt us."

"Hands up." The fox-faced man began to smile, enjoying this line of work more than anyone should.

Pinocchio and Mac complied while the cat-faced man disarmed each of them and tossed their daggers into the distance.

This wasn't their first attempt at theft, and each man knew his job. The cat-faced fellow acted as lookout while making sure that Mac and Pinocchio didn't make any sudden movements. Meanwhile, the fox-faced man was tasked with going through their satchels.

"They don't have anything but food. And water."

"Keep lookin'," his feline comrade replied. He kept his blade tight against Pinocchio's throat, seeing him as the only credible threat. "Where are you two going, anyway? All the way out here?"

"Up a hog's ass for some pork stew," Pinocchio said.

"Cute. That's cute. But I don't really care where you're going. I only care that you're here."

The flapping of leather and the shuffles of frustrated boots paused as the fox-faced man grew impatient with his search. "Nothing." He rejoined the other three, pointing his sword at Mac.

The cat-faced man kept one eye on his partner and the other on his captives. "Empty your pockets."

Mac and Pinocchio did as they were told, which ultimately didn't mean much. "What a waste," the cat-faced man said, digging his fingernails into his forehead. "What do you want to do with 'em?"

"Not much we can do with 'em." The fox-faced captor clicked his tongue to the roof of his mouth.

"Maybe I'm missing something here," Pinocchio said. "But you could just leave us be and go on your way."

The cat-faced man sneered. "And leave you out here to seek out the nearest watchmen? Tell them what we look like—what we're wearing—so we can end up swinging from the nearest gallows? I don't think so."

Pinocchio glanced around. "What watchmen are we going to flag down? It's the middle of the night in the coldest desert on the island."

Poked and prodded on the back by swords, Mac and Pinocchio were pushed away from the visible shelter provided by the shrinking bonfire. Mac's heart began to throb, and he found himself wishing that Jinni had come along for the journey.

The fox-faced man guided Pinocchio, struggling considerably in comparison to his partner in the matter of controlling his prisoner at sword point. "You made us waste a lot of time tonight. You practically brought less than nothing. Even your mules aren't worth this much trouble."

Feeling his life slipping further away, Mac came to grips that he wouldn't be able to brawn his way out of this situation. So he used his words.

"Wait." Mac tried to stop, but a solid jab forced him forward.

"Keep it moving."

Chapter 15

"If you're planning on killing us, I beg you to consider otherwise. My name—is Mac Seehus. My father is the king of Ithaca. And he'd be willing to pay a lot to get me, and my escort, home safely. You may have heard of my father. His name is Ot—"

Pinocchio pivoted to his right, safely wedging his captor's blade beneath his right arm. Pinocchio grabbed the sword's handle with his right hand, claiming a firmer grip than the man holding it. Simultaneously, his left fist slammed into the cat man's pointy nose, sending him to the sand.

Both Mac and the fox-faced man stood stunned as Pinocchio turned toward them both. The other captor tossed his sword to the chilly desert surface and dropped to his knees.

"Don't kill me," he said. "I'll do anything. Just don't kill me."

"OK," Pinocchio said, approaching the man cautiously. "You can start by emptying out your bag. I know you didn't take anything from our camp. So what do you got in there?"

Shaking, the man emptied the contents of his travel pack. "We weren't going to kill you. I swear. We were just going to scare you."

"Yeah," Pinocchio said, pulling the blade away from the man's throat. "That must be why you don't have anything in your pack but knives and rope." He went over each item, touching three lengths of rope and six knives as if checking to make sure they were actually there.

Pinocchio stood the man up and began to tie his hands behind his back. "Mac, you know how to tie a good knot?"

"Yeah."

"Go tie his hands like I tied this one's," Pinocchio said.

The man being held by Pinocchio started to cry.

"Oh, take it easy, ya big baby, before you piss yourself. I'm not going to kill you."

"You're not?" the man sounded like a young child.

"No," Pinocchio said in a soothing voice. "Just doing this to make sure you two don't hurt us tonight. Tomorrow morning we'll turn you loose and be on our way. You really do seem sorry."

"I am. I am!" the man exclaimed. "So sorry."

"Then let's all go back to the campsite and get a good night's rest."

The midmorning desert sun hovered as a heat wave started to burn off the cold of the night. Mac and Pinocchio packed up their camp as the fox-faced man and his feline-looking friend were beginning to wish they had been killed the previous evening. Their hands remained tied behind their backs while their necks were firmly noosed and tethered to the same tree branch. They each stood on a large boulder as their tiptoes bore the full weight of their bodies.

"You said you weren't gonna kill us," the fox-faced man cried out. "Goddamn liar."

"Hey, hey," Pinocchio said, firmly tugging down at the man's legs. "You fellas will be able to live nice, long, fulfilling lives. Just don't let your toes get tired." He looked up at the sky. "And as long as it doesn't rain out here. If it does, those stones you're standing on are going to sink like—well, they're going to sink like stones," he concluded with a chuckle. Pinocchio

Chapter 15

picked up a small rock and used it to inscribe a note in one of the boulders.

"We—tried—to—steal—and—all—we—got—was—this—lousy—rope." He stepped away and read it, satisfied with his penmanship. "Good luck, fellas."

Pinocchio strolled away whistling and joined Mac, who didn't yet have the moral range to know how he should have felt about what had just transpired. The two of them loaded their mules and rode off into the sunrise, ignoring the desperate pleas that finally hushed with distance.

Chapter 16

Pinocchio could see the remorse and sympathy in Mac's eyes. The downtrodden pace of the mules beneath them only exaggerated Mac's depressed jostling.

"Don't feel bad for those guys, kid. Let me tell you something. They were going to kill us. Anyone who threatens your life doesn't deserve your sympathy. And those guys were con artists. They know the best time to get sympathy is right after you've beaten them."

Mac didn't say anything, as he thought he would choke on the words, but he nodded in agreement.

"Right over that hill and past that open patch, you'll see a gate. Approach it slow. When they ask your business, tell them you're here to visit with the emperor and empress, and your father is Otis Seehus." Pinocchio smiled. "They'll know who he is."

"You're not coming with me?"

"No, sir. This is as close as I'm getting."

"Why's that?" Mac asked.

"I don't know if he'd remember me or not, but I don't exactly have that great of a history with the emperor."

"What happened?"

Pinocchio licked a smile onto his lips and tilted his head. "A long time ago, he came to South Nestor and visited a schoolhouse where one of my daughters went. Well, the emperor tells the story of Aladdin and how he went from being somewhat of a loafer to what he would go on to become.

"He hadn't gotten too far into the story before my youngest daughter blurts out, 'Aladdin needs to get a job and quit living off his mother.'"

Mac laughed.

"Oh, yeah. None of the adults laughed, but all the kids thought it was the funniest thing they'd ever heard. None of them knew that Aladdin—and the man telling them the story—were the same person. He turned beet red. It was humiliating. I'm lucky he didn't have me beaten in the street."

"Is that something I should be concerned about?" Mac asked, half grinning.

"Nah. He's no monster. Just moody, sometimes. But aren't we all? Best of luck, Mac. I'll set up camp over there, just past that ravine. Take as much time as you need. I'll be waiting here to guide you back."

Mac followed Pinocchio's directions over the hill. His mule grew curious at a small patch of vibrant vegetation, further slowing its already laid-back pace.

"Come on. Keep it mov—ahhh." Mac placed his hand over the side of his neck in response to the sting of a powerful bug bite. When he touched it, however, he realized the culprit was actually a dart tipped with some sort of sedative.

When Mac woke up, he was blindfolded and concealed from the neck up in a burlap sack. "Hello? Hello?"

Chapter 16

A stern, deep voice answered from the shadows. "What is your business here, young man?"

Mac was shaking his head, enraged by thoughts of Pinocchio. "I'm gonna kill him," he said under his breath.

"What?"

"Nothing. Nothing."

"What is your business here?"

"I sure hope I'm in the right place. My name is Mac Seehus. My father wa—is Otis Seehus. I'm here to see the emperor and empress."

The man responded with silence until his heavy footsteps clanked in Mac's direction. The mysterious watchman pulled his sword and cut Mac loose from the burlap sack. "You're Otis's son, huh?"

"Yes, sir. And I've come a long way to see the emperor and empress, so if they'd allow me to pay them a visit, I'd be indebted."

The watchman peeled off Mac's blindfold and looked him over. "I'm sorry I didn't see it before. I served with your dad in the war. He saved my life."

The lean man had a powerful presence that matched the gruffness of his demanding voice. "Follow me." Shaking off the emotional déjà vu, he guided Mac through an opening in the floor of the corner of the room and down a spiraling staircase.

In the dining hall of their heavily guarded log cabin, the Empress Helen sat alone at a lengthy table, staring at her water glass and tapping on her wineglass. The emperor burst through the door, just barely late. "You look so beautiful tonight," he said, resting his fingers against the silky olive skin on the nape of her neck. "Has anyone told you that lately?"

Odyssey Tale

She aggressively pinched his chin and pulled him in for a kiss. "They have. But not near as often as they used to."

"Oh, stop," he said, playfully. "I know for certain there's zero truth to that." Aladdin leaned in for another kiss, only to be interrupted by three drawn-out knocks from the room's only door.

He rested his forehead on her shoulder and nodded in frustration. "Never fails," he said. "Every time we're about to eat dinner. Every time." The emperor turned to the door. "What do you want?"

The watchman who had last spoken with Mac entered the room, armored helmet in hand. "I'm sorry to interrupt, Your Majesties. But there's someone here to see you, and I don't think you'll want to keep him waiting."

Helen turned to the door, curious.

"Well don't keep us in suspense," the emperor exclaimed. "Who is it?"

The watchman guided Mac through the door.

"Well, I'll be," Helen said. "Looks just like him, doesn't he, hon?"

The emperor stood up and grinned, completely taken aback. "It's uncanny. Pleasure to meet you, Mac. You can call me Aladdin. This is my wife, Helen. Please. Have a seat."

With full bellies and empty plates all around, Aladdin signaled the dinner servants to usher in more wine and the first dessert course. The elaborate feast had featured juicy, tender duck and sugary roasted carrots. Mac's curiosity began to pique, as all

Chapter 16

he'd had to eat that week were thin chunks of dried elk and drier bits of bread.

"I can't thank you both enough for your hospitality, Your Majesty." Mac turned to the empress. "Your Majesty."

Helen replied with a seated curtsy and smile before exuding pensiveness, circling her clanging spoon along the inside edges of a teacup.

"The son of Otis Seehus doesn't need to stand on formalities in this place. Please, call me by my first name," Aladdin said.

"And feel free to call me Helen. It's our pleasure to be hosting you, Mac. And I hope it's not difficult for you to break bread with me."

"Of course not," Mac said. "Why would you think that?"

"Your father. He helped organize the plans and orchestrate the attack that ultimately saved my life and the lives of everyone else the Trojan king had locked up in the castle. I don't even wish to entertain the thoughts of where I'd be right now if it weren't for Otis…but I think of you." Regret began to percolate within her rich auburn eyes. "I think of your mother quite often, and it pains me to know that his saving my life undoubtedly had a role in taking him out of yours."

Mac sat silent, unsure of how to respond.

"In any case," Aladdin said, looking to his wife with an adoring smile, "we're both very grateful. His sharp thinking and conception of the Trojan Horse—it saved a lot more lives than just hers.

"The Trojan king was a ghastly, arrogant man. But he was also a powerful man with a loyal army. Your father used the king's arrogance against him—and rendered that loyal army useless."

"I've heard a lot of stories over the years," Mac said. "But these past several days, traveling through your beautiful country, it's the first I've ever really understood what they mean to some people."

"It must make you proud," Helen said.

"It does. It really does."

"A great man." Aladdin raised his glass for a toast. "To Otis."

Mac and Helen raised their glasses and replied in unison. "To Otis." Several moments passed as all three savored the toast. Mac was the first to break the silence. "I don't suppose either of you know what happened to my father after the war?"

Aladdin sat up. "I'm afraid not. But he talked about you and your mom. A lot. Said he couldn't wait to get home to see you both...I don't want to scare you, Mac. And I don't want to give you false hopes. I'm hesitant to even bring this up, because I've never been one to put faith in thirdhand gossip. But there are rumors regarding his current whereabouts. And in certain circles, there is one rumor that seems to be more prevalent than the rest."

"Please," Mac said. "Go on."

Aladdin spoke in a hushed and delayed tone with subtle hints of fright. "You didn't hear this from me. But there's a black castle on the east coast of Calypso Island."

At that exact moment, thousands of miles from Mac and the emperor and empress's cabin, in a place where the sun hadn't yet set, Otis ran his rough hands through a cake of black dirt.

Chapter 16

The private garden was a sanctuary to him, as was the acre's worth of sweet corn varying in age. He had raised all of them from seedling to table. Damp bits of soil fell through the creases between his fingers before he patted them gently back into the earth. Otis hadn't aged a day and spent most of his time in this garden, collecting sun with the rotation of crops while looking out to the open sea.

Otis's youthful appearance, his garden, the corn, and all the emotional gratification that came with cultivation, however, were nothing more than a grand illusion. Otis was never confused about who he was or where. In fact, he had such a firm grasp on reality that his imagination was all he had left to keep him sane.

The reality of it was that Otis spent his days, nights, and everything in between confined to a narrow, empty sliver of concrete on the face of the Calypso Queen's castle. Where once stood the balcony of his luxurious private suite, the most recent layer of bricks had pushed him uncomfortably close to the edge. He might have accidentally rolled off the edge and into the rock-infested waters below, but harsh chills and whipping winds served as a constant reminder of the bloodthirsty fall awaiting such a mistake.

He was unshaven and unkempt and had aged considerably. His sharp, light-brown eyes gazed into the distance, failing to hide years of pain and heartache. Even a shaggy, goatlike salt-and-pepper beard covering half of his face wasn't able to hide the hurt.

The queen of Calypso Island was still every bit as lovely as the day Otis had met her. Even though she was over fifty years of age, time had preserved her youth with soft skin and thick layers of rich brunette hair. However, despite the ample wit and charm that matched her beauty, insecurities relating to her looks kept her from achieving true happiness. Otis's stubborn refusal to confess his love for her was also a strike to her ego.

Long, doe-like eyelashes bounced in the direction of her so-called magic mirror. She twiddled her thumbs and ran the glossy black fingernails of one hand over the other's fingertips, nervously initiating eye contact with herself.

"Mirror of magic, on the wall in front of me. When will Otis Seehus confess his love to me?" The queen closed her eyes and anxiously awaited a response from the reflective surface.

"His heart belongs to another," the mirror said. "As it always has. As it always will. But you already know this. We have this conversation every year around this time. Why must you insist on keeping him here? You say you love him. But this tortures him. And it tortures you."

"When you saw the sun come up today, did you ask yourself, 'What can I say that will get me smashed into little pieces?'"

"I cannot see the sun," the mirror replied coldly. "And you only make such veiled threats because you know I am right."

She turned her back to the mirror and paced about the room. After several quiet minutes, the mirror began to speak again. "Let him go," it said.

She turned to face it. "Stop."

"Let him go."

"I said stop it."

"Let him go."

With an ear-piercing scream, she reached for an apple-shaped stone paperweight on her nightstand and threw it at the mirror. It shattered as her shrieking ran out of steam. She quietly

Chapter 16

approached the thousands of tiny reflective shards, hesitant to look down. As she made eye contact with a scrambled version of herself, the mirror whispered once more. "Let him go."

"Please be quiet," she begged, tearing up. She placed her palms on her temples and pressed them inward, trying to squeeze the frustration out. After an exasperating sigh, she burrowed her face in her pillow, along with the tears welling up in her eyes.

"Please stop," she said, before crying herself to sleep.

Her beg had never sounded so desperate. Her mirror had never been so blunt. But what she hadn't realized, and what no one else knew, was that Jinni had snuck into her bedroom through her balcony as she ate breakfast. When she came back, he was hidden beneath her bed, where he used his mind's eye to enter hers. In doing so, Jinni was able to hear the mirror's voice and imitate it with identical tone and diction. It was an aggressive tactic, even for him. But Jinni had visited Otis's balcony just moments before. It was there where he found a beaten and broken man who was too afraid to leave on his own accord. Aware of the consequences that lie in wait should the queen notice a difference between her mirror's voice and his version of it, Jinni *felt* the highest probability of success within this particular strategy.

Chapter 17

Throughout his rather long life, Jinni had served in more wars than he could remember. For some of them, he had volunteered; in others, he was serving under slave's orders. But there was one common thread: regardless of the reasoning behind his participation, Jinni had a knack for solo assassin missions. His cunning, catlike maneuverability and stealthy attendance had caught dozens of high-profile targets off guard. Before they could even smell his breath, Jinni had already taken theirs.

While his abilities as a chameleon were a necessity to move around unnoticed in the Calypso Queen's castle, killing was out of the question, as it would draw the kind of attention and suspicion that would undo any progress he'd made while pretending to be the mirror.

As it had many times before, proper planning and decades of experience prevailed, and Jinni slipped out of the castle and through the surrounding forest unnoticed. Due to the overwhelming power of certain streams he'd taken to get to Calypso Island, Jinni guided his lifeboat along a different path.

He had spent three uneventful days on calm, balmy waters en route back to South Nestor Island and the Lost Boys, but before he could pat himself on the back for a job well done, he began to hear the water ahead screaming and pulling at the water gently guiding his boat.

"Great." Of course, getting there was easy. Jinni grabbed his oar firmly and dug into his seat as the lifeboat approached a waterfall. He took several deep breaths to brace himself for what was sure to be a sharp descent whose depth was still to be determined.

The initial drop wasn't all that remarkable, but once the lifeboat had taken the plunge, there was no end in sight to the raging waves smashing into one another and the cruel rocks craving flesh. Jinni, usually much cooler in such situations, succumbed to waves of panic as angry smacks from the aquatic cradle jolted the lifeboat.

"Come on," he said. From out of nowhere, the most significant wave up to that point threw itself over Jinni, landing enough in his craft to slow it considerably. "No. No. Come on."

The overworked vessel began to moan as the rocks reaching for the surface dug into its hull.

"Here we go," Jinni said, finally getting a glimpse of calm water. After two more gut punches to the lifeboat's tender portside, Jinni successfully guided it through the rough and into a large gentle pocket stretching ahead past his field of vision. He placed the oar at his feet, leaned back, and exhaled a breath of relief, then another, running trembling hands down a face that was still in shock.

"Wooooo," he yelled out. He was still unable to control his rapid rate of breath but began to relax his shoulders and the rest of his body before reaching back down for the oar. "Unbelievable," he said, nodding and looking ahead.

Chapter 17

Without warning, something burst from the water just in front him, stopping the boat—and the peace. Before he could pull a sword or dagger to stop her, the Sea Witch's face was inches from his own.

"Miss me?" she asked, showcasing her horrid green teeth.

Jinni reached toward his waist for a weapon, but his reflexes were no match for the scorpion-like strike of a tentacle wrapping around his throat. Just as quickly as she'd struck, she released him and retreated. Smiling, she slithered away and sunk beneath the surface with a deliberate pace.

Jinni's vision blurred, and his unconscious body fell limp in the lifeboat. He entered a vivid dream state, revisiting a tapestry of past traumas while simultaneously creating new ones. She left him alone out there in the vast aquatic space, at the mercy of her venom, the weather, and any other monsters lurking beneath the disturbingly still water.

A shiny bar of soap sat in the center of a sudsy bathtub until the delicate hand of Peter Pan's most current companion dunked it under the water. Her back rested against the clawed tub's porcelain wall while his rested on her welcoming breasts. She ran the soap over his bare chest and caressed his neck and shaggy hair afterward. He couldn't recall the last time he'd spent consecutive evenings with the same woman but found himself hoping the streak would continue.

"How do you know so much about Otis Seehus?" he asked, wrapping her left hand with both of his before planting a gentle kiss upon it.

"How do you *not* know more about him?" she asked. "You're the one on the rescue mission—so you say."

He could hear her grin form with her last words. "Everything about you is exquisite. You know that? Your skin. Your eyes. Even your name."

"Are you taking a piss?" she asked, wrestling with a giggle.

He looked down, taken aback. "No. What the hell kind of guy you think I am?"

"No," she said, smiling. "It means, are you messing with me?"

"Oh. No, I'm serious. I think your name is lovely. And I've never heard it anywhere else."

"That's because it's a nickname—a moniker that I acquired. The night of my first performance, some drunken asshole sitting in the back yelled out, '*When-dee-ya* take your clothes off? I ain't payin' ya to tell stories.' My stage name has been Wendy ever since. My real name is Moira Angela."

"Moira Angela," he said, enunciating. "Even more beautiful than I could have possibly imagined."

"You are *the* biggest bullshitter this side of the island."

"I'm serious," he said. "It is. And you never did tell me how you know so many Otis stories."

"I'm a traveling storyteller," she said. "You know that."

"You know what I mean," he said, playfully tossing a handful of bubbles over his shoulder. "There's a lot of traveling storytellers. Not all of them know as much about Otis Seehus as you do."

"Popularity, mostly," she said. "When people ask to hear stories about the Trojan War, it's him they want to hear about.

Chapter 17

Him and Achilles. Sometimes Robin Hood. Maybe one day they'll want to hear stories about the great Peter Pan."

Peter grinned. "They'll be hard up for stories if that's the case."

"You're still young," she said. "There's time for you yet. And you can't be a Lost Boy forever."

Peter's smile washed away with her comment. Wendy could feel his mood shift despite being unable to see his troubled face.

"But that's not a bad thing. Especially when you consider what they're doing tonight—compared to what you're doing tonight."

"Don't think for one second that you have any idea what I'm doing tonight, Moira Angela." He turned to face her and leaned forward to kiss the dampness of her ear and neck. "But just for fun—guess how long I can hold my breath." He slowly burrowed his forehead into the suds, disappearing into the water. She closed her eyes and grinned, unleashing several more giggles. One thing was for certain: none of the other Lost Boys were doing what Peter was this evening.

The violet sky carried a hodgepodge of voices and indiscernible conversations over the docks and on the deck of the stationary *Elvira*. One, Two, and Tootles sat in a lopsided circle open to Nibs, who was pressing his thumbs into a corncob pipe.

"So is it tobacco? Or something else?" One asked.

"And why's it green?" Tootles wiped the gloss from his face. As it was unseasonably humid that night, the moisture carried by the sticky evening air refused to absorb the damp layer accumulating on his skin.

"The girl who sold it to me said it was like tobacco but way better," Nibs said, frustrated that he had to explain himself further. He finished packing the pipe, growing impatient with their lack of faith, but he began to question his own after a quick whiff of his fingers triggered an involuntary scrunch of the nose.

"It better be," Two said. "It smells like a skunk's asshole."

"That's probably your asshole you're smellin'. Crick-shy mooncalf."

"What the hell did you just call me?"

"Take it easy," Nibs said. "Just bustin' balls." He pulled a match from his breast pocket and sparked it to life before placing it over a small corner of the open pipe. He took several puffs and passed the pipe to his left, leaving a tiny black blemish in the otherwise pea-colored herb. A chalky breath of burning plant scorched the back of his throat, causing him to double over and release a violent, unruly cough. Everyone stared in silent horror.

"Are you all right?" Tootles asked.

With his arms wrapped around his shins and his knees digging into his chest, Nibs rocked back and forth. He couldn't stop coughing but was able to ease the increasing concern for his wellness with an enthusiastic thumbs-up.

"Pass that pipe, and give me a match," One said eagerly.

The four of them passed the pipe and book of matches around as they normally would a bottle of whiskey, surprised by the increasing euphoria, peace, and lightweight depth saturating the air and conversation.

"What I want to know," Nibs said, with lead-filled eyelids. "One. How did they find this stuff? Two. How did they know

Chapter 17

how to grow it? And three. How did they know that burning it and breathing in the smoke would make you feel like this?"

"I thought you were talking to me and him for a second," One said.

"What?"

"You were like—One—blah, blah, blah. Two—blah, blah, blah." Two's eyes were practically closed as his ear-to-ear grin quickly turned to a laugh.

"Were you seriously not listening?" Nib's asked.

"You lost me when you started talking about your round earth theory," One said.

Nibs sat up with a passionate hostility. "If it was flat like all you assholes say, there would be so many more stories about ships falling off the edge. You hear more stories about the Sea Witch than you do about ships falling off."

"How would any of the stories get back if they fell off the earth, dummy?"

"Eat a dick," Nibs said. "I was done with this conversation five minutes ago."

The bunch sat still long enough to let the dust of the bad vibes settle. "Where's Slightly tonight?" One asked. "He'd like this."

"Not sure," Tootles said.

One, hesitant, looked over both shoulders and lowered his voice. "Have you guys ever seen Slightly...go home with a guy?"

"I have," Nibs said. He began to smirk, then giggle, causing a chain reaction of laughter.

"I walked in on him with a guy once. Here on the *Elvira*," Tootles said.

The laughter was contagious.

"Why you ask, One?" Nibs asked. "It bother you?"

"Nah," One said. "I wouldn't say *bother*. I think it's a bit weird, and I can't help but think it'd be rather painful. But to each his own."

The group's laughter collected and swelled. Tootles contained his for a moment but never let go of the wide grin being smashed by his chubby cheeks. "The poor bastard he brought back sure sounded like he was hurtin'."

At this point, the group's laughter boiled like a pot of water, taking on more heat. Even people in town were starting to hear the faint collection of cackles.

"Slightly has a great big hog too," Tootles added, wiping a tear from his eye.

"How the hell do you know that?" Nibs asked.

"I walked in on him changing one time."

"Christ Almighty, Tootles," One said. "Don't you ever knock?"

Two sat up and looked toward Nibs. "You should pack another pipe. This stuff is great."

A familiar voice entered from a distance. "There she is," Slightly said. "The *Elvira*." The group turned and opened their squinting eyes just enough to see Slightly approaching with a male counterpart who had a similar build and facial features.

"What are you non-pussy-gettin' losers laughing about?" Slightly asked, never stopping en route to his room. "And what are you doing back so early?"

"Nibs got some sort of special tobacco from a girl in town. Want to try it?"

"No thanks," Slightly said, twitching his nose at the lingering foreign smell.

Chapter 17

"Who's your friend?" One asked, his smile about to burst with laughter.

The question was met with the aggressive slam of the downstairs hatch. Once Slightly and his new friend were out of sight, the laughter hit an entirely new level.

"Oh, I have one. I have one," Tootles said urgently. He glanced over at the orange-and-white-striped cat. "Do you think that Cecil can see things we can't—like gods, or ghosts…or trolls?"

The following morning, Nibs awoke, feeling as though someone had lined the roof of his mouth and the back of his throat with carpet. He stumbled toward the nearest barrel of drinking water and scooped out two full ladles before being distracted by a rhythmic tapping coming from somewhere nearby. He moved with purpose throughout the vessel, searching it inside and out. He couldn't pinpoint the tapping, but he knew it wasn't coming from any of the other Lost Boys—all of whom were still fast asleep, scattered about everywhere but their beds. The only other living soul up and about was Cecil, licking remnants of a late-night milk bottle from Tootles's lips.

Tap. Tap. Tap. There it was again. *Tap. Tap.* Nibs stepped over Tootles and looked over the *Elvira*'s starboard side.

"Oh shit," Nibs said, turning toward the comatose bunch. "Guys. Wake up. It's Jinni."

Jinni was as dead to the world as the rest of them and looked ten times worse. The stingers injected into his neck were clearly visible, despite the expanding cherry rash surrounding them.

It had worked its way down his chest and up past the curve of his chin.

"Jinni." The increased volume of Nibs's voice woke everyone else on board while its urgency galvanized them into hurrying over. Collectively, the bunch raised Jinni's boat and carried him to his bed as he shook and spewed gibberish in the midst of what seemed to be a harrowing nightmare.

Slightly's fingers were steady and precise with a pair of rusted tweezers. He pulled the first of many stingers from Jinni's neck and placed them in a glass jar before rolling him over and realizing that there were twice as many scattered across his back.

Within the dreadful, hallucinogenic slumber, Jinni kept repeating himself. "Don't put me back in there," he shouted, tears streaming out the bottom of his closed eyelids. "Please don't put me back in there."

"Man. These things are in there good," Slightly said. He removed two more turquoise stingers from Jinni's back, struggling to win the tug-of-war with the tender flesh.

"Don't put me back in there. Please. Please don't put me back in there."

Chapter 18

Otis's wrists and ankles had been shackled to the head chair at the Calypso Queen's dining table. He guessed it was sometime early in the evening but wasn't sure, as he'd spent most of the day soaking in the sunrise and tending to the garden within his mind. His uninvited, unkempt beard dangled close to the table's edge while his eyes screamed out in fear of his next punishment. What could this be about? It had been years since he'd been allowed in this room.

The queen entered with a smile but was met with a gloomy stare from Otis.

"What do you want?" he asked.

"You're always so angry," she said.

"Don't act like you don't know why."

"I've been doing some thinking this morning," she said. "I've been doing a lot of thinking on a lot of mornings as of late. And as much as I love you, and…as much as I wish you could see that the two of us are meant to be together…I'm not getting any younger. I was so focused on ruling this kingdom with the perfect king by my side, I failed to remember, or maybe I chose not to. It'll never work if that king doesn't want me by his." The fight to hold back tears quickly cemented itself as one of the fiercest battles she'd ever had to endure.

"I know…that you've been sending out messages," she said, pausing to swallow a sad lump occupying her throat. "I feel dumb for even saying this, but I honestly thought that if enough time passed, you would forget all about the life you had in Ithaca. I know now that's never going to happen. And I don't have the time to wait for you to do something you're clearly never going to do. If leaving is what you want, you may go."

"Are you serious?" he asked. "This isn't a test? Or some trap?"

"No. No test. No trap. You are free to leave. When you do, go to the dock on the north end of Ogygia Village. There will be a small vessel ready for you. I'm sorry things didn't go differently for us, Otis."

Otis looked at her in disbelief. Was it really going to be this easy? She stepped back into the hallway, shutting the door behind her before leaning in to share whispers with two loyal guards. "When he's ready, escort Mr. Seehus to the front gates, and let him go."

Concealed by ominous iron masks, the guards' collective curiosity went unnoticed until one of them spoke, only to make sure he hadn't misheard. "Your Majesty. Are you certain?"

"Do not make me repeat myself," she said, with furious pupils hiding behind a calm demeanor.

"Of course, Your Majesty. My apologies."

"Before he leaves, I need you to get a message out to the Sea Witch. Let her know that Otis will be shipping out from the north docks. Tell her to be on the lookout for a black vessel with a red stripe on the bottom."

Chapter 18

"Your Majesty. I must beg for your forgiveness, as it seems I'm having trouble trusting my own hearing. I have to ask again, just to confirm. Are you certain this is what you want?"

"No." The emotional dam holding her tears finally cracked, allowing one to fall, painting her cheek with a trail of eye-liner. She turned away from the guards. "But do not make me repeat myself."

"Yes, Your Majesty, I will get the message to her mermaids at once."

Despite its dense and bustling population, the island of Calypso was a relatively small chunk of land. As a result, the castle was visible from almost every vantage point thereon. Living in the shadows of royalty served as a constant reminder to the adults that someone was in charge and living much higher on the hog than they were. But the kids, ambitious and eager with imagination, saw something else.

Little boys would make believe they were knights, basking in the prestige that attaches itself to one's armor when he's wielding a sword in defense of Calypso's homeland. Meanwhile, little girls were arguing over who got to be the queen during their playtime. The perks included illusory access to the most beautiful silks and linens in the world, servants readily available to handle any task, regardless of its pettiness—and, of course, the crown, often made of paper, twigs, twine, or flowers.

Many little girls pretended to be queen. While most would eventually grow out of the phase, there were a handful who would not. Some girls spent their entire lives preparing and expecting to one day be in the position to be noticed and courted by that generation's prince. The current Calypso Queen, ironically, had not been one of these little girls.

Her childhood had been rich with imagination, but daydreams of pampered life in a towering castle filled with servants weren't for her. Instead, her days consisted of acting out life as the woman who raised her, her great-grandmother. She'd scurry about the yard, frantically collecting seedlings and moving them from spot to spot, repeating, "Oh my lord, oh my lord."

She and her great-grandmother lived alone in a small cottage hidden by acres of forest and the orchards they lived on. The lush soil surrounding the modest domicile held so many apple trees that the air smelled like cider most of the year. The sweet nectar attracted the friendliest of honeybees and visitors from the surrounding area and beyond. Everyone, from impoverished peasants to affluent royalty, indulged in at least one slice of pie while collecting a bushel or two of honey-sweet apples. Deep reds, tart greens, and rich golds dangled in a magnificent tapestry of flavor. It also provided a considerable living.

Around the Calypso Queen's thirteenth birthday, her great-grandmother's age and occupational limits were becoming more noticeable. Her mind remained just as sharp as always, but the rest of her just couldn't keep up. Arthritic fingers and crippling back pain kept her from even the most basic of daily chores.

Finally, one night she went to sleep and didn't wake up. Her great-granddaughter was devastated, but intimate knowledge of the business and the mental maturity necessary for its demands had her ready. Problems arose fast, however, as the area's residents began helping themselves to free bushels through all hours of the day. Their blatant and disrespectful disregard for the young girl's birthright was brought to the attention of the king and queen.

Chapter 18

She pleaded for their help, but it was promptly decided that thirteen years of age was much too young to handle all those apples alone. For her troubles, the young woman was shipped off the island and placed in a reformatory for girls.

Within days of her transport, her great-grandmother's property was appropriated by the king and queen and made available for public use and consumption. During this time, the fruitful orchards in which she'd spent her youth—and in which she expected to spend time with her own great-grandchildren—were consumed and depleted by the island's ungrateful residents.

On the other side of the world, she was hardened by the strictest of teachers with the singular goal of churning out midwives. The wrathful whip of a switch on her neck and tops of her fingers helped her forget her old name. Once she was finally willing to admit that her new name was her real name, she was allowed to grow her hair back out. Life with the tyrannical mistresses really became quite easy for Daisy after that.

After seven years of school, and eight days before her twenty-first birthday, the vile group of women who'd beaten and shamed her into submission those early years were gleefully offering her a position to become one of them. She requested some time to think about it, and much to her surprise and delight, they told her to take as much time as she needed. She could return anytime. A job and room would be waiting.

She took that initial time and dedicated it to travel, returning to her native homeland, pining to see what had become of the orchards where she'd grown up. After a rough and bumpy five-month stint on the open seas, she stepped on the rich Calypso Island soil for the first time since it had been taken from under her feet. She was unsure what kind of emotions to expect, or if any of it would still be there.

She soon discovered that both the house and the orchards were exactly where she'd left them. The orchards, however, had been scorched. Bare, desperate branches reached to the sky and cried out for help, but the charred black soil cradling each one consumed more life than it supplied. A stream of tears filled her eyes and slid down her cheeks. Only one tree still showed signs of life. It was charred like the others but held a handful of ripe and healthy apples varying in color.

The house was wrecked. It had been vandalized and burned and was leaning on itself, looking as though a stiff breeze would soon put it out of its misery. She stepped over the threshold gingerly, not wanting to disturb the walls. The inside was filled with crunchy leaves, empty bottles, and other various articles of trash. There was no pride or shame motivating visitors into caring for the remnants and litter scattered about the once-proud home.

The only article of furniture that hadn't been completely destroyed was her grandmother's mirror. The subtle gold shimmer of its frame was now drenched in permanent soot, but the reflective surface was every bit as clean and shiny as it ever was. That was about the time she began to hear it talk. It was a bit more hushed and a lot more frightening, but the mirror's voice was eerily reminiscent of her late great-grandmother's. And it only wanted one thing: revenge.

Just as Daisy was wrapping her mind around the fact that her great-grandmother's mirror had just spoken, someone outside inadvertently caught her attention. The portly stranger seemed

Chapter 18

to know her way around, loading up on the choicest of apples from the lone flourishing tree.

"Hello," Daisy said, approaching from behind.

The startled stranger perked up, looking as proper as the bonnet carefully strapped under her wrinkled chin. "You're on private property, miss. Run along now."

Something inside Daisy's heart shifted. "Private property?" she asked, grinning.

"Yes. Belongs to the king and queen. You must be soft in the head, or new to the island, if you don't know that. Either way, you best be moving."

"And how do you know it belongs to the king and queen?" Daisy asked.

"Because I work for them. Been their nanny for over fifteen years. Now I have done told you more than once. You need to leave."

Daisy glared, turned away, and left.

The nanny, little more than mildly annoyed, turned back to the tree, carefully examining each apple before violently plucking it from its branch. She turned around twice, thinking she heard footsteps, but neither time did anyone or anything besides the breeze enter her field of vision. As she redirected her attention back to the tree for one last grab at the apples, the shadow of Daisy raising a shovel above her head began to cast over the unsuspecting woman.

The woman awoke tied to a chair—and in such shock that she failed to notice the gaping cut leaking from the back of her head.

"I am about to ask you a series of questions," Daisy said, opening and closing a set of pliers cradled softly in her fingertips.

"And if you answer them correctly—no, if you answer them honestly—I promise, from the bottom of my heart, that you can be on your way, and the two of us will never cross paths again."

"And if I won't?" the panicked and angry woman uttered.

Daisy gripped the pliers in her left hand and squeezed them shut. "People don't realize how sensitive their thumbs are to pain."

Daisy did not need to apply as much pressure as she'd expected, and the woman gave up more information than was necessary. It turns out that the elderly woman had just returned from an extended sabbatical and had yet to visit the castle. She was picking these apples to surprise the royal family with fresh cobbler. This trivial tidbit may not have seemed like much at the time, but it would prove to be crucial for Daisy's next move.

By the time the interrogation was over, Daisy had all the pertinent information necessary to set in motion a plan she'd only thought of within those moments. Unfortunately for the woman she had detained, Daisy had to go back on her promise of letting the woman go on her way. To have this woman leave and tell the king and queen what had just transpired would not have been an issue had Daisy just left the island. But Daisy wasn't going anywhere. And one bad apple spoils the bunch, as they say.

Dressed in the disguise of a woman thirty years her senior, Daisy approached the Calypso Island castle. With a large dish of apple cobbler warming the weaves of her basket, Daisy entered, acting as the former nanny's cousin. She offered condolences and delivered the news that their nanny had fallen ill and passed during her sabbatical.

Chapter 18

With heavy hearts and trusting palates, they invited Daisy in and gobbled up every last bit of her cobbler. The king, queen, and teenage princess practically licked their plates clean, but the preteen prince was not one for apples, so he declined. So pleased with the rich dessert, and hearing of her education and experience, the queen offered Daisy a job on the spot. She would serve as a nanny and midwife, should the aging couple decide to have more children.

One year later, to celebrate her first anniversary as their hired confidante, Daisy baked another batch of the cobbler. This one, however, tasted somewhat off. The king went down first, clinging to the fragile handle of his porcelain coffee cup until it shattered in his hand. The queen watched him until she clutched her chest and went down. The prince leaped out of his seat, rushing to his mom first. "No. No. What's wrong with them?"

The prince had been so focused on his mother and father that he failed to notice when his sister stood up and placed her fingers against an increasingly irritated throat.

"Oh my," Daisy whispered in her ear. "Your snow-white skin is turning green, my dear."

The young prince dug his forehead into his father's lifeless chest while clinging to his mother's nearest arm.

"You did this," he yelped. "It was your cobbler."

"That couldn't have been it. I had just as much as they did," she said, pointing to her empty plate. She was telling the truth, but she left out the part where she'd strategically eaten from a section that hadn't been poisoned.

"You're right," he said. "Who did this? Who would do something like this?"

"I don't know. But I've seen this happen before, and we have to keep what happened a secret."

"What? Why?"

"I know the timing isn't ideal, but as of this moment, you are king. And if you don't keep this from getting out, people are going to think you did it."

"Why would they think that?" he asked.

"Because you stand to benefit the most."

"My whole family just died in front of me," he asked through falling tears. "How did I benefit?"

"You are the king now."

Defeated, he calmed himself. "I would never do something like that just to be king."

"They don't know that. And many of them would. So they're not going to believe you." At a time when the new king needed someone most, Daisy was there to guide him.

"Well, what do I do now?" he asked.

She pondered in her pride, already knowing the answer and feeling good about her control over the young man. "You need to tell the servants and the guards—that someone has just waged war on Calypso Island."

Thousands were slaughtered in the battles that followed Daisy's counseling, but one thing remained perfectly clear: there was a new king on Calypso Island. With his trusted maternal figure always at his side, the king matured into a rather fine young man. But on the night of his twentieth birthday, Daisy retired to her quarters for the night and didn't wake up the following morning. The king was devastated and spent the first couple of days alone and in silence.

Chapter 18

But with every death comes new life, and at the funeral, the most beautiful woman came to pay her respects. She was in her mid to late twenties, but her tan cherub cheeks and shroud of freckles made her look much younger. Her black hair was sleek and shiny, and her eyes were so kind—and familiar.

She introduced herself as Daisy's niece and offered a gentle handshake. After a brief conversation, the king was elated to discover that many of their interests and ideals were shared. Not only that, but the young woman was well versed in several subjects in which he had a recent interest.

At a time when the king needed someone the most, Tamber was there to fill the void that Daisy had left behind—and then some. Three months later, Tamber was the queen. She always seemed bubbly and glowing with love. Little did her young king know, however, that she was more tickled to be using her given name than she was with her royal status, or him.

Their first year together went as many first years go, but on their first anniversary, the queen learned something about her king that caught her by surprise. While lying in bed, she dug her teeth into the crispy flesh of a bright-green apple. He hopped in and took it from her, taking a bite from the other side.

"Since when do you like apples?" she asked in a teasing tone.

"I've never—disliked apples. At least not their flavor."

"Well, what don't you like about apples, if it isn't their flavor?" she asked with a smile.

"When I was a kid, there was this orchard not too far from here. Beautiful. Apple trees stretching as far as you could see in any direction. We were there picking some one afternoon, and I got stung by a bee. A lot of bees, actually. It seems I'd stumbled across a hive. I cried, of course, all the way home.

The next day I demanded my father burn the orchard to the ground. And he did."

The queen appeared a bit rattled but was aghast inside. "But your father loved apples. Why would he do that?"

"Becuase he loved me more than he loved apples. And he wanted to keep me happy. It seems so silly to think about now that I'm older."

"Looks like we're still discovering things about each other," she said, playfully inviting him under the sheets.

Suddenly, his mouth began to go dry, and his tongue began to itch. Soon after, he was bent over and couldn't stop coughing.

"If I had known you were going to take a bite from my apple," she said, "I would have just put it on the other side."

"Put what on the other side?" he asked, choking and scraping his tongue against his teeth in a feeble attempt to relieve the itch.

"The poison I put in your tea earlier," she said. "It's the same one I put in that cobbler when you were just a little boy."

His eyes widened as he struggled to draw in one last breath. Then he fell to the floor with a heavy thud.

"Happy anniversary. My king."

Her revenge had been slow and ice cold. But it was ten times sweeter than the sweetest apple in the world. Once it was over, however, and she had taken the castle from the people who had taken her home, she realized that she had spent the better part of her life chasing a life she never wanted to begin with.

Her powerful lust for revenge had clouded her judgment and made her forget what she really wanted—a life like her great-grandmother's. It should have been a simple yet busy life, sowing seeds, picking apples, and baking cobblers and pies.

Chapter 18

She wanted a family who loved her. Kids, maybe a dog, but first and foremost, a companion. A man—someone who could protect her with his bare hands and didn't need an army of loyal guards. Someone who could kill and cook her a meal, and promptly spoon-feed her dessert in bed. A lean man with brawny shoulders and a baby face hardened by battle, but receptive to romance. A man who couldn't be corrupted or compromised into wavering in his love for her, regardless of time apart. A man they sang songs about. A man they told stories about. A man like Otis.

The Calypso Queen reflected on her most pivotal life moments on the cold, narrow balcony she'd forced Otis to endure for the last several years. He was no longer there, but she could feel him. His presence lingered in the air. It was as though he'd left a large piece of himself out there. She couldn't see it, but its power to control her mood was just as dominant as that of Otis in the flesh.

"I still don't know why I couldn't make you love me here—in this lifetime. But that's OK. We can rule the seas together in the next one."

The Calypso Queen closed her eyes and stepped over the edge of the balcony. She didn't scream. She didn't regret it. Knowing that she and Otis were destined to be together, the Calypso Queen had done her part. Now it was up to the Sea Witch, waiting somewhere off the coast, to kill Otis and complete the final chapter of Queen Tamber's destiny.

Chapter 19

Right around the time the Calypso Queen plunged from her balcony, Penelope was looking out from her own balcony. She wasn't about to jump, nor had she thought about it. She was falling in a different way, killing herself slowly. She told herself time and time again that this was going to be the last bottle. She'd reach the end, feeling good about her dwindling need for another. But the final sips were never able to put her at ease, as last sips should. And once the warmth dissolved, there was no way to go about her day. So many moments were spent in a trance, thinking about that distant sweet smell of roasted poppy seeds—almost chocolaty. And getting a good night's sleep? Forget it.

Still, no matter how badly Penelope craved the next bottle, once she had it in her possession, she would sit and stare for a good long while before taking that first pull. It was almost as if she had to convince herself that she could do it. She could control it. She even felt as though she didn't want it. Then, the first sip would start the cycle all over again.

Throughout her lifetime, Penelope had heard from a handful of people that the ability to have a baby does not make one a mother. This is true. For far too long, she wasn't a mother to

Mac. She was just some woman who lay about most of the day, only sober between the hours of noon and two o'clock in the afternoon. Despite her good advice, and having been right about most things, Penelope's own mother was an awful woman. She used to chase Penelope around the house with sheep shears, threatening to cut off her hair. She did once. Penelope promised herself that she was never going to be that kind of mother. But she turned into something worse. She was neglectful and conceited, and for reasons unknown to her, she still had people who loved her. For that, she would be eternally grateful.

As she looked out from the balcony at a beautiful day that was about to be wasted, someone knocked on her door. Clio was a loyal friend and a retired servant. Clio had known Otis since he was only a boy and had a heavy hand in his rearing. When Mac was born, she taught him many of the same life lessons and morals. She spent many of her waking hours in the castle, trying her best to conceal her resentment for the so-called suitors.

Their boorish manner and mindless vandalism of the castle bothered her thoughts even when she wasn't around. Had she known how bad Penelope's lust for laudanum had gotten, Clio would have smacked her sideways and tied her to her bed. There, Penelope would have remained until she had expunged that poison from her blood, until it didn't cry out for more.

"Clio," Penelope said. Her eyes were most lucid this time of day. Otherwise, Clio might have known something was wrong. "How are you? How have you been? Please, come in. Can I get you something to drink? Tea? Coffee?"

Clio tilted her head slightly before looking deep into Penelope's eyes. It was a look Penelope would never forget. It was as if Clio didn't recognize her—as if Clio had come

Chapter 19

to speak to Penelope, and the woman standing there was just some imposter.

"What is it?" Penelope asked, puzzled, and perhaps hostile as a result of her shame. Clio stepped in, hesitantly, leaving the door cracked behind her.

"It's Mac."

"What about him?" Penelope asked.

"My cousin. She works down at the docks. He saw Mac. About a month ago, he left with a Lost Boy crew. Apparently, he's out looking for Otis."

"That can't be," she said.

"I'm sorry I didn't say something sooner. I just found out myself."

"That can't be," Penelope repeated. "Can't be. I just saw Mac." She shuffled through her recent memories like a stack of playing cards. When she came to the realization that she hadn't seen him in over a month and didn't even know it, Penelope began to feel ill.

There is no greater love than the one a mother feels for her children. Motherhood is constantly changing. Even when all the right things are done at all the right times, most mothers will question and second-guess everything they do. It's sacrifice; it's heartbreak; it's unconditional love. It's rewarding and challenging all at once. It's exhaustion from sleepless nights when she knows her child is hurting, and she's helpless because there's nothing she can do to make it better. It's all those things and more. And, admittedly, it took Penelope much too long to learn all this.

When one thinks about what she's willing to do to provide for her children and protect them—it's almost animalistic. Mac was Penelope's cub, but she was far from behaving like a mother bear. She burst into tears and buried herself into Clio's loving arms. "It's OK," Clio said. "He's gonna be fine. He's a strong boy, like his daddy."

"You're right," Penelope said, calming down. "We have to keep this a secret as best we can. Who else knows?"

"I'm not sure. I already told my cousin to keep quiet, and I trust him. But if anyone else knows, it's just a matter of time before it spreads like fire."

"Thank you, Clio," she said. Penelope's tears had finally subsided.

Out in the hallway, around a corner and well within earshot, Eury took a mental note of every word exchanged between the two. A satisfied smile laid claim to his face as he left before someone saw him eavesdropping.

Clio stayed with Penelope that day until dusk, refusing to leave until Penelope convinced her that she'd be OK alone, successfully hiding helplessness, shame, and a heavy heart. Penelope reached under her pillow for the fresh laudanum bottle she'd acquired that morning and carried it out to the balcony to catch the last few moments of sunset. It provided just enough light for her to watch the bottle fly upward from her hand before crashing into the calm sea below. It was the last time she'd ever touch a bottle of laudanum.

Several days away from Calypso Island, in one of the colder parts of the ocean, a large passenger ship traveled north on a predetermined route that would stop along several island chains.

Chapter 19

Ithaca was one of its ports. As they had been ordered to do, the Calypso Queen's most trusted guards passed a message out to the Sea Witch using her network of trusted merpeople.

The Sea Witch slithered gracefully through the icy depths, lighting the black around her with an eerie turquoise hue. Bobbing her torso and tentacles to move forward, she looked up and caught a glimpse of a black ship with a red stripe running down its center.

"Otis." She grinned, looked up, and shifted her trajectory to slant upward, stretching and spreading her tentacles behind her until they were one hundred times their original length. Keeping pace with little effort, she ran her fingers over a tiny spot on the bottom of the hull before endless locks of glowing tentacles groped over the rest. Each one, searching for weak spots, attached like a parasite and began digging into the soft dimples of the ship. As she rooted in further, the captain, who was about to go to bed, turned to his first mate. "Why are we stopped?" he asked.

Most of the ship's occupants were asleep in their bunks or were in their rooms preparing for sleep. Only a handful lingered on deck. The adults were discussing how cold the water must be while the children made use of their visible breaths by pretending they were adults having a smoke. Suddenly, everyone stopped what they were doing and stood in silence, stoned by the glamour of the alien fluorescence glowing beneath the ship.

Once the Sea Witch's outreached tentacles had completed their penetrative assault, she closed her eyes and began to twist them around. The ship moaned in pain. Moments later, the sound of cracking wood filled the air, only to be interrupted by the panicked screams of waking voices.

Angry tentacles sliced through each deck, sending the still-waking residents running in one direction, only to be met by another tentacle. She dissolved the ship. Bodies, beds, and splinters were all that remained in the frosty water. And she carried no more emotion about it than a god would feel by stepping on an anthill. These little mutants were ants as far as she was concerned.

She hurriedly searched through every man, killing each one she concluded not to be Otis with the swift strike of her tentacle. The women and children were left alone to freeze to death. All in all, there were one hundred and one souls on board who didn't live to see the following day.

Enraged that none of them were Otis Seehus, as the Calypso Queen had promised her, the Sea Witch ran her fingers through the frost accumulating in her blond hair and calmed her nerves. This was no time to be irrational. Maybe he was supposed to be on board, but circumstances within or beyond his control hat kept him from boarding. Maybe he didn't trust the Calypso Queen and didn't want to fulfill travel arrangements she'd arranged for him.

"I wouldn't trust her if I was him," the Sea Witch said, casually glancing at a baby doll as it floated by. "What an ugly little doll."

The Sea Witch floated away from the wreckage to a place less cluttered—a place where she could think. Keeping only her torso above the surface, she slid through the water and glanced up at the bright mixture of stars. *There are only two main routes that can get him to Ithaca from Calypso Island. If he didn't take this ship, does that mean he won't be taking this route?*

Chapter 19

She ran her palms over her face once more, still gliding, still thinking. Steam poured from her skin and trailed like ghosts in her wake as she continued to drift farther from the shipwreck. "What to do? What to do?" She ran her rough tongue over her green teeth and licked her salty lips before lowering into the icy abyss.

The ocean can be a lonely place—the loneliest place. If you're in it long enough, especially alone, it'll do things to you. It'll make you see things. It has no regard for your well-being. But truth be told, for the most part, it probably doesn't even know you're there. This makes it all the more terrifying how much of a stranglehold it'll put on your emotions, especially fear—whether it's fear of the unknown monsters lurking beneath the surface or that of the vast sky and its unpredictable weather. While the massive stars glisten across the slow-moving sky, seemingly spying for some entity that doesn't have your best interests at heart, the vessel moans out, breaking the deafening silence and making your heart spike.

As the sun set on Otis and his stolen vessel, he hadn't been able to shake the feeling that his current reality was actually a dream. He also pondered the thought that he had died and had entered some sort of afterlife or underworld, as current circumstances didn't allow him to believe this was any sort of heaven.

Unable to sleep, he approached a large wooden wine barrel sitting in the central stern and grabbed a ladle resting on its lid. He raised the lid, plopped in the ladle, and shot back a large gulp. His bitter reaction should have kept him from drinking the rest. He never was much for wine. But he scooped out two more gulps before replacing the lid and going to his cot to lie down and look up at the open sky.

The Calypso Queen, he thought. *What is she up to? And what, if anything, will she do when she finds out I wasn't on that ship?* Otis began to think about the people—the children—he saw getting on that ship. "Oh, no." He felt a cold, remorseful shiver and closed his eyes. "What did she do to that ship?"

As the dawn sun turned the insides of Otis's eyelids orange, he sat up and walked to the stern, popping a lid off a different barrel. This time, it was the water. He cupped a splash between his palms and rinsed his face. Beads ran down his beard and back into the barrel before he brought up another couple of handfuls. Digging his wet fingertips into his eyes, he felt the vessel come to a sudden stop.

The force brought him forward a few steps, but he remained on his feet, confused as he looked over the ship's ledges and then the bow. Fifteen to twenty feet in front of the vessel, a thick cluster of blond locks rose through the water's surface.

Otis was overcome with fright and curiosity, but he blushed as the smooth skin of her neck, shoulders, breasts, and abdomen followed behind the beautiful face of the Sea Witch. Once her waistline had barely broken the surface, she locked herself into place, holding his vessel still with her unseen tentacles.

"Hi there," she said, her green teeth front and center.

"You're not real," Otis said, quickly convincing himself that this was indeed a dream.

"Sorry, love. But I am. Have been as long as they've been talking about me."

"No. No. This is just a bad dream. You are just a dream."

Chapter 19

"That's good," she said. "This will be a lot more fun if you think you're dreaming."

"And why's that?" he asked.

"If you think you're dreaming, you might be able to actually convince yourself that you're about to wake up. When you don't, I'll get the best fight I can out of the great Otis Seehus."

"How do you know who I am?" he asked.

"Honey. I've been waiting for the queen to turn you loose for some time now. I can't believe she actually did it."

"What are you talking about?"

"I'm talking about you, war hero. They can't say I'm just a myth forever. One of these days, I'm going to kill enough of their heroes, and they're going to know, once and for all, I was here. And I was real. And I was always better than the best of *you*."

"Who's *they*?" Otis asked.

"Who isn't?" She sneered. "Why weren't you on that ship? A lot of people had to die for you. I would have let at least half of them live had you been on there, where you were supposed to be." Her words grew angrier. "You have any weapons on board?"

"Yeah," he answered.

"Get them ready, war hero. Let's see what all the hype's about."

Otis remained still, waiting for her to reveal something, anything, about her personality that he could use against her.

"Go on," she said, reassuring him. "Get whatever you need, and do it fast because I'm not going to say it again."

Arrogance.

Otis gathered two swords, a bow, and several arrows before tapping the knot on the rope attached to his anchor. He raised a sword in each hand.

"OK, then," she said. "Here we go."

Several of her tentacles rose from under the water, swarming and swatting him. He batted them off with the razor-sharp swords, sending slices of tentacles and detached stingers about the deck. This didn't anger her. She actually seemed somewhat amused, as her regenerative limbs replaced any that he happened to chop off.

"What else you got?" she asked, running her tongue over her mossy teeth. He picked up his bow and fired an arrow at her face. She caught it with her left hand. He fired another. She snagged it with her right.

"Oh, Otis. I don't know if I'm shocked or disappointed that this is all you have to offer."

Finally, Otis threw a lasso over her head, wrapping her torso and pulling her arms tight against her side. Still carrying a look of amusement, she let loose another smile and raised her dripping tentacles from the water and into the air. After a brief pause, she slammed them down on the deck, causing the vessel to burst in several spots, sending splinters into the air and provisions into the water. The vessel's anchor slid between the jagged crevices of the deck and splashed in the water. Only then did she realize that the anchor was attached to the other end of the rope that Otis had used to wrangle her.

The anchor sank and jerked her down with such force that Otis had just enough time to get into position, hopping onto a wine barrel and praying that his timing would be flawless. Sinking rapidly, she used her tentacles to free herself from the

Chapter 19

lasso and swam back up with a fury. She saw Otis's legs dangling in the water next to the large wine barrel. Suddenly, those dangling legs disappeared, shrouded by a growing purple cloud. As she came up for Otis, the sweet violet nectar filled her nostrils and made her eyelids go weak. She sank back down into the abyss with a grin affixed to her lips, and her tentacles retreated to their standard size.

Otis wrapped his arms around a nearby piece of the vessel and held his breath, only able to hope the wine had worked. He began to kick his legs away from the scene and spent the next few minutes percolating in the fear that she was going to yank him under. She never did. Through all the commotion, one of her tentacles had scraped a shallow flesh wound into his neck. He rubbed the painful mark with his right hand, causing the pain to grow worse with touch.

"Ow," he said, weakening. He repositioned his arms and their grip on his floating chunk of debris. His vision grew blurry, then black.

Chapter 20

Jinni lay on a cot in the *Elvira*'s belly, as gravity's brawny shove weighed him down. His eyes opened slowly, bothered by the thumping coming from above on the ship's deck. After concluding that it was One and Two going best seven out of ten in a series of competitive sprints, Jinni knew the noise wasn't going to quit anytime soon. He let out a sigh, rolled onto his side, and placed a pillow over his right ear. Peter, sitting in a nearby chair, startled Jinni's attempt to get more rest.

"There he is," Peter said. "Glad we waited an extra day."

"Mac back?"

"No. Not yet."

"How long was I out?"

"Few days."

Jinni tried to rub the itch from his eyes but only made it worse as he forced his legs off the edge of the cot and sat up.

"You OK?" Peter asked.

"Yeah. Will be."

"Must've been a wild trip."

"You could say that." Jinni grew concerned with the lack of energy following his awakening.

"So...uh, now may not be the best time to ask, but I'm gonna anyway. You find out anything about Otis?"

"Yeah," Jinni said, closing his eyes and attempting to shake the pain between his temples. "I know where he is."

"You heard where he is, or you *know* where he is?"

"I know where he is. I saw him. I talked to him."

"Really?"

"He's on Calypso Island. Being held by the queen."

Peter, midblink, kept his eyes shut upon hearing this news. "Are you serious?"

Jinni nodded.

"Of course, he's on Calypso Island," Peter said as if this journey had reached its worst-case scenario. "Well, what now? What's next? I suppose you want to keep going with this."

"No. We're not going there," Jinni said, much to the surprise of his young captain. "I can't go back." Jinni stood up and suffered a dizzy spell paired with weary legs.

"Whoa, whoa." Peter stepped forward and grabbed his shoulders, helping to guide him back down. "You all right?"

Jinni raised his eyebrows. "I dunno. I've never felt like this before. It's strange."

"Go back to sleep. You just need some more rest, is all."

"That's probably it," Jinni said, knowing that it wasn't. "Hey, before you go. Don't tell any of the other guys about this."

"How come?"

"If Mac comes back empty handed, I don't want one of them to let it slip and give him a reason to keep going with this."

"Fair enough," Peter said. "Anything else?"

Disheartened, and potentially more emotional than usual as a result of his withdrawal from the Sea Witch's venom, Jinni

Chapter 20

began to confide in Peter in a way he hadn't up to this point. "I hurt, Pete. My skin hurts. My insides hurt. Even my soul feels like it's crying out in pain. Like there's some…problem, deep inside me, struggling to correct itself. I feel—"

Peter could see Jinni struggling to find the right word. "Human?"

Jinni nodded, downtrodden, and released a small amount of stress with his next breath. "I'll never forget the first time she got ahold of me."

"Who?" Peter asked.

"The Sea Witch."

Shell-shocked, Peter dropped his jaw and raised his eyebrows.

"It was like she was a toddler, and I was her new toy," Jinni continued. "She took pleasure in the fact that her stingers could only hurt me. There was this…admiration in her eyes. Like she finally found someone—something she always wanted. But it feels different now when she gets me.

"Time was, I'd seek her out for a game of cat and mouse, just because I was bored, feeling adventurous. I don't know if I've done it too many times, or I'm just getting too old to fight off her venom, but everything feels so much different now."

"What are you saying, Jinni?"

Jinni gently pressed his left hand against his belly. "Nothing," he said, realizing he'd said too much. "Her poison makes me chatty. Just need to get some more rest—like you said."

Peter nodded, struggling to hide the concern on his young face. "You do that. Holler up if you need anything."

Up in the crow's nest, Nibs's gentle paintbrush was guided by the glimmering night sky he was attempting to capture on paper. He dipped his brush into a cup of water, captivated by the dark-blue cloud as it dispersed in the once-clear liquid until Peter's head and slender shoulders peeked over the ledge.

"He OK?" Nibs asked, never looking away from the painting.

"I dunno."

"He gonna live?"

"I dunno," Peter said disconsolately. "I think so. But there definitely seems to be somethin' wrong with him, or his magic, or both."

"Really?" Nibs set his brush down.

"Yeah. There's something else, though. But ya can't say anything to the other guys."

"What is it?"

"Jinni says Otis is being held captive on Calypso Island—by the queen."

"Oh."

"Yeah."

"He sure?" Nibs asked.

"He seemed pretty sure."

"So we're not going then? Right?" Nibs asked.

"No. Big no."

"That's a bummer. I was lookin' forward to meetin' him," Nibs said, turning half his attention back to his painting.

"Otis?" Peter grinned.

"Hell yes!" Nibs exclaimed. "They'll be telling his stories and singing his songs for centuries. We were about to be part of one of the most important chapters. Arguably *the* most important." Nibs looked up at the sky once more for reference before peeking back down at the early stages of his painting. "So what's our next move?"

Chapter 20

"Don't have one yet." Peter stood up and crossed his arms. "For now, just enjoy our downtime until Mac gets back."

"How long's that gonna be?"

Mac wasn't expected back at the *Elvira* for at least another few days, but after only one night as a guest of Emperor Aladdin and Empress Helen, Mac double-timed it back to the South Nestor coast. Both he and Pinocchio were eager to make it back.

Pinocchio was missing his wife and daughters, and Mac was one bread crumb closer to finding his father and excited to share what he'd learned with Jinni and the other Lost Boys.

The two of them arrived on the edge of town just after dusk in the exact spot from whence they had left. After a quick goodbye, they parted ways, both grateful to have met the other and to have been a part of two generations of fathers and sons working together. While they hadn't encountered any obstacles on their journey back as they had on the way there, Mac had to make a small jaunt through town before he could count his blessings. It was there, within the busy grid of the market square, where he was spotted and recognized.

Of the three men sitting together, John was the only one who caught that initial glimpse. "I'll be. Look who's out, all alone."

"Who?"

The other two men squinted in the distance before one of them lost interest and took a swig from his stein.

"It's one of the Lost Boys that cut us off on the way here."

A giddy Mac had tunnel vision en route to the *Elvira*; otherwise, he may have noticed his attackers closing in on him after leaving the busiest part of town behind. They trailed closely before dispersing and sneaking ahead. They got into position, hidden by the cloak of a pitch-black alleyway. The moment Mac had stepped within their grasp they pulled him into the darkness.

The three of them would go on to beat Mac severely. His face was pounded to a bruised and bloodied pulp while everything from the neck down suffered through an array of jabs, cuts, and more bruises.

"Please. Please." It was the only word he could spit out. "Please."

After a harsh half a minute, two of the three men decided that they'd had enough. They could plainly see that Mac had as well.

"No." The man with whom Peter Pan had the original dispute declared, "I ain't done with him yet."

"Come on, John. You give him much more, and you're gonna kill him."

"Pity," John said unfazed.

"Think about the watchmen."

"Their only concern right now is the boats comin' in. No one'll bat an eye for this little twerp. Not by the time we're gone anyway." John sneered at the two men. "If you two aren't going to help, then get the hell outta here."

As they walked away, John took a moment to collect his breath. Mac lay in a pool of blood and saliva. At that moment, above the pain, above the thought of impending death, Mac thought of Penelope. In one quick flash, he was weighed down

Chapter 20

with a life's worth of regret. He regretted that he wouldn't have a chance to tell her goodbye. Even more so, he regretted all the times that a simple spat between the two of them had escalated into a memorable argument. He thought of times he had hurt her feelings with his careless choice of words and shed a tear at the thought that these moments would sum up her memories of him. All he ever wanted was to please his mother—and make her proud. And now he was about to leave her, alone.

"Get up," John said, pointing his sword toward Mac's chest.

Mac was drained but used what was left of his energy to stand up. Glaring at John, Mac confidently spat another mouthful of blood.

"Turn around, tough guy."

Mac turned around slowly.

"Move it," John said, dashing a glance over his shoulder. He poked Mac in the back with his sword, guiding him deeper into the alley.

"Are you going to kill me?" Mac asked, seemingly delirious.

"Do you really wanna know?"

Mac stopped. "No. Please don't kill me. I'll do anything you want. Please, no."

"Shut up," John said with another jab of his sword. "You ain't talkin' your way outta this one, Lost Boy. Now get scootin'."

He jabbed Mac in the back once more. That's when Mac widened his eyes and performed the tactic that his new pal Pinocchio had taught him in the desert.

Mac pivoted to his right, guiding John's blade under his arm and grasping the sword's handle. While fighting for control with the dumbstruck John, Mac curled his left fist and planted it firmly into John's unprepared cheek.

Odyssey Tale

Within the darkness, the thud of John's body and the clang of his sword gave birth to a new man: Mac Seehus. The young champion knew he would never live up to the name created by his father, or the stories people told of him. But Mac did know that this moment was important. And if they ever did tell stories of him as they did his father, this moment would belong entirely to Mac.

He had been beaten into mush, in more pain than he knew to be possible, and as close to death as anyone has ever been without meeting it—not once, but twice. But something funny happens to some people when they're as close to death as Mac was at that moment. They realize, more than ever, they want to be alive.

Chapter 21

Back on the *Elvira*, Jinni sat on the edge of his bed suffering from a fever, only finding relief from the occasional wipe of a damp rag. He remained silent in the dark, running the soothing cloth over his neck and face while listening to the indiscernible chatter coming from the Lost Boys on deck and directly above his room. All of them lay scattered about, bathing under the blazing high-noon sun.

"Keep wearing dirty underwear, and that's exactly what's going to happen," Nibs said, directing his comment at One.

Peter, losing patience, sat up. "Enough. We're done talking about this." He started to close his eyes and lie down but was startled by Tootles and his reaction to something Peter hadn't yet noticed. Peter, along with everyone else, looked over to see what had Tootles so taken aback.

It was a beaten and bloodied Mac. He was tired, sweaty, grimy, and wearing a well-deserved stubble that hadn't been there when they'd last seen his young face. Peter looked him over, making a note of the spiderweb cracks on his raw knuckles and the dry crimson that had leaked and blackened.

Slightly approached Mac, getting into his face and pawing gently at his most visible wounds. "Holy shit. Are you OK?"

"I'm fine," Mac said.

Slightly, still concerned, eased away.

Peter could see through the surface wounds and knew that the young man who stood before him was not the same young man he'd seen off. Mac was gone. And this strange, young, stout man carried a pearl of wisdom and way about him. It was painful wisdom that one can only ascertain with a harsh test that breaks the very fabric of comfort and spirit that once made that person who he was. The Mac in front of them now was cold, harsh, resilient, and much more determined. Nothing—and no one—was going to stand in his way.

"What's the other guy look like?" Peter asked, letting out a playful grin.

Through bruised yet confident cheeks, Mac replied with a mischievous and red-toothed grin. "Where's Jinni?" he asked, trading the smile for a more puzzled expression.

"Downstairs," Peter said. "Resting."

Peter's glum tone and the quiet, emotional response by the Lost Boys was cause for concern.

"Is that bad?" Mac asked.

"It's a long story," Peter said. "He'll have to fill you in on the details."

Mac nodded. "I've got some details for him as well."

"Yeah?"

Mac nodded again with more vigor. "I know where he is. I know where my father is."

"Yeah?"

"A small island called Calypso," Mac said.

The Lost Boys recoiled in horror.

"What? What is it?"

Chapter 21

"Calypso Island?" Tootles asked. "The emperor said those words? Calypso Island?"

"Yeah," Mac said with a shrug. "So?"

"Calypso Island is a dangerous place," One said. "It's hostile. And the queen there is—"

"Insane," Jinni said, ascending from the stairs.

"Queen?" Tootles asked. "What about the Sea Witch?"

"Sea Witch?" Mac asked mockingly. "Don't tell me you guys have gone superstitious on me now. She's not real."

"Yes. She is," Jinni said.

"I can't believe I'm having to sell you all on this. You wanted a payday; you brought me all the way here for the chance at a payday. And now that we get confirmation that my father is still alive and that payday is a certainty, you guys come at me with stories about scary queens and sea witches. Come on."

"Don't be like that." Jinni closed his eyes and crossed his arms.

"I'm not being like anything. I'm just saying. If you guys don't want to come, I appreciate all you've done up to this point. I really do. If you don't want to go any further, I understand. And I won't hold it against any of you. But I'm going to get him."

"How you plan on getting there without us?" Jinni asked.

"Without this ship?" Peter added.

"I'll figure it out," Mac said. "I suckered you into bringing me here, didn't I?"

"Yeah. Big man," Jinni said. "Got it all figured out now."

"I didn't say that. And this isn't about me being a *big man*. It is and always was about finding my father. This is the closest I've ever been to reaching out and touching him. I don't care if there are a thousand crazy queens on Calypso Island, each with her own personal sea witch. I'm going to get my father—with or without you. I figured, from all I've learned about you guys, that you'd understand what this means." Mac looked down at his knuckles. "What I've done to get here. What you guys have done to get me here. And how close we are now." Mac paused and realized that his plea for sympathy from the Lost Boys did little in terms of value. None had much of a reaction to his emotional display.

"Ya know," Mac went on. "I never believed it when I heard people say bad things about Lost Boys. But now I know they were right. You're nothing but a bunch of bandits claiming false moral high ground. You really don't give a good goddamn about the people you claim to want to help unless there's an easy guarantee it'll line your pockets."

Peter stepped forward. "Jinni already told you once, Mac. We were all slaves most of our lives. We're—"

"Yeah, yeah. You're done doin' shit for free. I know. But no one's asking you to do anything for free. I know you were in this for the reward from the start—all of you. But we're as close as we've been. The reward is still there. It'll be yours for the taking. And the glory. But we're gonna have to go through Calypso Island for you to get it."

"Nope. Sorry," Peter said unapologetically.

Mac curled his lips, ready to let words and fists fly.

"I was there, Mac," Jinni said. "I was in the castle. I spoke to your father. Directly." Jinni's words fired through the air like an arrow, striking each of the Lost Boys before settling on Mac's chest.

"You what?" Mac asked. "When were you planning on telling me?"

Chapter 21

"I wasn't sure I *was* going to tell you. But your father—he isn't who he once was. He looks like a frail old man. And scared. So scared. Poor bastard wasn't even convinced I was really there. Thought I was a ghost. Or part of some dream."

"No. You're lying," Mac said, growing red.

"Afraid not, kid."

"No. No. If I'd have been with you…if he had known that I was out looking for him, trying to—"

"I told him all that, Mac. I told him everything. It didn't matter a lick. Said he couldn't explain it, but he couldn't leave without permission. I got the distinct feeling that he was—afraid. There was no question there. At first, I thought he was afraid of me. That my helping him was some sort of a trick or trap. But it was her. He was afraid of her and what she'd do if she caught him trying to escape."

"Who?"

"The queen," Jinni said, with a shiver. "She's the one who's got him."

"I still don't believe you. I might not know my father, but I know he wouldn't turn down the chance to escape. No. No way. I don't know who you talked to, but it wasn't my father."

"I really wish it wasn't."

"Tell me what he said, then. So far, all I've heard is a lot of bullshit about what you think he was feeling. What did he say?"

The personality in Jinni's face disappeared, and he stood like a statue as Otis's voice began to speak, with a crescendo of emotional outpouring.

"Tell him I'm sorry. And tell Penelope I'm sorry. Tell Mac he's officially the man of the house now, and that I'm proud of the man he's become. Tell him that…not many sons get a chance to live up to the names their fathers make for them, but he has the potential to do exactly that..." Jinni shed a tear. "But I have to stay. I can't leave here without permission."

After several moments of silence, Jinni's soul returned to his face.

"Bastard." Mac wiped the sad tears from his eyes as a few angry ones stepped into their place.

Still shaken by Jinni's metamorphosis, the Lost Boys gave Mac their undivided empathy.

"For what it's worth, he couldn't explain why he needed her permission," Jinni said. "Just that he needed it. Like he was being held by some kind of spell or invisible gate. I know I said it was just a feeling, but I could see in his eyes that he was petrified to get caught by her. Like it'd happened once before. And the punishment was severe."

"Did he say any of that?" Mac asked. "Or is it just another feeling?"

"Just a feeling."

"That's what I thought." Mac hung his shoulders, defeated. "Some hero. The great, brave, magnificent, charming, witty..." he said with showmanship. "Otis," he said, deflated.

"Sorry, Mac," Jinni said. "Unfortunately, sometimes that's part of growing up."

"What's that?"

"Learning that your father isn't the man they said he was."

Mac got himself cleaned up and into some fresh clothes. He rested on a hammock under the shade of closed eyes but couldn't

Chapter 21

catch any sleep as his mind raced with resentment. Much like Otis had once pictured his family moving on and being happy without him, Mac pictured his father living the good life with a new family and a new castle.

Life there must be good. Dad must be happy. How could he turn down a perfectly good opportunity to escape? Jinni talking about feelings, and spells, and invisible gates. What a load of horseshit. Who wouldn't seize on the opportunity to leave somewhere they were being kept prisoner unless they wanted to be there?

The question burned like an iron brand on the back of his neck. *Nobody—that's who.* But the question was just too big for Mac at the time, as was the answer.

As Mac sat alone, sulking and growing more resentful of his father's cowardice, his father's unconscious body lay limp on the damp sand of a desolate beach. Suddenly, his mind jolted the rest of his body awake, forcing his tense eyes open. For a moment, everything from his neck down was paralyzed until his lungs filled with life, and he was able to sit up.

"Ow." Otis gently brushed the tips of his fingers over the sand sticking to his arm and the shallow scratch from the Sea Witch's stinger. Seething, he struggled to curb the pain coming from the cherry-red rash spreading rapidly around his wound.

He stood and patted himself down, only to be startled by a small, malnourished white rabbit scampering across the sand. It was the type of incident that would have been forgotten about within the hour. But there was something peculiar about this particular rabbit. He was dressed in human clothes. Donning a sleek three-piece suit, the rabbit was either running to or from something and paying little mind to the dents and scratches being picked up by the pocket watch chained to his back right paw.

"*Now* I've seen everything," Otis said, watching the debonair critter scamper into the nearby woods.

Moments later, Otis saw exactly for himself what the rabbit had been running from, as a flock of jumbo king crabs pitter-pattered through the coarse sand. The fleet proudly carried human skulls for shells and sounded as though they were walking on fiddle strings as their claws stabbed the earth with each step forward.

Otis was overcome with an eerie feeling, complete with a spine-soaking chill as the last and smallest crab tailed behind with a child-sized skull. As creepy as they were, however, they all ignored Otis. Following the exact path and opening that the rabbit had taken into the woods, they organized themselves into a single-file line and disappeared into the brush.

Otis apprehensively stepped in line behind the small crab and followed it through the open patch. Once encumbered by the shadow of that first tree, Otis could feel the inviting embrace from a collection of trees nearby. The seemingly visible presence of their age and wisdom was euphoric. Despite the lack of light, brilliant and vivid colors chimed out from the lilies, orchids, tulips, roses, and wildflowers that had been intricately placed throughout the heavenly landscape.

Still feeling a bit delirious, Otis couldn't shake the feeling that the trees and flowers were watching him, studying his movements and consciously aware of his presence—maybe even his thoughts. *Curious*, he thought, smiling.

"Oh. Hello," a strange and gentle young voice called out.

Chapter 21

Otis turned to his left and noticed a narrow yet rapid stream that hadn't been there before, where a seven-year-old girl was cleansing her hands. With a mess of back-length hair and cheeks overflowing with freckles, she seemed eager to see Otis and acted as if she had known him for a number of years.

"Hi there," he said. "What are you doing out here all by yourself?"

"I'm not by myself. You know better than that."

Puzzled, Otis looked around, seeing no life except for the surrounding collage of vibrant vegetation.

"What happened to you?" she asked. "You're soaked."

He raised his eyebrows. "I was sailing home." He remembered bits of what had happened but struggled to find the words or any proper order in which to let them out. Despite all that had happened, all he could muster was, "The Sea Witch. She sank my boat."

"I see she got your arm there," the little girl said. "That's no good."

"You're telling me. Her venom hurts."

"That's not all it does."

"What else does it do?"

She stared up and tilted her head.

"Am I going to be OK?" Otis asked.

"I don't know," she said, smiling and looking just as confused as he.

"Well, where are we?" he asked. Otis raised his palms to the sky and twisted his slender torso to the left and right. "Am I dreaming? Am I...did I not make it? What the hell is going on here?"

"I don't know," she said. Her smile hit Otis in such a way that he thought she was antagonistic. But in reality, there was no reality.

"Well, what *do* you know?" Otis asked, changing his tone from concerned to frustrated.

"Show me your eyes," she said.

"What?"

"Your eyes." Her voice elevated. "Show me your eyes."

Still feeling as though he was being toyed with, Otis appeased the young girl by standing still and facing her. She gazed into his eyes curiously, tilting her head back and forth before her face froze in terror.

"What? What do you see?"

"There's something…wrong with them."

"What? What's wrong with my eyes?"

She looked around, scanning the area to make sure no new parties had arrived. "They're seeing things that aren't part of your universe," she whispered.

"Who?"

"Your eyes."

"I don't understand," he said, more puzzled than before.

"You're in a rabbit hole now. At the bottom, in fact. And it's one you were never meant to be in. Here. Drink this." She handed him a small bottle labeled "Drink Me."

"What's it going to do me?" he asked.

"Why is a raven like a writing desk?"

"What?" he asked.

"Why is a raven like a writing desk?"

"I have no idea. Why?" Otis looked at the bottle as if expecting to find the answer.

Chapter 21

"Drink it," she said. "You'll get all the answers you're looking for."

Otis hesitated but eventually brought the bottle to his lips and took a tiny sip before slipping into a convulsive coughing fit. Liquid began to pour from his mouth so fast and so thick that he couldn't take a breath. He dropped to his knees in a panic as the stream grew heavier and faster. He looked up to her, asking with his eyes why she felt the need to poison him. Her eyes closed, revealing two more eyes instead of eyelids. Then she leaned forward and whispered. "Climb."

Otis's closed eyes popped open, and water burst from his mouth, catapulting him from the dream world. Violent ocean waves rolled ashore, inches from his feet, as he lay in the damp, gritty sand. The rich, earthy aromas of pine trees and marigolds played peekaboo with the inside of his nose as the hum of a billion honeybees lay claim to the beachfront. Otis had no idea where he was, and less of an idea as to how he gotten there—and he was paralyzed from the neck down.

Chapter 22

The *Elvira*'s next several days blended together as one while passing by in the blink of an eye. In the span of that time, Mac was offered—and accepted—a job from Peter Pan as a more permanent crew member. It was really a sweet deal for all parties involved. Mac could ride with them as long as he wanted, provided he continued performing his duties. Peter told him that in twelve to fifteen months, they would be returning to Ithaca, at which time Mac could either part ways with them, or he could stay on as crew.

After loading up on provisions and enjoying one last night of drunken mayhem, the *Elvira* set sail for North Nestor, using the island's west coastline as a guide. Mac had performed his duties for the day and kept to himself on what was quickly becoming his favorite hammock. Previously, the Lost Boys had thought of Mac more as a passenger—a privileged prince who had all of life's goodies and none of its hardships. However, now that they were about to label him a peer and spend significantly more time with him, his reserved demeanor and social skills were noticeably incompatible with "Lost Boy culture." His choice of few words, and how he spoke them, rubbed them the wrong way. And none of them, least of all Peter, expected Mac to make it.

Needless to say, teenagers are moody. And the pendulum of their moodiness is as unpredictable in pace as it is in direction. As Mac's slender back dug into that hammock, the resentment he felt toward his father was reaching such a peak that it began to bring into question his relationship with Penelope. *When was the last time she acted like a mother?* He couldn't remember.

He could remember the smell of laudanum on her breath—sometimes vague, more often rich. He could remember all the times she'd pawned him off on one of their servants when she didn't have the strength to get out of bed or face the sunlight. But he couldn't remember the last time she'd acted like a mother. That's when he realized, much like he had with Otis's words spoken by Jinni, the person Mac had left behind wasn't her. Who Penelope had been for the better part of his life wasn't really his mother. His true mother had been the bottle clutched within her fingers. Once he made this realization and understood that his parents weren't the parents they should have been, something inside him clicked, when, before, it would have snapped.

Belowdecks, and finally sleeping fewer than twenty hours a day, Jinni was finally nearing full recovery from the Sea Witch's near-lethal injections. Once darkness had overtaken the dusk, Mac got out of his hammock and walked downstairs. Despite Mac's footsteps being silent and Jinni's eyes being closed, Jinni could feel his presence in the room.

"I don't suppose you're down here to tell me a bedtime story," Jinni said.

"I wanted to tell you first," Mac said. "Then I'll tell Peter."

"Tell me what?" Jinni asked, sitting up.

"I'm not going any further with you guys. I'm going to Calypso Island. I have to. I know it may sound stupid, but I

Chapter 22

can't just leave family behind like that...I won't be able to live with myself if I know that I could have done more to help him and choked when I had the chance."

"Well," Jinni said, disappointed. "If that's how you feel. Pete's not gonna be happy about it. It's not every day he offers someone a job. But it is what it is. And he'll get over it. So will the other guys."

"Thank you." Mac nodded.

Mac packed what few items he had in a satchel, strapped his sword and dagger to his belt, and went upstairs to tell Peter of his decision. Peter was indifferent, for the most part. If he had shown any signs of caring, it was only because he had lost the pool he and the other guys had going on how long Mac was going to last as a crewmember. Tootles was the only one who had bet that it would be less than a week.

"Are there any ports we can stop at tonight so you can let me off?" Mac asked. Peter and every other Lost Boy reacted to Mac's question as if they thought he had been joking. Tootles and One even began to giggle.

"No," Peter said. His stern tone was over the top, to the point of being comedic. "There aren't any ports we can stop at tonight."

"But I thought you said—"

"At no point in time did I ever say we'd be making any special ports so Princess Mac can get off the boat. Tootles, did I say that?"

"No."

"Nibs. Did you hear me say anything of the sort?"

"No, sir."

"I didn't think so," Peter said. "We won't be making port until we reach North Nestor Island. Until then, you'll perform your duties as they were assigned to you." Peter cracked a smile and started hamming it up with the other guys. "Are there any ports we can stop at tonight?" he asked in a mocking tone. "Get the hell outta here."

Fuming, Mac wanted to tackle Peter and bury his fists into Peter's smug face. But a cooler, more rational head prevailed. While Peter and the Lost Boys continued to snicker and smirk at Mac's expense, he walked away from their condescending eyes to the *Elvira*'s starboard stern. He tightened his satchel, secured his dagger, and grabbed two logs from a pile of firewood. Unnoticed, Mac lowered the logs into the water and carefully placed his sword on top of them. He slipped into the surface and watched the *Elvira* sail on without him.

Jinni, sensing that something was off, bolted upstairs to find Peter and the Lost Boys still yukking it up. They had moved onto another subject, oblivious to the fact that Mac was gone.

"Where is he?" Jinni asked, panicked.

"Probably went back to his hammock to cry some more," Peter said. "I'm not his au pair."

Jinni looked back and saw that the hammock was empty. "No, he's not. Where'd he go?"

"I don't know," Peter said, trying to mellow the mood. "He's gotta be around here somewhere."

"There he is," One yelled out, pointing at the *Elvira*'s wake.

"Son of a bitch," Peter said. "The little brat jumped overboard."

"Drop the anchor," Jinni said.

Chapter 22

"No," Peter said. "And don't ever give me a command again. To hell with him." Peter proceeded toward the back of the ship to share his thoughts with Mac. "Good luck. Spoiled prick."

Jinni brought up a bag of provisions and got the lifeboat ready.

"What the hell do you think you're doing?" Peter asked.

"I can't let him go to Calypso Island alone. He's gonna get himself killed."

"Who gives a shit?" Peter asked. "I think the world will survive with one less prince running around."

"I have to help him."

"Since when?"

"I'm sorry, Pete. I just can't let him go alone."

"Then don't," Peter replied, coldly.

Jinni held a stone face and didn't answer.

"You wanna get yourself killed on Calypso Island?" Peter asked. "Be my guest. You can even take the lifeboat." Peter said these words as if he had won the argument. But everyone knew that if anyone other than Jinni had challenged Peter, the result would not have been the same.

"Thank you, Peter," Jinni said.

"If by some miracle you don't get yourself killed, we'll be on the north port of Nestor Island for three weeks."

Jinni nodded and quickly loaded up in the lifeboat, not wanting to draw out the goodbye with fear that Peter would change his mind. Just as Jinni was about to break loose from the *Elvira*, Nibs called out and stopped him.

"Not you too." Peter's tone was that of a disappointed parent.

"Come on, Nibs," Two said.

"Sorry, guys. But it's not every day you get a chance to meet a real-life hero, much less save one. See y'all at North Nestor. Have an ale and two whores ready for me."

Jinni waited for Nibs to grab a few sticks of beef jerky, water, weapons, and a small bottle of wine.

Once Jinni and Nibs had caught up to Mac, Nibs initiated the conversation. "I swear Nestor Island has the ugliest mermaids I've ever seen."

"Piss off, Nibs," Mac said with a middle finger.

"Mac. What are you doing?" Jinni asked.

"I have to go to Calypso Island. I have to."

"Yeah. Thought you meant you were gonna go once we'd reached port. Why don't you let us take you back to the ship? You can think about everything—really think about it."

"No time," Mac snapped back.

"I already told you—"

"I know what you told me, Jinni," Mac said. "And I believe every word of it. But he's not himself right now. What he said—him staying there—it's not him. Something's controlling the real him, so I can't abandon him now. The same can be said about my mom." Mac felt a weight lift from his shoulders.

"Get in the boat."

"No," Mac said. "I'm not going back to the ship."

"There's something you should know…I didn't exactly leave your dad behind after I spoke to him. I did try something else. Whether or not it worked, I still don't know."

Mac raised his eyebrows and leaned forward, resting his arms on the boat. "What did you try?"

"The queen of Calypso Island…has this mirror." Jinni went on to reveal the last remaining secret he'd been keeping. "And

Chapter 22

if she truly swears by its every command, request, and opinion, it stands to reason that she's going to free him—if she hasn't already."

"And how do you know she hasn't already?"

"I don't. But that's information that will travel fast. We won't have to go to Calypso Island for it to find us."

Mac looked east toward the vast, hungry sea that awaited his next move. "I'm still going. He's been cooped up all these years. You said yourself, he seemed scared. It's hard to say what kind of mind tricks she used to get him under her control. When he gets out, he's going to need a friendly face to help him home. How many more secrets you got in that big magic brain of yours anyway?"

"Mac," Jinni said gently. "Get in the boat."

"No. I'm not going back to the *Elvira*."

"Get in," Jinni said, reaching his hand toward Mac. "I'll take you. I'll take you to Calypso Island."

Mac, Jinni, and Nibs spent the next several days in close quarters and exposed to the elements. A clear midnight sky guided them quietly into Calypso Island's foggy and humid coastline. The three of them settled on a secluded bank hidden by fallen tree branches, thick swarms of brush, and mosquitoes.

"Ow. Damn," Nibs said, smacking his neck.

"Shhh," Jinni said, with a finger on his mouth.

They stepped off the boat as silent as the calm waters that had cradled them on the way in.

"Follow me," Jinni whispered. Nibs and Mac followed closely behind, mirroring their guide's every move. Jinni stopped and turned around. "Shhh. Don't move." He tiptoed ahead. "Something doesn't feel right here." He stopped and turned around once more. Nibs and Mac stood frozen like frightened goslings. "Climb this tree. Don't move, and keep your mouths shut. I'll be back in a minute."

Before Mac and Nibs had even taken their first steps up, Jinni was gone. He had disappeared into the woods, feeling uneasy without the slightest inkling as to why. He was right to be worried, however. The cause of his uneasiness was the glowing energy of raw, war-torn land. It was as abundant in the air as the ozone rolling over the moonlit moss. Calypso Island was officially in the midst of a civil war.

First, the queen had gone missing. Several guards swore up and down that they had seen her go into the guest quarters after dinner, but no one had seen her come out. Then, several days later, it was discovered that a passenger ship was attacked and torn to shreds, leaving over one hundred Calypso Island residents to freeze to death in the icy waters. In many minds, there was little doubt. Calypso Island was under attack.

The panic wasn't limited to inside the castle walls either. Every guard and servant who had been loyal to the queen remained so after her disappearance. Not only were her military and security units on the lookout for the nonexistent threat from somewhere overseas, but they were also skeptical of their own residents' intentions more than at any other time in the island's history.

As a result, vigilance had become the number-one priority. Different patches of land surrounding her castle that weren't

Chapter 22

normally under surveillance were now under the eagle-eyed foot soldiers ready to defend her honor. Of course, all this information was so new that it hadn't yet reached the *Elvira*. Otherwise, Jinni might have taken another route to the castle. With light and quick footsteps, Jinni scampered through roving hilltops encumbered with trees that blacked out the moonlight. He didn't feel any sort of human presence, just the musical mixture of communication between birds, crows, and wild turkeys.

"Stop right there," a stern voice called out from the dark. "By order of the queen."

Jinni stopped, stood still, and held his breath. He had been around long enough to know that sometimes it's better to plead your case with the authorities than to run. This, however, was not one of those times. Within the blink of an eye, Jinni turned around and ran for his life.

"Stop," the voice called out again. "Fire."

Jinni was already running as fast as he could but somehow picked up speed as the whoosh of zipping arrows fired past and around him. Feeling their nips, he juked, twisted, bent, slid, and ducked all the way back to where Nibs and Mac were waiting.

"Oh, shit," Nibs said, seeing Jinni's panicked silhouette sprinting into eyeshot.

"Ruuuuuuun!" Jinni yelled.

Mac and Nibs scurried down the tree, landed hard on the ground, and started running toward the boat. Jinni and multiple relentless waves of arrows followed behind. "Go, go, go," Jinni yelled.

He, Nibs, and Mac sprinted as fast as they could, nearly losing balance and running themselves into the ground several times. The arrows felt to be moving in closer with the potentially slow hand of death, but water and the boat were finally in sight.

"Nibs," Jinni said, keeping his breath despite the sprint. "You're gonna take the left paddle. Be ready to haul ass."

"Check," Nibs said. He slid beneath a fallen tree and popped up onto his feet, seamlessly accelerating back to his original pace. "Ow. Damn," Nibs yelled. His face went pale with terror as he reached back, clutching the sharp sting in his right leg. After another half step, he fell to the ground, sliding face-first through the dirt.

"Get up," Jinni yelled.

"I can't," Nibs said, trying to pull the bloody arrow from his leg, failing to make it budge. "Ow. Shit, that hurts. You're gonna have to go ahead without me, Jinni. Don't let 'em get you too."

Jinni looked at Nibs and Mac, then toward the war cries closing in all around. After a moment of struggle, Jinni helped Nibs guide one arm around himself and the other around Mac. They carried him onward. By some miracle or other force of good nature, all three made it back to the lifeboat without any additional wounds. Jinni and Mac plopped Nibs inside and paddled with maximum effort while Nibs affixed his eyes to the blacked-out tree line resting over their seemingly sluggish wake.

Fueled by a superhuman supply of adrenaline, Jinni paddled so hard on the right side that he was forcing the boat left. He shoved Mac aside and took over the left paddle, desperately trying to place distance between the lifeboat and shoreline.

As the rain of arrows pounded down on the water behind them, Jinni eased up on the paddling and sighed with relief, allowing himself and the boat a rest. Mac was still in a slight

Chapter 22

state of shock but was coming around. Nibs seemed to be visibly relieved, too, letting out a nervous but reassured giggle.

The gentle momentum that carried their boat came to a sudden stop.

"Oh no," Jinni said.

Thump. Thump. Thump. Overcome with dread, Jinni, Mac, and Nibs looked at the bottom of the boat and felt chills wrap around their shoulders and backs. *Thump. Thump.* Jinni reached down for his belt and pulled out his sword. Mac and Nibs did the same. *Thump.* They each readied their stances, Nibs struggling more than the other two.

"Jinni," Nibs whispered. "What do we do?"

"Fight. And whatever you do, don't let go of that sword."

Just as the boat began to moan and creak, Jinni dove headfirst into the water and swam away.

"Jiniiiiiii," Nibs shouted.

As Jinni diverted attention from the lifeboat, a trail of wake followed behind. As the wake nearly caught up to him, Jinni rose from the water, encased by the grip of several stringy, twisting tentacles.

"Hey there, stranger," the Sea Witch said, rising from the water. The more Jinni struggled, the tighter she squeezed.

"Ya know," she said. "There's something remarkably different about you, isn't there? I thought I felt it last time, but I wasn't sure what to make of it. Now I know. It's your blood. It used to reject my venom. I used to be able to feel it. Fighting—like a proud Titan in the heat of battle. Now, it just feels like a man's blood. A weak man's blood, at that."

Her tentacles reeled Jinni in, but before she could indulge in the spoils of her next kill, Nibs launched into the air and landed on her back. Finally having freed the arrow from his leg, he drove it into her shoulder. She craned her neck as the tentacles holding Jinni tossed him aside, and two others swatted Nibs. He splashed into the water as the Sea Witch pulled the arrow out of her shoulder.

"That was rather unpleasant," she said. She tossed the arrow aside, treating it and her wound as nothing more than a minor inconvenience. "Where did you come from? Are you a Lost Boy too?" She approached the helpless Nibs and raised him from the water with a mess of tentacles, keeping his limbs spread open and wrapped separately.

Frozen by a sheet of terror, Mac watched from the lifeboat, wondering when she would notice him.

"Ahhhh!" The universe of pain in which Nibs was navigating was unlike anything he'd ever endured.

"Hurts, doesn't it?" the Sea Witch asked. "As my stingers penetrate your weak flesh, the venom makes your blood feel as though someone set it ablaze. And even though you're submerged in an endless supply of crispy cool water, you'll never be able to put it out. It'll just burn, and burn, and burn, until there's nothing left—but ashes."

Her tentacles gave him one unbearably tight squeeze before releasing their grip. Lifeless, Nibs sank into the abyss with the arrow.

"How about that?" she said, looking down as Nibs sank deeper within his watery grave. "Now you really are a *lost boy*. Where were we, Mr. Jinni?" she asked, letting out her sinister green smile and yanking him under the water. Skimming just under the surface, she looked back and saw Jinni struggling to remain conscious. "Boy, you are getting weak."

Chapter 22

Suddenly, an imposing purple cloud overtook the area, churned by the speedy craft from which it seemed to be coming. It was the *Elvira*, and she was traveling alongside a thick trail of wine.

"Get another barrel ready, Tootles," Peter yelled out.

Beneath the water, the Sea Witch was overtaken by two tiny streams that trailed off the mass of purple haze and entered her nose. Her eyes grew heavy, and her grip loosened, releasing Jinni back up to the surface. One and Two roped him aboard while the Sea Witch sank. Docile and without a care in the world, she gazed up at the endless collection of rippling stars and dropped even further as the *Elvira* sped away.

One and Two pulled Jinni over the edge and plopped him on deck. Slightly immediately started performing his initial series of medical tasks. One and Two then proceeded to pull Mac aboard and resecured the lifeboat.

"I'm fine, Slightly," Jinni said, annoyed. "She didn't even sting me."

"Where's Nibs?" Peter asked, knowing without knowing.

Jinni stood up, struggling to recollect his strength.

"Where is Nibs?" Peter repeated, raising his voice, looking to both Jinni and Mac for an answer.

Jinni looked down at Peter's feet, then up to his teary eyes. "Nibs didn't make it."

Peter struggled to let in a new breath and fought, even more, to let it out. "Did you see his body?"

"What does it matter? There's no way he—"

"Why can't you just answer me?" Peter screamed. "Did you see his body?"

"Yeah."

Peter took heavy steps toward Jinni and tried to shove him several times.

Jinni didn't budge. "There's nothing I could have done, Pete. Nibs jumped in to save me."

"You saw his body, didn't you?" The first of Peter's tears began to fall. "Why didn't you do that…thing you do? Jinni."

"It doesn't work like that, Pete. It's never worked like that."

Peter waved him off and stormed away, intentionally bumping his shoulder into Jinni's arm while passing by. "This is your fault," Peter said, pointing an angry finger at Mac.

"Peter," Tootles said.

"Let's get him back to Ithaca. Before he gets anyone else killed tonight." Slightly, One, Two, and Tootles watched disapprovingly as Peter stomped belowdecks.

"He didn't mean that, Mac," Tootles said.

"Doesn't mean it isn't true," Mac said.

Chapter 23

In a location unbeknownst to Otis, he woke within the soft grasp of a cloudlike bed. He disentangled himself from the thick comforter and silky sheets and examined the dim room, taking note of a large dressing wrapped around his arm. Hanging near the bed was a fresh change of clothes with a small note attached to the front.

> Dear Stranger,
> If tonight happens to be the night you wake up, please join us in the ballroom. We are having a party and would be delighted by your presence. If you are not feeling up for it, please remain comfortable as long as you like.
>
> Sincerely,
> King Calvin and Queen Elaine

Otis was overcome with delight at the note's final line. He had known King Calvin and Queen Elaine, and they were friends, even having attended his and Penelope's wedding. Otis stepped outside his room and into what seemed to be an endless hallway. The party was reaching its peak, and the noise was undoubtedly coming from the right. Once he'd reached the end of the hallway, a grand staircase led him down to the ballroom. Chitchat, live music, and hundreds of dancing townspeople between the ages of five and seventy enjoyed a vast, wholesome party.

Remarkably approachable despite extravagant, flamboyant crowns and wardrobes, King Calvin and Queen Elaine mingled with their gracious guests. Otis wandered in the room, swimming inside his borrowed outfit. He tried to blend in as best he could but was spotted immediately by his hospitable hosts.

"So. He's alive," King Calvin said, grinning.

Otis stopped and approached them softly.

"Thank goodness," Queen Elaine added. "We were really starting to worry about you."

"I suppose I have you two to thank for the lavish accommodations."

"You're very welcome," King Calvin said. "Think nothing of it. I'm Calvin and this beauty here to my right is my wife, Elaine. We are the king and queen here. But you don't have to address as such. Pleasure to meet you, mister…"

Elaine locked eyes with the mysterious stranger and watched him closely as he toiled over the answer.

Having been punished severely for both lying about his name and telling the truth about his name, Otis wasn't sure how to answer. He knew the king and queen. And they had been allies in the Trojan War. Observing the surrounding crowd, however, Otis couldn't shake the paranoia that comes with knowing

Chapter 23

that a favorite hiding place of enemies is among those who think they're friends, so he decided to lie—sort of.

"Otis," he said hesitantly, looking around the room and noticing a plethora of rose-filled vases. "Ross. Ross Otis."

Otis's stumbling didn't go unnoticed by either of them.

"Well, Mr. Otis," Elaine said. "Do make yourself at home as long as you like, and enjoy the party. If you're hungry, we've got plenty of food. If you're thirsty, you couldn't be in a better place than you are right now, and if you're eligible—refer back to what I said about being thirsty."

"How long have I been here?" he asked, smiling bashfully at her last remark.

"We found you on the beach the morning before yesterday," Calvin said. "Your eyes were open, but it didn't look like you could move all that much."

"That scratch on your arm," the queen added. "I've never seen anything like it...what happened?"

"I'm not sure...So what's the occasion?" Otis asked. "This is quite a party you've got going here."

"You must be far from home if you're not familiar with this party," Calvin said. "We throw it once a year."

"And every year more people show up," Elaine added. "On this day, fourteen years ago, the biggest war this country has ever been involved with came to an end."

"Fourteen years," Otis said. "You must be talking about the Trojan War. That certainly is something to celebrate." *Fourteen years. Has it really been that long?*

Otis stood dejected for a moment, drawing even more suspicion from his royal hosts, causing them to exchange a private glance while he looked down at the busy dance floor. "Well.

Thank you again. But I am—" As Otis looked up, a large eerie painting caught his eye. It was a little girl—the same little girl he had been led to by the white rabbit. "Who is that?" Otis asked, growing frightened and having no idea why.

King Calvin put his arm around the queen. "That's our daughter, Alice," he said, deflated. "She was taken from us a few years back."

"I'm so sorry," Otis said. "I can't imagine."

The energetic party did little to drown the silence percolating between the three.

"Do you have children, Mr. Ross?" Elaine asked.

"I have a son."

"What's his name?"

Otis rubbed several beads of sweat off his forehead and grew pale. "His name? I'm sorry. I'm not feeling all that well," he said grabbing a lump in his throat. "Would you excuse me?"

"Of course," Calvin said, stepping aside.

The two watched Otis stroll away, casually studying the room, as though he'd eventually be quizzed.

His failure to disguise half truths as whole ones urged him to get away from the king and queen, fearing their continued line of questions would reveal his true identity. He sought out and meandered to the nearest exit. Down a small flight of stairs on the back side of the extravagant castle, velvet sand awaited. The private beach was lit by a full moon and several lonely bonfires struggling to survive an onslaught of clashing whirlwinds. The bonfire farthest from Otis, however, was thriving as if fueled by the huddled energy of the dozen or so people standing nearby.

Chapter 23

Closest to the fire and illuminated by its chaotic dance, a blind man with a tattered robe and dark spectacles reflecting the flames had everyone captivated.

"Robin Hood," Otis whispered.

With a cold and demanding tone of wisdom, Robin Hood continued his impassioned anecdote. "Everyone was as scared as they'd ever been. No exceptions. Especially the younger fellas. They knew we were outnumbered. They knew we were outarmed. And there was a lot of doubt as to whether or not the horse was going to work. It was plain as day on all their faces. But the great Otis Seehus had this strange ability to put ease into everyone's mind.

"I know all of you have heard of Otis. But has anyone ever met him?" Robin awaited an answer, only to be answered by silence. "Well. Otis was the kind of person we used to refer to as a high-tide guy. The men's morale was always high when he was nearby or had any involvement with plan or strategy. And that evening, with what was sure to be the most important battle any of them would ever fight, he did what he always did and put ease into their minds.

"He said, 'I know, up to this point, it hasn't seemed like it's a fair fight. Well, so far—for us—it hasn't been. It hasn't been a fair fight. They've outnumbered us, they've outfoxed us, and they've got a lot more gadgets than what we're able to bring to the table. To put it bluntly, they're the favorite. They *are* the favorite. But the upset is always in the mind of the favorite, and there's one thing that we have that they're not going to be ready for: the surprise. I know some of you are scared. I'd be lying if I said I wasn't a little scared, too. I'm a little scared before all of 'em. Always have been. That probably won't change until I'm

Odyssey Tale

too old to fight. But my desire to live keeps me brave in battle. My desire to see my wife and son keeps me brave in battle. So tonight, when you encounter your enemy out there and show him the surprise of his life, he's going to be more afraid of this fight than you ever thought you could be. And you're going to know it because it'll be plain as the white in his eyes.'"

Robin paused with emotion and wiped a tear from his cheek.

Otis looked around the crowd and noticed some of them were crying as well. He didn't know it at the time, nor would he have been able to comprehend it, but Otis Seehus was a famous man. Had someone told him at this moment that he was a household name, and that the term *Trojan Horse* would be used literally and figuratively for centuries to come, he would have deemed that person mentally unfit.

Robin continued. "Otis told us that a man's arrogance is only fueled by the weakness of other men—which, in turn, means that arrogant men, by definition, are weak. 'The Trojan king and his soldiers are the most arrogant in the world,' he said. 'They know we're vulnerable right now, but if we present ourselves as weak—convincingly—they'll no longer see us as a credible threat. But you can bet your ass, and the one on the guy next to you, that we are a credible threat. They have no idea what kind of monster they're about to let through their gates… but they will soon enough. Because the upset is always in the mind of the favorite.'"

The fire's reflection raged in Robin's spectacles. The audience ranged in age, but all of them swelled with a patriotic pride at this soldier's presence and willingness to share his stories. Once the dust from his words had settled, many from his audience approached him with ear-to-ear smiles and asked for

Chapter 23

his autograph. The only man who didn't seem to share in their giddiness was Otis. He lowered his eyes to the sand and disappeared from the reflection in Robin Hood's spectacles. Otis thought that he'd slipped away unnoticed, but Calvin had been studying his reactions from afar and growing more concerned that he may have a rogue wandering his party.

Once away from the bonfire and entirely out of sight, Otis found a private spot on the thunderous beach and looked out to the raven-tinted sea. "I'm coming home, Penelope. I'm coming home to you and Mac just as fast as I can."

At this time, Penelope was two days removed from her last sip of laudanum, and even though her concern was solely on Mac and Otis, she was still feeling the effects of its dissipation. On those rare occasions when she let her bottles get low, much of her day would be bothered by this very thought. *When can I get another one? How should I spread this remaining amount for consumption? When will you do what you are always thinking about, and quit?* All these questions haunted her, but that last one made her really think. Penelope didn't feel like she wanted it anymore. If anything, she felt as though she had a tiny demon living inside her, and his sole purpose was to acquire the next sip.

The first morning Penelope had decided not to feed him turned out fine. But once she'd reached a certain point in the day and realized that a major part of her routine was gone, she started to feel a little restless. At first she convinced herself that it was really just the flavor she was missing, maybe the smell.

Smelling empty bottles and their caps only made her want that feeling more.

By day two, her sheets were filled with sweat, and her night was empty of sleep. She got out of bed the following morning earlier than usual. She wanted the flavor. She needed the relief. Nonetheless, Penelope stayed strong and resisted, reluctantly allowing her mental state to slip further into an emotional limbo in which she couldn't maintain balance. She told herself repeatedly that this was all a matter of time and dosage. These morbid feelings of turmoil and sporadic jabs of pain stabbing the inside layer of her skin were all inside her mind and would go away with time.

Penelope stepped outside for some much-needed fresh air and looked over her balcony at the blushing predawn sky. "Otis," she said, looking out at the calm sea as violent waves crashed on the rocks below. "Where are you?"

"Hello, Penelope."

Startled, she stepped away from the railing and glanced toward the direction of the mysterious deep voice. "Oh," she said, still shaking the surprise from her voice. "Eury. What are you doing in here?"

"I'm sorry to just barge in like this, Penelope. But I'm afraid I've got something to discuss with you, and I can't imagine you're going to like what I've got to say."

"What is it?"

"I'm afraid I've got some rather bad news about Mac."

Penelope's heart stopped. The worst feeling she'd ever had up to this moment was a brief stretch of time in which Mac was as moody as she'd ever seen. Penelope could tell that something was eating him up inside, and she didn't know what it was.

Chapter 23

What's worse, he didn't think highly enough of her to share what had been bothering him. Not being able to help when she could clearly see that Mac was hurting from pain that was well below the surface was one of the most excruciating experiences she'd ever had to endure.

"What about him?" Penelope asked.

"He's out on a Lost Boy ship sailing the open seas, looking for Otis." When Eury uttered these words, Penelope was convinced the ones to follow would include something about Mac's death, but they never came.

"Oh my." She tried to express some form of shock, but stage performing was never her strong suit. "Thank you, Eury. I...I..."

"If you need anything, you know where to find me," he said in a quiet, comforting manner. He left the room and shut the door behind him, releasing a foul smile.

Penelope returned to the balcony and looked back out to sea. She knew it was only a matter of time before others learned of this information and shared it with her in hopes of earning her love and respect. The grim reality, however, was that the further this information spread, the more danger it would bring to Mac. They knew he was becoming a man and that he was not going to lie down while they stumbled over one another trying to steal his birthright. After several moments, she sighed. *Think, Penelope. Think.*

"Otis," she said with more desperation in her voice than ever before. "Where are you?"

Chapter 24

Shying away from the crowd gathered around Robin Hood, and the bulk of the party's guests in the ballroom, Otis kept to himself and wandered the halls as best he could without arousing suspicion. Eventually, he reached a room with an open doorway somewhat off the beaten path.

Once inside, Otis looked over a variety of colorful portraits. Beneath all of them were plaques featuring the person's name and years, ranging from their birth to their death, unless they were still living, of course. Upon closer examination, Otis soon realized that each of the men hanging on the wall had one thing in common: they were high-ranking military officers who'd served in the Trojan War. Sure enough, one in particular happened to stand out.

A young "Otis Seehus" stared ahead into the mysterious distance with a studious look while the half-constructed Trojan horse stood tall behind him. The plaque stated the correct year of his birth, while a question mark signified the year of his death. Fearing that someone would come in and recognize him staring at his own monument, he promptly left the room.

He started back toward the party, stopping to admire the myriad of paintings and portraits he hadn't yet encountered.

In a busy hallway that opened up to the dance floor, another portrait jumped out at him. Otis stared up at the painting, then looked over to King Calvin speaking with a guest. Otis looked back up at the painting, then back to King Calvin.

"Heh," Otis said, amused.

The painting was that of a massive, hairy beast, standing upright like a man and wearing an outfit identical to the one King Calvin happened to be wearing on this particular evening.

"Something, isn't it?" a familiar voice asked.

"What's that?" Otis replied, looking to see who had sneaked up and concluding with a double take.

"Love," Robin Hood said. "And the effect it can have on a person. The way you think. The way you behave. Decisions that you make. People are always trying to show me pity because I'm blind. Their attempts to avoid making it obvious only accomplish the opposite. I can always hear it in their condescending voices. But I've discovered it's the ones who never figure out the true meaning of love that need pity. Whether they choose not to feel it, or just can't. They're the ones who are walking this earth truly blind."

"I'll drink to that." Otis looked the man's face up and down. "You're Robin Hood, aren't you?"

"Indeed, I am," Robin said, grinning. "Do I know you?"

"No. Name's Ross. We've never met before, but I'm a big fan of yours. I know how important you were in the war—keeping the men's spirits up."

"That's kind of you to say, Mr. Ross."

In the dance hall, the music stopped. A boisterous, muscular man in his midtwenties cupped his hands to his face. "Let the games begin!" His deep, burly voice nearly made the floor

Chapter 24

rumble, while the entire crowd showered the man's announcement with applause.

"What's this?" Otis asked.

"Follow me," Robin said. "I take it this is the first time you've been here for a party."

Robin led Otis down to the private beach on the back side of the castle, where a group of fifty or so strong and feral men ranging from their late teens to their late twenties stood in a sloppy single-file line that led to a sign-up sheet. Two hundred or so of the party's guests had no intention of signing up but were starting to gather around to watch the upcoming festivities.

"Every year, toward the end of the night, anyone who wants to show off their strength and cleverness can sign up for the games," Robin said.

"What are the games?" Otis asked.

"There's a handful. Javelin, fencing, archery. And every year, they come up with a different puzzle. But—it all ends with the discus. There are five events in total. You can sign up for one event, or you can sign up for all five. If you win all five, you get thirty-three pounds of gold and sixty-six goats. But no one's ever won all five. Care to sign up? Sounds like you've got some youth left in that voice."

"Unfortunately, *some* is about all I got," Otis said, observing the youthful strongmen playfully engaging one another in line.

A meathead in his midtwenties en route to the line, stepped between Otis and Robin, shoulder checking the both of them. "Hey Robin, you going to sign up this year? Or is your boyfriend going to have to win it for you?" The cocky alpha laughed all the way to the line and then cut to the front.

Seething over the intentional shoulder check, Otis looked toward the meathead, now ribbing and giggling with the other men in line.

"I like to think otherwise, but it seems to be a young man's world," Robin said with sorrow.

For the next several hours, a wide variety of men took their turn. The meathead, whose rise from obscurity made him a fan favorite, had dominated the first three games and edged out what seemed to be his only real threat during the fourth, which was the puzzle course. After he had officially taken four of four games, and with the discus supposedly being his specialty, talks of all five were bouncing around the crowd.

He stood in line for the discus sign-up. The youthful testosterone surging through his veins had him ready. He was on top of the world, already spending that gold in his mind. But Robin and Otis broke his concentration, attracting his wrath once again. As it had been before, the meathead's attack was directed more toward Robin.

The meathead closed his eyes, extended his arms forward, and mockingly walked in place.

A few of the nearby competitors snickered. Otis was enraged, leaving Robin behind to approach the meathead.

"What do you want, lover boy?" The meathead pouted his lips.

"Before this day, if someone told me that there were people out there over the age of fifteen that make fun of blind people, I'd tell 'em they were full of shit. Then I met you." Otis buried his eyes into the meathead's, knowing that youth was the only real attribute this pompous reprobate had in his corner. "That

Chapter 24

man may not have his sight, but he accomplished more when he was your age than you will for the rest of your life."

"You want to step over there and handle this like men?" the meathead asked. "I'd be glad to fight you. At the very least, I can accomplish that today."

"No," Otis said, still not backing down. "I don't care enough about that to bruise my fists over it. He's not my kid, and he's not weak. Doesn't need me to fight his battles. Or assholes like you. So know that this isn't going to be about him. I just don't like you."

"What are you talking about, gramps?"

"I'm going to teach you a lesson in humility and respect."

"How's that?"

"By throwing a discus further than your simple ass. You can kiss your gold, and those goats, goodbye."

"Is that so?" the meathead asked, raising intrigued eyebrows.

To build hype and draw more of a crowd, the men who read off the names were sure to place the meathead and Otis as the final throwers, and in that order.

The meathead wrapped his stocky fingers around the bronze disc and closed his eyes. The tiny sliver of nervousness he did carry was overshadowed by giddiness. He had seen every throw he had to beat, and he knew that there was no way some old man was about to outthrow him. The meathead took a deep breath and calmed his mind, confident that he himself was the only person who could stand in his way. He took one more deep breath, spun around, and launched the discus into the night sky. His feet landed perfectly within a chalk circle. When the discus finally landed, its distance had undoubtedly toppled that of the previous first-place holder. The crowd went wild with applause.

Odyssey Tale

He turned toward Otis and walked away from the thrower's circle. "All eyes on you, gramps. Good luck."

The crowd settled as Otis stared at the disc in his hand, wondering when he'd last held one, unable to remember.

"You gonna kiss it or throw it, old man?" the meathead asked.

Otis took a deep breath.

"This ought to be good," the meathead continued. "I think he really is gonna kiss it."

Otis closed his eyes and took his deepest breath of the day. He looked over to the meathead, winked, and kissed the discus. After two spins within the chalk circle, he whipped the discus two times higher than the meathead and one and a half times farther. The meathead, other strong men, and spectators were stunned silent until everyone burst into another round of applause.

"How did you do that?" the meathead asked, his jaw still in the sand. "That was. I mean—that was. You threw that further than anyone here can see."

"Foul," the field judge yelled out.

Otis looked down at his foot. It had just barely broken the chalk fault line.

"Yeah!" the meathead yelled out in celebration.

"Your throw doesn't count, sir. I'm sorry." He was an older fellow who was genuinely remorseful and had been secretly pulling for Otis, having had some personal stake in the outcome of youth versus wisdom. While it pained him to have to be the one to say something, the simple fact was that Otis had stepped over the line. However unpleasant, however disrespectful, that

Chapter 24

young man had earned his gold prize and the first perfect score in the party's history.

As the field judge announced the young man's win by default, only a few in the crowd let out some uninspired claps. The meathead, initially too excited to contain himself, jumped up and down with joy. The crowd's lack of response and immediate dispersal took the wind from his sails, until he saw Otis.

With a smile and another shoulder check, the meathead squared up with a visually disheartened Otis. "Thanks for makin' it interesting, old-timer. I should probably give some of this gold to you for helpin' me out back there, but I ain't gonna." The meathead cackled away as Otis accepted the loss gracefully and let time guide it further into the past.

Otis scanned the crowd in search of Robin, but Robin was standing behind him.

"There you are," Otis said. "Win some, lose some, I guess."

"In all my years, I've only known one man who can throw a discus far enough to draw a response like that," Robin said. "And it's probably no coincidence that you sound exactly like him. Your name isn't really Ross. Is it?"

Otis lowered his eyes to the beach. "No."

"Then I say it's high time you tell us who you really are," Calvin said, stepping in. "And while you're at it, maybe you can explain why you got so sad when Robin was telling his story earlier. Yeah, I saw that." Calvin looked around, realizing he had attracted a lot of attention and sent it all in the direction of Otis. "I think all of us deserve to know why you show so much remorse while listening to a story that makes us swell with pride."

"You've been so nice and generous," Otis said, still looking down with shrugged shoulders. "I suppose I wouldn't be a very good guest if I wasn't willing to be honest with you. I'll tell you who I am. And I'll tell you my story. But I have to warn you, it's not an easy one to tell. I can't imagine it's an easy one to hear. My name Otis Seehus. I'm the king of Ithaca, and I fought in the Trojan War."

The crowd reacted with a verbal gasp.

"To those of you who don't know me, I was part of the stealth team in the wooden warhorse. The horse…it was…I helped come up with the idea. The war went on longer than any of us had anticipated. There didn't seem to be any signs of it stopping. And then, it was over within the blink of an eye."

Over the next two hours, Otis captivated an audience that gained members by the second while never losing a single one. He told everyone how he'd been taken prisoner by a vile pirate named Captain James and how he'd been scooped up by fishermen, sold as live bait, and almost fed to a python before the queen of Calypso Island kept him prisoner for over a decade. By the time Otis had finished telling his story, his throat was sore, and his voice was raw, as he'd spoken more words in that hour than he had in the previous sixteen years combined.

"I'm not really sure what happened after that. I just remember waking up on the beach and feeling tired. Really, really tired. Then I woke up here. And I'm sorry. I really am sorry that I lied about who I was. But after everything I've been through, I just want to get home with as little attention as possible.

"I've heard that absence makes the heart grow fonder, but I wonder—if my wife thinks I'm dead, did she move on? If so, will my son ever see me as his true father? He was only a

Chapter 24

newborn when I left. Now, he's almost a man. I don't even know what he looks like."

Without warning, a small child began to sob and heave uncontrollably.

"Aw. I'm sorry," Otis said. "Please don't be sad."

"That's the saddest story I've ever heard," the child said, struggling through the tears.

"It's going to be OK, though. Because I'm going home."

"You certainly are," Calvin said. "Anything you need. A vessel, provisions. Wine. It's all at your disposal. We are going to get you home."

The fire continued to rage by the beach, and all eyes remained so affixed to the great Otis Seehus, that no one noticed the curious pair of mermaids who had been eavesdropping from the water's edge. If there was one stereotype of mermaids that rang true far more often than not, it was that they loved to gossip. And war hero Otis Seehus being released by the Calypso Queen after thirteen years of captivity was a juicy, juicy story. In fact, some merpeople knew of places where a story that juicy had monetary value.

Chapter 25

King Calvin made good on his promise to provide Otis with a vessel and provisions for the journey back to Ithaca. According to the most up-to-date maps, which the king also provided, Ithaca was only a two-month trip from port to port. The king provided four months' worth of food and water and six months' worth of wine.

Otis stepped aboard his new vessel and loosened the ropes, keeping it tethered to the seasoned dock. The sweet smell of sap burst from the handcrafted pine vessel, despite having been coated with several glossy coats of cherry varnish. As Otis floated away from the dock unhurriedly, he looked ahead to the calm sea. Even though his rather recent encounter with the Sea Witch was something taken from him by amnesia, he still felt uneasy as the land mass faded from sight.

As the setting sun plastered the sky with every shade of pink and blue, the uneasy nerves that had sent him off the island were starting to settle. Further decompression from his release, and the expulsion of Sea Witch venom from his system, was helping him regain confidence. While the maps and provisions were great, nautical know-how he feared he'd forgotten was as fresh in his mind as it ever was. The very first night, he was using celestial markers with confidence as a map to guide him home.

As the continuation of calm waters guided his vessel deeper into the night, Otis opened a barrel of wine and ladled some into a contraption placed on board, courtesy of King Calvin. It was a tubelike device that had been affixed to the back of the vessel, capable of holding several gallons' worth of wine. Attached to it was a smaller, more flexible tube running out the side and emptying into the ocean at the behest of a time-release mechanism.

The design was a brainchild of Mr. Geppetto, and one of the many innovations he would be known for during the war. Its sole purpose was to provide libations for the Sea Witch, should she place the ship that carried it under attack. He never gave the device an official name, but over the years, one caught on. It was known simply as "the antidote."

It was a smash hit with more affluent ship captains, due to its light weight, durability, and functionality. It was explicitly designed for crews to save time and keep themselves free for other, more mentally demanding tasks. But often times it turned into a joke, with much of the wine being drunk by crew members readily awaiting the stream with a mug or open mouth.

Only a handful of people knew the Sea Witch to be real, and a vast majority didn't take her existence seriously. She was little more than a myth, even to those who had heard her tales from credible sources. It was just too unfathomable for most to believe in such horrid things.

With no further tasks to speak of, Otis ladled one last scoop from the wine barrel and slugged it down before getting comfortable on the vessel's only hammock. He closed his eyes but

Chapter 25

wasn't able to get any sleep. As if beamed into his mind from some telekinetic projection, Otis thought back to random moments from his and Penelope's time together. There were funny moments. There were private moments. And there were visceral moments that brought tears to the bottom of his eyes as the weight of all the years he had spent away eroded his conscience. A mass of questions bounced around in his mind, many more than once. But the one he kept coming back to, and the one he was most nervous to learn, was "Do they still love me?"

The night sea could be a lonely place, and especially scary to those less experienced with the sights and sounds one might encounter. The eerie echoes of whales crying, the candy-covered songs of sirens, and hostile shrieks of merpirates all had the potential to break the silence and peace at any given moment. Otis kept his guard up but allowed his mind to relax and reflect on nostalgic moments that ran parallel with a carousel of bright traveling stars.

In the Sea Witch's cold, dark grotto, a preteen merman swam in from the cave's underwater entrance and emerged to find the Sea Witch sleeping. Her top half rested on a slick, rocky portion of the floor while her billowing tentacles danced slowly below the surface. The neon-sapphire hue they emitted was the only source of light within the dark lair.

The young merman approached slowly in a nonthreatening manner until a glowing tentacle whipped up and wrapped around his petrified young throat.

"You wanted to see me?" the merman asked, trying to remain calm.

"I did," the Sea Witch said. She opened her eyes and turned toward the merman, still holding him tight. "How are the great Otis's travels coming along?"

"He…uh…"

"Well, don't hem and haw around. Spit it out."

"Otis is already less than a week away from Ithaca. He left sooner than we thought, and he's moving much, much faster than we originally projected."

"King Calvin and Queen Elaine have the best shipbuilders in the world, but even that doesn't explain how he's moving so fast." She released the grasp of her tentacle, freeing her young guest before swimming over to a large crate. Using her hands and tentacles, she sifted through an array of mementos she'd accumulated over the years. "I won't be able to get to Otis before he reaches land," the Sea Witch said.

She placed four or five hand-drawn pictures of Otis over several mysterious documents before rolling them up and stuffing them into a large glass bottle. "Be careful with this stuff," the Sea Witch said, corking the top. She extended her tentacle and the bottle within its grasp. The young merman's trembling hand accepted it. "I can't stress enough how bad it'll be for you if you lose, or damage, the contents of this bottle," she said. "Do you understand?"

"I understand."

"I need you to get this to some humans that I can trust—humans who aren't afraid to get their hands dirty. I need you to find a ship called the *Jolly Roger*. Ask for the captain, James."

Chapter 25

She shared her infamous green smile and sent the young merman on his way.

Chapter 26

Somewhere in a remote part of the ocean, a massive, luxurious warship sat still in calm, peaceful waters. In the comfortable, oversized bed sitting dead center in the captain's quarters, Captain James lay, massaging each side of his forehead with his fingers, humming a repetitious tune. It was something he often did to relax after a long day.

He was in a so-so mood this evening, but as of late, he'd actually been down, feeling that time had left his best moments in the past and that life had little, perhaps nothing, left to offer. He had reached middle age. No amount of coffee could keep him from feeling tired all the time. No amount of whiskey could drown the feelings of sorrow long enough to help him sleep. When his back wasn't bothering him, it was his knees. The one on the right popped and clicked with every stair he climbed, and the left felt as though something was grinding it away.

He couldn't relate to his men anymore either. Their brand of humor was juvenile, and he was constantly feeling as though their inside jokes were making him the figure of ridicule. Every time he assumed this to be the case, he reacted with the rage of a proper pirate captain, and every time, they all looked at him as though he'd lost his mind. When such offenses used to call for a death sentence, these days he had lost his grip on the reality of what it took to keep a crew loyal. And he worried that sentencing the wrong man to death would ultimately result in his own.

Whenever they stopped at port now, the best whores paid him little mind. They didn't care that he was the captain of the magnificent *Jolly Roger*, as they had once upon a time. Now he was just a weird old man that the better-looking and younger crew members had to tolerate and take orders from.

Late one rainy night at a random location offshore, Captain James was about to rest his head when a large glass bottle rolled down his wooden stairs and into a corner bedpost.

A chill wrapped around his neck and ran down his back as he recognized the bottle's unique shape, and immediately knew where it had come from. Feeling his heart pirouette, as it hadn't done in years, he grabbed the bottle and twisted it open to reveal its contents.

"Otis Seehus," he said, skimming and mumbling through the first document. "Blah, blah. Ithaca. Blah, blah." He picked up another document. "Blah, blah, blah. War hero. Blah. Personal." Then another. "Blah Blah. Riches beyond belief... now we're cooking with whale blubber."

Twenty years earlier, he would have leaped about the cabin, overcome with joy. But at this age, he didn't expect to live long enough to enjoy the reward she was promising. He knew that a task like this, pulled off successfully, however, could be a great send-off for the twilight of his career. And if he were to make his crew rich, retirement would be filled with glory. He'd finally have their undying respect and loyalty. They'd tell stories and sing songs about him for years to come. And he could finally retire—on top.

Chapter 26

Captain James stood up and stepped into a pair of slippers before spreading the papers over his desk. He shook a pair of spectacles open and looked over several worn maps and a few hand-drawn pictures of Otis from when he was in his mid to late twenties.

"Where do I know him from?" Captain James asked. He studied the drawings at various distances from the glasses resting on his nose. "Otis Seehus. Otis. Seehus. Otis Seehus. Doesn't ring any bells. But I know that face. I know, I know, I know that face. Where have I seen you before?" He looked closer. "No. No. It couldn't be." Captain James grabbed a nearby feather and drowned its tip in an ink jar before scribbling over one of Otis's portraits. "Impossible."

The captain's erratic scribbling came to a stop. Suddenly, the song he had been humming for the past several days was no longer stuck in his head. He looked over the marked-up picture. A beard and cage had crudely been scribbled over young Otis's likeness.

"Nobe."

It had just reached lunchtime on the *Elvira*, and emotions over Nibs's death were still running too high for any of them to hear the grumble jumping from belly to belly. Mac's stubble was growing thicker but still was clearly the stubble of a teenager. His tanned face soaked up more sun as he leaned against the railing on the ship's bow, gazing at the path ahead and unable to shake the feeling he'd been carrying since seeing the Sea Witch. He'd never watched anyone die before, and there was no doubt in his mind as to whether or not Nibs was dead when he hit the water.

Mac was starting to beat himself up, replaying the event and watching himself cower in fear. Nibs's death began to weigh on him, to the point that he began to wonder when the Lost Boys would start to agree with Peter and hold him responsible. The more Mac watched the scene unfold in his young mind, the more he wished that he could travel back to that moment. He would have done anything in his power to stop it. And he was hurt and disappointed when he awoke each morning, only to find that he'd moved forward another day instead of back.

Up in the crow's nest, Peter sat alone and questioned the validity of his current universe as well. It was increasingly difficult to accept the fact that Nibs was really gone. No more teasing him or getting bashed by his witty responses. No more sending him into a crowd of pretty girls to make introductions. No more paintings. No more late nights discussing the meaning of life, the universe, and maritime politics over a bottle of whiskey. *Just no more.*

Peter's emotions inspired a tickle to pinch his nose, which nearly caused him to cry, but the shuffles and steps of someone climbing up snapped the young captain out of his disconsolate gaze.

"Mind if I join ya?" Jinni asked, stepping in.

"Of course not. Have a seat…sorry I shoved you."

"Don't mention it."

"I know…knew…Nibs better than anyone," Peter said. "And you were right. There was nothing you could have done. Even if it was a stranger getting attacked by the Sea Witch, he still woulda dove in headfirst. Just the kind of guy he was."

Chapter 26

"I sure wish I could've saved him." While Jinni didn't prefer that Nibs had died, something in his psyche made him care very little. Perhaps it was his age, or maybe he just thought differently than most of those around him. But Jinni wasn't all that bothered by these sorts of human emotions. Oftentimes, he struggled to find the words that would fan out the smoke of their release. "I don't know if this helps at all, but back when I was a young man, about your age, I traveled to Atlantis for the first time."

"Really?"

"Oh, yeah," Jinni said. "It was wild. None of us had ever seen anything like it. The lights. The colors...the women. It really was wild. Late one night, I went into a bar by myself. Just wanted a steak, potato, and some ale. Maybe a little privacy. So I went to this little place off the beaten path owned by a guy from the Americas. You know how you and the fellas come from Cherokee Country...this guy came from a place he called Navajo Country.

"For some reason or another, he started talking about times he'd traded with them and technology they used. And eventually, he started talking about their language. They had six or seven words for everything under the sun and nine to ten for everything that's not. But one word that had no translation was *death*.

"He said, 'Of all the places I've traveled, and all the people I've traded with, they're the only ones that ain't gotta word for death. The closest one they have translates roughly to *not here at the present moment*. As if here is just some...place we visit for a short time.'"

"That sounds nice," Peter said. "But. Unfortunately, we do have that word in our language. And I know I'm young, but

I've had to watch a lot of my favorite people die over the years. Ain't none of 'em have been easier than the last. But I think I can take a little comfort if I think of 'em in terms of not being here at the present moment."

"You OK then? We OK then?" Jinni asked.

"Yeah."

"I'm gonna head back down," Jinni said, standing. "If you need anything, just holler down."

Peter nodded as Jinni began his initial descent.

"Land!" Tootles shouted out from on deck.

If it were up to Mac, the *Elvira* would have sailed through the night, but with Ithaca being four weeks away with no stops in between, Peter wanted to treat himself and his crew to a one-night stay on land. Mac, eager to get back home, didn't leave the *Elvira* while they went into town for drinks and companionship, nor did he get any sleep that night. Then, the next morning, much to his chagrin, Mac would learn that the *Elvira* would be docked for at least the next three days. Time stood still.

He spent all of his time on the ship, lying under the sun, attempting to breathe his anger away and failing with a lack of patience. On what he was told would be the final night at port, Mac stood on the stern, watching the ripples. He had a throbbing suspicion that when the morning finally hit, Peter would decide to stay for another day, or two, or week.

"Dammit," Mac said, under his breath. He stared back down at the water. For a moment he was able to clear his mind of all thoughts and just gaze upon the tiny waves. That's about the time something burst through the water.

Mac recoiled in horror but returned to the ship's edge when he realized that whatever it was that had burst through was of

Chapter 26

no threat. He looked down and saw the top half of a middle-aged mermaid sitting idle in the water.

"Is this the *Elvira*?" the mermaid asked.

"Yeah," Mac said hesitantly.

"Is Jinni on board?"

"I'm here, Athena," Jinni said, stepping into the conversation.

"I was hoping I hadn't missed you."

"What's up?" Jinni asked.

"That guy you're looking for—Otis. He's on a small vessel right now headed for Ithaca. Not sure how far he's gone, but he is on water."

Jinni's eyes widened. "How did you find this out?"

"The Sea Witch," the mermaid said. "She's put a bounty out on him. Dead or alive."

Otis awoke to an area shrouded by fog. It looked like dusk but felt like dawn. He stood from his hammock and walked around the hazy vessel, trying to get any kind of visual of his surroundings.

Thump...thump. Otis watched as the thumps scraped the bottom of the boat, moving from front to back. He looked over the stern, relieved to see that a random tree branch had been the source of the forbidding sound.

He turned back toward the bow. Suddenly, the vessel began to shake and shudder, coming to a halt and sending him face first to the deck. He closed his eyes and buried his fingertips into the wood, waiting for the vessel to splinter and disappear beneath him. He cringed, waiting. But nothing happened, and the air remained silent.

He opened his eyes calmly and stood up. As if afraid to wake some sleeping giant, he slowly approached the bow and looked down through the fog. The vessel had burrowed itself in the moist sand of some mysterious beach. "Thank the gods," he said, hopping out the front and into the spongy sand greeting his feet. "Great. Where the hell am I now?"

As he observed the area, each step brought forth more sunshine. The beaming rays' refusal to be ignored sent the fog on its way at a rapid rate. That's about the time the beach's tree line came into view. It wasn't just any tree line—it was an olive tree line.

Otis dropped to his knees and burrowed his forehead in the sand, just as the vessel's bow had done moments before. He kissed the ground and scooped two handfuls of ocean water to his face before running his fingers down his shaggy cheeks in joyful disbelief. "Ithaca." Tears welled up in the bottoms of his eyes. "Ithaca."

Between the mental torture caused by the unknown whereabouts of her only son, and the physical anguish caused by the lack of laudanum in her life, Penelope wasn't getting much sleep around this time. She'd never make it through the night, and only once or twice during the day would she doze off, only to be jolted from her slumber an hour or so later.

As the fog cleared for Otis down on the beach, Penelope was still in bed, guarded from the sun by two large drapes. She

Chapter 26

opened her eyes slowly until she realized that someone was in the room with her—in bed with her. Penelope rolled away from the strange man in a panic until she realized who it was. Aside from casting the most disturbing of stares on her sleeping face, she was certain he hadn't done anything to her, so she was able to keep calm while still backing away.

"Eury?"

"I was just watching you sleep. You really are quite lovely when you sleep."

Her shock packed its way into a lump in her throat where it clung. "Wh-what do you want? What can I do for you?" Penelope stood up and walked across the room. She didn't know why, but she felt the need to undo the drapes and allow the sun into the room, as if it were somehow going to protect her in the event that he decided to become physical.

Eury stood with a nonthreatening presence while his didactic expression carried something of a neutral tone. "I was down by the docks last night, and I learned some things."

"What did you learn?" she asked.

He turned to her, offering a soft face. "You may want to sit down for this, Penelope."

"No, no," she cried. Penelope threw herself into Eury's arms, pressing her tear-streaked cheeks into his chest. "He was my only son. How could I let this happen?"

"Penelope. Calm yourself," he said. "I'm sorry; I should have been clearer. Mac is fine."

"Oh," she said. "Are you certain?"

"As far as I know, Mac is alive and well and on his way back here right now."

"Oh," she repeated, wiping her eyes. "Well, that's great news."

"Yes, it is. But it's not all great," he said. "You remember when I told you he went out looking for Otis?"

"Yes."

"Well, he found him. Sort of. Penelope, I'm sorry to be the one to have to tell you this, but Otis died on an island called Calypso. It was sometime after the war. I'm so sorry," he said.

Penelope felt a new wave of tears gather in her eyes, but none of them fell. It was almost a relief to hear Eury break this news. At the very least, she knew that Otis wasn't suffering somewhere. On a more self-interested level, she was relieved that he hadn't fallen out of love with her, or lost interest in the life the two had built together. For so long she had refused to believe that Otis was dead, while so many people tried to tell her otherwise. This was the moment she finally let it all go.

"Is there anything you'd like me to get you?"

"No. Thank you," she said.

"Is there anything I can do? You want me to leave? You want me to stay? Whatever it is, you say the word, and it's done."

"I think, for now, I'd like to be alone."

"Absolutely," Eury said. "You got it. And again—if you need anything, you know where to find me."

"Thank you, Eury. You're a great friend."

Insulted by the patronizing label, he let out a smirk and squared himself in the area separating her from the door.

"You see, that's where you're wrong, Penelope. Whether or not you realize it, or want to admit it, we're much more than friends."

Chapter 26

His friendly demeanor was gone. He was imposing, intimidating, domineering, and all-around antagonistic. It was as if he'd been waiting this whole time to reveal his true nature and shed the skin of the Eury whom everyone knew and seemed to enjoy.

"What do you mean?" she asked, failing to prevent the dismay in her heart from making its way into her voice.

"If you and I were just friends, I don't think I'd stop those guys downstairs from killing Mac when he got back here."

"Why would they do that?" Penelope asked, now struggling to control her breathing.

"I guess, somehow, they got wind of his little journey, and why he was out on it. And let's just say, if Mac is old enough to go looking for his dead daddy, he's old enough to fight for his crown. When he gets back here, that's exactly what he's going to have to do."

"No. He won't. There's still plenty of time for me to choose a husband. And if Otis is dead, like you say, what threat does Mac pose? He's just a boy."

"A boy who understands that his crown is being threatened. Going out and looking for Otis was just the first step. Since it didn't work, he'll move on to another. Any way you slice it, that puts me, and all those guys downstairs, in something of a quandary. Wouldn't you say?"

"This is still my castle, and my time to decide isn't up."

"Maybe not. But people are getting very impatient with you, Penelope. A lot of people. And I know you like to use that little shroud of yours as an excuse—and how it's not done yet, but, say, where is that shroud?" Eury looked around the room, only pretending to care.

"I keep it tucked away in my dresser when I'm not working on it," she said, defensively.

"I see," he said, not believing her. "Well, if you were serious about finishing it before getting remarried, I suggest you finish it soon, because sooner than later, if you don't choose a husband, one's going to choose himself."

"Get out of my room. And don't come back." She pointed an angry finger at the door.

He grinned. "Don't get mad at me, Penelope. And seriously think about this before you send me away. Weigh your options. We'd make a good match. And I'd treat you like the queen you are. Maybe one day there will be a time and place where women aren't so limited on who they can and can't marry. But you live in this time. And you live in Ithaca. And if you want your castle to stay your castle, you're going have to choose one of us."

Eury turned toward the door and peeked over his shoulder to let out one last smirk. He had Penelope right where he wanted.

Chapter 27

When the fog had cleared enough to see where he landed on Ithaca, Otis was relieved, as the spot didn't warrant much traffic. He gathered the most valuable of his provisions before stashing them in some tall grass and wrapped himself in a fresh brown robe—one of several gifted to him by King Calvin and Queen Elaine. Even though this was his home, Otis knew that a lot could happen in thirteen years, and should there be someone new wearing his crown, his life would be in immediate danger.

There was a decent chance he wouldn't be recognized under the beard that covered the most recognizable parts of his face. But he needed more. It wasn't enough to go unrecognized. He had to make sure he was ignored. So he reached down into the lush dirt keeping the olive trees fed and smeared just enough on his face to achieve the look he was going for.

They won't look at a bum.

Every step closer to the castle made it grow in size, but for every one step Otis took toward it, the castle seemed to take two steps away. The pace of his heart increased rapidly while his breaths became more challenging to bring in. He was just about to break the barrier of town when he took a moment to collect his poise. There was no telling how much had changed, or if these next few moments were to mark the beginning of something—or the end.

As he took in his first full view of the castle and the small town in front of it, Otis noticed little change aside from cosmetic. Many of the street vendors were still in operation, or their children had taken over. The colors of their signs and platforms were seasoned and rickety.

Otis stepped through the crowd, feeling as though everyone's eyes were recognizing him all at once. In truth, his disguise was working to perfection, as not a single person had purposely looked his way. Skittish and visibly paranoid, Otis approached the stairs as a man who was up to no good. There was no one standing guard on the front steps, but Otis expected to be greeted by at least three bulky men, demanding to know his intentions once he'd made it inside.

"Penelope," he said, before knocking on the door. "If anyone asks, I'm here to see Penelope. She's a cousin. No, she's a—"

Otis stopped thinking aloud, as he'd realized he was making it too complicated. He needed to find a neutral way to approach this conversation, so he decided that if need be, he'd present himself as a messenger "here on behalf of distant family of Penelope." And to give his lie validity, Otis knew of a place where Penelope actually had family. He figured that if someone else had taken over the castle, there was no reason to assume this grungy third-party messenger had any loyalty to her.

Otis knocked on the door, getting no answer. After a few curious moments, he looked around to make sure no one was staring and placed his ear on the door. The sound of shattering glass was surrounded by hearty laughter and chitchat.

Chapter 27

"What the hell?" Otis asked, slowly cracking the door.

He stepped over the threshold and looked around in astonishment. Random men were scattered about, slamming full steins of ale, filling the air with smoke from their stories and tobacco, and treating the place as something in between an outhouse and saloon. No one noticed him standing there in disbelief. Otherwise, someone might have seen that he was about to break down right there.

He used his imagination as best he could to block them from sight and picture his castle as it was when he'd left it. It was quiet, clean, wholesome, and nothing short of heavenly. Otis was able to keep any tears from falling. Then he saw the dog. Grace was the sweetest and most docile black Lab anyone could ever have the pleasure of meeting. She loved Otis very much. Her first several months there, the two of them would wake up during the predawn hours, eat breakfast, and play for hours. He worked with her, taught her tricks, and even though it took her longer to control her jumping than anything else, eventually, she got it figured out.

That poor puppy adored him, and when he went off to fight in the war, she'd watch the front door of the castle every day, patiently waiting for him to return. For those first few months, it broke Penelope's heart to hear her whining for him. After several months she stopped whining, but she never stopped watching that door. And when he came in for the first time in over a decade, her graying face lit up. If her haggard legs didn't have so much trouble carrying the rest of her, she might have broken the rules and jumped up on him.

"Grace." Otis crouched down and let a tear slip from his eye as he hugged the dog, emotionally accepting her jubilee of licks. "How are ya, girl?"

Her once-rambunctious tail used to sway high and proud, swinging wild in every direction. In recent years, however, it hung in a sad curve, finding little reason to wag. After those first whiffs of Otis's hand and wrist, everything changed.

Despite the unusual scene between Otis and a dog that was usually on the wrong end of a smack or kick, still no one noticed him standing at the door. He held her floppy ears between his thumbs and forefingers and gently gave them a pinch before standing up and moving farther inside.

"Hey, anybody know where Eury is?" a husky male voice asked.

"He's upstairs," another answered. "With Penelope."

A handful of men let out suggestive laughs as Otis looked up to his and Penelope's bedroom door. At that moment, Eury was walking out of the room, smiling. Otis saw this and glared, assuming the smile was for something other than conversation. Eury, perhaps feeling the sting of Otis's seething eyes, returned the stare for several moments before looking away and retiring to his own suite, as if having lost interest.

Otis had known things were going to be different in some way, but he didn't expect that things would be so confusing. *Who the hell is he, and who the hell are all these guys?* He looked around the room, utterly disgusted by the lack of respect being shown to his home. Drinks were spilled, glasses were smashed, and several flocks of flies indulged in a buffet of rotting food on the floor. Otis wanted to shout out in anger. He wanted to kill each and every one of these men for invading his home, and

Chapter 27

he wanted to do it before sunset. But he knew that if he reacted with the same rage he carried in his gullet, he would be the one who wouldn't live to see the night.

Just as his internal top was about to blow, he saw Penelope emerge from their bedroom door. She was just about to rest her arms on the banister when she looked down and saw him looking up. Even from a distance, his gaze bore deep into her eyes. He was experiencing a whirlwind of emotions.

Penelope slowly strolled to the top of the staircase. Looking and feeling as though he was being carried by a cloud, Otis approached the bottom of the staircase and started to ascend as she walked down.

"Queen Penelope," he said. She previously wouldn't have thought it possible, but now that they were face to face, he looked even deeper into her eyes.

"Hello, sir," she said. "And what, may I ask, is your name?"

Otis was dejected, but he regained his composure just as quick as it had left him.

"Are you a friend of my husband's—or my son's?"

"Yes. I mean, no. I mean…I knew your husband," Otis said, feeling the words pour in as if given to him by someone else. "I served with your husband. I was in the wooden horse with him—in the war."

"The Trojan Horse," Penelope said.

"Yeah," Otis said. "The Trojan Horse. I, uh…just thought I'd stop by for a visit."

"I'm sorry, good sir. But it looks like you've come a long way for nothing. Nobody's heard from Otis, and he hasn't been around here for years."

Otis's concern revealed his identity, just a bit. "I see," he said. "And what's this about your son? He's not here either?"

"No. He snuck out and went overseas to find his father. Word is he's on his way back, but I'm afraid he's going to come back disappointed. Everyone around here believes Otis to be dead."

"What do you believe?" Otis asked.

Penelope thought long and hard about that question and what it meant. She'd answered it for herself so many times that she really didn't have the strength to answer it for someone else. But she did it anyway. "I'm not sure anymore. It's been a long time since anyone's asked me that. It's getting more and more difficult to believe he's alive. I'd like to think that if he were, he'd have found a way home by now."

Otis closed his eyes in despair, but the coverage of his beard helped to soften the tone of his true feelings. "Well. If he is still alive, anything keeping him from you and Mac is keeping him against his will. I know there's nothing he wanted more than to get back here to you. He loved you and Mac very much. You two were all he ever talked about. All the time. He mentioned that he missed your laugh and the way you always had the most adorable nicknames for him."

Penelope couldn't hold back the tears any longer, but when they came, they came softly and only visible to Otis.

"And he mentioned this twinkle you used to have in your eye when you looked at him," Otis continued. "He said the thought of it could get him through anything. No matter what, it would all be worth it. Even if he only got to see that twinkle one more time…It was nice talking with you, ma'am. But I should probably get going."

Chapter 27

"The pleasure was all mine," she said, wiping away the final tear. "You are welcome here anytime."

Otis nodded and went back down the stairs before approaching the front door. Away from her, and away from the central cluster of sloth and drunkenness, Eury stood with a couple of pals and watched Otis leave.

"Who was that?" Eury asked.

"Who?" one of his pals asked.

"The guy that just left. Guy in the brown robe."

"I don't know. Looked like a bum to me."

"He was talking to Penelope," Eury said, hints of jealousy escaping his words. "He was talking to her for a while."

"He just left," the other pal said. "Want us to go take care of him?"

"Nah. That's all right," Eury said. "But there's something about him that seems…familiar."

Chapter 28

As much as it pained Penelope to admit, and as much as she despised Eury's threats, she knew he was right. As long as the appointed elders of Ithaca controlled the destiny of their castle and fortune, neither Mac nor herself would truly be safe. While most of the invasive suitors wouldn't dream of usurping the castle by means of violence, or defiance of the elders or the gods, there were still plenty who lurked like sharks approaching bloody water. Each day, they grew more impatient with the process and less concerned with the prospect of having to face the gods. Living in that castle, enjoying its amenities day after day, year after year, some of the men began to feel that any punishment they would have to suffer in the next life would be well worth the lifestyle acquired in this one. *If there is a next life*, many thought.

If the suitors didn't fear the gods, the elders didn't stand a chance. Should they disapprove of such behavior, the suitors could just kill them and make way for the next batch. While this thought wasn't one they'd spent much time entertaining, it was certainly in the back of every elder's mind.

Penelope certainly didn't want that. The elders had been so kind, appeasing her every request when it came to the timeline of getting remarried. They had been sympathetic and patient with the delayed progress of the shroud she wanted to make in honor of Otis. Any of them could have accused her of taking advantage of their kindness and making a mockery of her own request. If any of them had known she'd actually finished it, and it had been sitting in the top drawer of her nightstand for the past three years, they would have birthed kittens.

Not long after starting the shroud, Penelope realized that she was working much too fast. As the days came and went, she slowed her pace but was still moving too fast. So she slowed her pace even further, but on top of that, every day she would unravel half of the day's progress. It was a trend she would continue for the next ten years.

Initially, Penelope had assumed and daydreamed that different elders would stop by to check on the shroud and how it was coming along, but none of them ever did. Even after she'd finished, she waited for someone—anyone—to stop by and ask about it. But no one ever showed.

The morning after a disguised Otis stopped by the castle to visit, Penelope lifted the shroud from its place in the nightstand and took it to a rocking chair on the balcony, where most of it had been embroidered. She sat and unfolded the magnificent cloth monument, recalling specific details the laudanum had rendered blurry.

A strange scratching noise shot over from the balcony's ledge. She kept her eyes on the shroud and leaned forward to set it at her feet, exchanging it for a bow and arrow concealed beneath the rocker. It took a moment for her sight to maneuver past the teenage stubble before she recognized the cautious smile.

Chapter 28

"Hey, Ma," Mac said, holding his hands up on either side of his face while his eyes pointed back at the arrow's tip. "It's me. Please don't let that go."

She stood up and ran to him before rearing back and smacking his cheek sideways. It was the first and only time she'd ever hit him.

"Don't you ever leave like that again, young man. Do you understand me?"

"I'm sorry," he said, with a genuine timbre. "I won't. Promise."

"So...did you learn anything about your father?"

"No," he said, still eager. "But I met a whole lot of people that he either inspired or helped during the war. He's a hero—everywhere I went."

"So you didn't hear anything about what happened to him?"

"No," he said. "Nothing like that."

A mother can always tell when her child is lying, even though sometimes she'll pretend not to.

"Look, Mom," he added. "I know you've done what you could since Dad's been gone. But it's difficult to fight an uphill battle, especially by yourself. And that's exactly what you've been doing all these years."

"What are you saying, Mac?"

"I'm not sure, but I think I'm in a position—or getting close to being in a position—where I can help. I know that we can't keep waiting around on Dad. And I know you don't want to marry any of those slobs downstairs...I can help. I can help get rid of these guys. Then maybe you can find someone who actually deserves to marry you—for you. Instead of some asshole who just wants to live in this castle, and off your fortune."

He walked to the ledge of the balcony and sat on the rail.

"Just make sure you don't finish that shroud in the next few days," he said.

Penelope looked down at the completed shroud but couldn't tell him the truth. If anyone ever found out, if he were to accidentally let it slip in some conversation, it would've put both of their lives at risk.

"I know growing up here hasn't been easy," she said. "Especially without your father. But ever since the day you were born, my entire life has been dedicated to one purpose. And that's keeping you safe—until you're old enough to keep yourself safe."

"Now it's my turn to keep you safe, Ma."

She glanced back at the shroud, then up to where Mac had been standing. He was gone. "You're not that age yet."

Only moments later, Mac and Jinni walked on a remote beach and were about to pass a beggar man. Nearly looking past the mud on his face and the drabness of his brown robe, Mac locked eyes with the stranger and felt as though he was looking at the same sad eyes he'd seen in the mirror. While the rest of this shaggy man shared little resemblance, the likeness of their eyes was uncanny.

"Mac." Otis stood still, stunned to silence.

"Dad?" Mac asked. "Is that really you?"

"Yeah," Otis said. Tears began to stream down his heavy eyes. "It's me." After a long, heartfelt hug, Otis finally released his grasp. He leaned back and clapped Mac's shoulders within

Chapter 28

his palms. It really was like looking in a mirror, albeit one that had the ability to enhance the powers of youth. After the tears had settled and the hugs were done, the air remained ripe with a raw sentiment. Otis took in a deep breath, finally leveling his emotions.

"It's you," Otis said, just now noticing Jinni.

"I told you I was one of the good guys," Jinni said with an arrogant yet friendly smile. "Glad to see you made it out."

"It's so great to finally meet you," Mac said. "We have a lot to catch up on."

"You have no idea how much I've pictured this very moment—thinking it was never going to happen," Otis said, feeling another round of tears moving in.

"I know, Dad. I know. And I wish it weren't this way, but before we can celebrate, we've got some work to do. At the castle."

"Yes," Otis said, shifting to a more hostile tone. "I just came from the castle. What in the hell is going on there, and who are all those guys?"

"I'll explain everything."

"I hate to interrupt, fellas," Jinni said. "And I know this isn't exactly the busiest of spots, but neither of you should be out in view of the public right now."

"No one recognized me at the castle," Otis said.

"That doesn't mean they won't out here," Jinni replied.

Otis nodded. "You're right. I've set up a small camp. It's not far. Follow me." Without warning, a swarm of raindrops poured from the cloudless sky. A flash of lightning lit the beach, sending a clap that ricocheted and rumbled off every standing surface.

"Actually," Jinni said. "We have a place. Indoors."

"Great," Otis said as the rain picked up. "How do we get there?"

Through a raging monsoon and a narrow channel that led to Ithaca's main docks, Jinni and Mac paddled the *Elvira*'s lifeboat back to her home. Otis sat in the back with a pensive look that only grew more so, as incoming rain drenched the three of them relentlessly. Since the Lost Boys had a reputation to uphold, they came and went as they pleased, exaggerating those first few drunken nights. For Mac, the lifeboat was the only way to go to and fro without anyone knowing he was on the island.

As the soaking-wet trio climbed aboard and claimed shelter belowdecks, Peter was the only Lost Boy who had decided to stay in for the evening. He was alone in his cabin trying to sleep. He thought the sneaky visitors were there to steal—a thought that was only confirmed when the first face he saw in the darkness belonged to Otis, disguised as a vagabond.

Peter pulled a dagger from his belt, taking a deep breath and getting ready to pounce. "Stop right there."

"Relax, Pete," Jinni said, bringing a lantern to life. "It's just us."

With groggy eyelids and a cross demeanor, Peter looked the three of them over. "What…we're takin' in bums now? What the hell is this?"

Jinni smiled. "This is Mac's father. Otis Seehus."

"Well, shit," Peter said, taking note of the brown robe and grubby appearance. "So much for us getting paid."

"Don't worry," Otis said. "You'll get paid. Mac's told me all you've done for him. For us."

"Yeah?" Peter asked.

Chapter 28

"From the bottom of my heart, I just want you to know how grateful I am."

"You're welcome," Peter said. "But let's get back to the getting paid part."

"My fortune is being looked after by elders that I appointed some time ago. Right now, they control it, but once I have access to it, *you'll* have access to it."

"Why don't you go talk to them now?" Peter asked.

"It would draw too much attention," Otis said. "I need to be…strategic in how I reveal my presence here. But rest assured, once things are back in order, you'll be compensated generously."

Slightly, Tootles, One, and Two burst down the stairs. The drunken cluster reeked of cheap whiskey and burned tobacco, and all seemed to be laughing at the funniest thing any of them had ever seen. But as it often did, Peter's mood controlled the mood of the room. And when they saw their captain looking as serious as he was, their laughter lost its momentum.

"Fellas. Meet Otis," Peter said.

They all tripped over one another, making obnoxiously drunken introductions. After several stern, fatherly looks from Peter, they all sat down and got quiet.

"And how long until things are back in order?" Peter leaned forward and interlaced his fingers.

"I don't know," Otis said. "All depends."

"On what?" Tootles asked.

"Tootles. Shut up. On what?" Peter asked.

"If you fellas are interested in one more job, I got one that'll pay enough to keep you set for several lifetimes. But it is going to be dangerous."

"What even makes you certain you still have a fortune?" Peter asked. "Those guys up there in your castle. It seems they've been chipping away at it for some time."

"No," Mac said. "They haven't. They haven't even scraped the surface."

"And how do you know?"

"I've overheard the elders share this information with my mom."

"I did pretty well for myself when I was just about your age," Otis said, with a smile of friendly arrogance. "If you guys help me get my kingdom back, you'll be able to do whatever you want, whenever you want. You're just going to have to have a little faith." Otis looked over the group, taking note of their builds. "And a lot of training, from the looks of it. I'd be willing to bet there's not one in the lot of you who can fight worth a shit. Except maybe you," he said, pointing at Jinni. "But you're no spring chicken, are you?"

Peter took a deep breath and leaned back in his chair. "So what's your plan?"

"Don't have one yet. But I'm thinking. In the meantime, how well are you boys conditioned?"

"Conditioned?" One asked. "Like when we get paid for a delivery?"

"That's commission, retard," Slightly said.

Otis smiled and stood up. "What do you say we all go for a little run?"

Chapter 29

Before any of the Lost Boys were willing to run anywhere with Otis, something they often referred to as "turkey" needed to be discussed. Otis, being the master negotiator that he was, and Peter, being surprisingly easy to please, had come to an agreement that satisfied both parties. At the time, Peter didn't understand exactly what kind of wealth comes with being a king. Otherwise, the Lost Boys might have earned double. But, as promised, Otis agreed to pay them more than enough to make it frivolously through an ample number of lifetimes.

As the predawn hours were beginning to approach, Otis led Mac, Jinni, Peter, and the remaining Lost Boys to a secluded spot on the beach several miles from where Otis had landed. Before dedicating his thought to "the plan," Otis needed to see precisely what kind of talent he had employed.

"First things first," Otis said. "We are all going to go for a little run."

Peter and the Lost Boys let out a collective grumble while Mac and Jinni both kept still with stoic faces.

"I thought you were payin' us to fight," Peter said. "What are we supposed to accomplish runnin' around, wasting energy?"

"If you want paid, you're going to have to do what I say. And you're going to have to trust that everything I say is in the best interest of this group. I'm not gonna ask you guys to do anything I'm not willing to do. But I'm not going to waste good gold on a lot of inexperienced street fighters."

"OK." Peter shifted his hands over the front of his hips. "How long is this little run going to be?"

"Two, two and a half miles," Otis said. "You guys think you can handle that?" The words tickled every Lost Boy except Jinni, to the point where they took turns doubling over.

"Yeah," Peter said, trying to hide his smile among a chorus of snickers. "I think we can handle it."

Had this been a little jaunt around the beach, the Lost Boys would have been right to laugh. But Otis had led them to a place known to locals as Edgewood Hill. It was a place where Otis once had exercised in preparation for the endurance needed in battle. The grueling uphill jaunt wasted the most finely tuned athletes to ever attempt its upward stretch.

Just as Otis had suspected and hoped, the run minced his new hires. Looking as though they'd been doused with buckets of water and breathing cramps into their winded bodies, everyone made it to the top without having to stop running—except for Tootles. He had to walk those last two miles.

As the pink sun guided their walk down the steep slope of Edgewood Hill, Peter had to stop and throw up. "That hill get the best of you there, Lost Boy?" Otis asked.

"Nah," Peter said, spitting out one final chunk. "Shouldn't have had those raw oysters for breakfast."

Chapter 29

The friendly yet sarcastic tone made Otis grin. "Well, rest easy. It won't be the hardest thing you do all week, but it'll be the hardest thing you do today."

"You mean there's more?" Tootles asked, panting.

For the next several hours, Otis made them perform drills in hand-to-hand combat, fencing, archery, general battle tactics, and strategy. He made Mac sit off to the side for anything in which one of the Lost Boys could physically hurt him, be it accidentally or on purpose, but Otis was pleased with Mac's eagerness to learn and be a part of what was happening at that moment.

It didn't take long for Otis to figure out that Tootles was the best with a bow and arrow by a long shot, One and Two were the best fighters, Slightly was the smartest and had the coolest head under pressure, and Peter was the most agile, best overall athlete, and most skilled swordsman.

Otis also noticed that Jinni was nearly an expert in all of these areas, but likely trending downward and on the wrong half of his age. Jinni knew it too. His best performances were long behind him. Otis understood, all too well, how ferocious time's appetite could be.

Otis was a natural leader and quite gifted in the arena of coaching. He always had an uncanny understanding as to which guys he needed to pull aside for a heart-to-heart, and which guys he needed to shove face first in the dirt with a series of screams to both ears.

One thing that became apparent was that the Lost Boys as a team were better at fighting than they were at anything else. But they were still street fighters. Their rudimentary knowledge was based entirely on what they'd learned from being thrown in the fire. They'd never had any real training up to this point.

Otis started them off with a few fundamentals. He taught them how to properly hold their fists and the importance of accurate footwork, and he couldn't stress enough the value and underutilization of rib shots. "They're effective. They hurt like shit. And they're distracting. Every second that your opponent concentrates on that pain, that's one second they're not concentrating on you or the fist that you're about to slam into their jaw."

Otis fine-tuned their swordsmanship, offering advice and general criticisms to everyone. "Hold it like a man, Tootles. You look like a new bride grabbin' a tally-wacker for the first time. One! How many more times do I gotta tell you? Don't come down like that. Your grip is going to slip, and you're going to cut your leg and bleed to death. But I guess you're a redundancy anyways, so what difference does it make? I don't know why I'm surprised, Two. I should have known an exact replica would be just as useless. Slightly! What the hell are you smiling about, ya jerk-off? You just got yourself killed. Again. Peter. That wasn't quite as pathetic as your last try. But it's still for shit." And to finish the day properly, Otis told everyone to run up Edgewood Hill once more.

"What the hell?" Peter asked, soaked with sweat and still breathing heavy from the last swordfight.

"Yeah," Slightly added. "You said the hardest part of today was over."

"It is," Otis said, adding a smile. "You've already done it once. How much harder can it be a second time?"

Everyone made it through the second run, albeit at a slower pace than before. This time, Tootles walked the final two and

Chapter 29

one quarter miles. Once everyone had made it back to the bottom, they scattered about, lying down and sitting and enjoying rest more than they ever thought one could.

Otis sat off to the side with Jinni, silently rebuilding his energy reserves and relieved to see that his new hired soldiers still had enough of their energy to be joking around and in good spirits, even after the gauntlet he had just put them through.

Once their day was officially over, the younger Lost Boys and Mac jawed back and forth, arguing over who had performed best throughout the day, letting out an occasional laugh. Jinni and Otis were close by but tucked away with some element of privacy as a crow landed nearby and began to caw. Soon after, two more crows cawed from opposite directions.

"Their communication system is fascinating, isn't it?" Otis grinned. "Makes you wonder what they're saying."

Jinni returned the smile and picked a few blades of grass from between his tired legs. "When I was younger, I was always told that crows were a bad omen. Then I met someone who told me that when crows go out of their way to talk to you, it means the coast is clear."

"Whose coast?" Otis asked, raising his eyebrows and rubbing his knees. "Gaaah. My knees feel like there's two little people living inside them. And their purpose in life is to stab me to death from the inside. What hurts on you?"

"Everything," Jinni said. "Look. I know more about you than these guys do. I know how clever you are. I guess—what I'm getting at—do you really still have your fortune and plan on paying us, or are you just saying that so we'll go along with this and help you?"

Odyssey Tale

"I know you don't know me, so my word can't mean much. But I promise that even if all those guys at the castle stayed here for another fifty years, living off my wealth, they still wouldn't scratch the surface."

"Man," Jinni said, baffled that such concentrated fortune could exist. "How did you accrue such wealth at such a young age?"

"It was all in here," Otis said, proudly tapping a forefinger to his temple. "Military strategy."

"Military strategy?" Jinni asked.

"That's right. Years before the Trojan War, I had the ear of a very powerful person. I was one of several advisers who offered up my opinions and knowledge on the opposition, different strategies, terrain mapping. I helped out as often as I was asked, saving both lives and resources. Eventually, I saved enough lives and enough resources that I was named king of Ithaca and given more gold than any one hundred men could need for one thousand lifetimes—or so they phrased it. So yeah. I'm not gonna rip you guys off."

"What was his name? The powerful person you advised?"

"Was a her. Queen Rapunzel."

"Rapunzel," Jinni said curiously. "I think I've heard of her."

Otis dusted off his knees and stood up. "All right, listen up. Gather around. Today was a good first day, but we've got a lot of work to do before you're ready. And to be completely honest, my opinion of Lost Boys has really gone into the shitter. But I'm the one paying for that opinion, so don't take it personally. With just a little more hard work and some fine-tuning, you guys will be able to put the man in Lost Boys."

Chapter 29

Slightly grinned at the remark while One and Two exchanged sideways glances.

"I don't think that came out how you wanted," Peter said, holding back a chuckle.

For the next two weeks, this was their routine. By the end, they had only broken the surface of their true potential, but Otis had them leaner, meaner, and bursting with more true confidence than their cocky demeanors had allowed before. Otis even offered himself as something of a father figure, something they desperately sought, whether or not they knew it. The best fatherly advice he had to offer didn't pertain to physique or battle, however. It was about how a man should treat a woman. It wasn't complex advice, but it was accurate.

"You definitely wanna treat 'em right," Otis said to the attentive ears surrounding that night's campfire. "If not, when you grow up and get married and start having kids of your own, your wife will only give birth to little girls. And they're all gonna grow up to be the most beautiful women in town."

"You're boshin' us," Peter said.

"No, no. I swear," Otis replied, holding his hands up. "I've seen it happen personally—*hundreds* of times. And the worse you treat the romantic interests in your life, the prettier your daughters will be," Otis added.

"*Bull.* Shit."

"Fine. Don't believe me. Just remember this conversation when you've got six or seven daughters and they're each being chased by six or seven guys just like you."

Peter stared into the fire and looked as though he was going to be ill.

Odyssey Tale

The next day, Otis allowed everyone the day off for some rest and relaxation. He also asked Mac to join him for a campfire dinner so the two could share some much-needed alone time. Since their introduction, they hadn't had a chance to speak one on one. As time slipped further ahead, both felt increasingly awkward, initiating what was sure to be an emotional conversation.

In silence, the two of them sat on opposite sides of a fire hidden by trees. Otis wasn't sure where to begin, but once he got going, he wasn't sure where to stop. "I've been looking for the right words, and I'm still not sure I found 'em. But for what it's worth, I'm sorry. I don't know why, but where I was, and who was keeping me. It all felt like some weird…dream. I had plenty of chances to leave. But there was always something in the back of my mind that wouldn't let me. Like a spell, or some invisible gate.

"There were times where it was just the two of us. Out for a walk where I could have run away. Or in the kitchen. One time, she handed me a knife and immediately turned her back to me—like she was daring me. And I wanted to. I really did. I wanted to take that knife and drive it into the back of her skull and leave that place. But every time she did something like that, it felt like she was two steps ahead, hoping she could catch me, just to show me how bad it'd be when she did."

Mac felt remorse, realizing something that he hadn't before. "You don't have to apologize, Dad."

"Holy shit," Otis said. "Holy shit!"

Chapter 29

"What?" Mac asked. "What is it? What's wrong?"

"Nothing's wrong," Otis said, leaping from the stump he'd been sitting on. "It's brilliant. It really is brilliant."

"What? What the hell are you going on about?" Mac asked.

"I have a plan."

"Yeah?"

"Yeah." For a moment, Otis became lost in his own prophetic nod. "I have a *great* plan."

Elsewhere, in a private cove lit by a small but sturdy bonfire, Jinni, Peter, and the Lost Boys sat in a circle. All eyes were on Jinni as he was the one who had invited and led everyone out there. They passed the time with idle chitchat, not pressing him, fully aware that he'd get to his topic when he was good and ready.

"I know we've only been riding with each other for a couple of years now, so there's a lot you still don't know about me. My past. My beliefs. But I'm sure by now, you've all noticed that I'm not as strong as I was when we first met. I've noticed it too. It feels like it takes an eternity to heal from anything. I'm sluggish. I'm moody." Jinni put his head down and ran his frustrated palms up and down his face.

"The magic in me. I know it's one of those things that you all know about, but we never really talk about. It's as strong as it's ever been. The magic will never expire. But I am—expiring. And when I'm done, that magic will roam this world aimlessly, causing chaos wherever it goes. But…if I choose to remove the magic from myself and give it to you guys, it'll be able to serve you for a very, very long time. Until you expire."

Odyssey Tale

Everyone understood the magnitude of what this meant, but Tootles understood more so than the others. "Jinni," he said, leaning forward. "Are you saying what I think you're saying?"

Jinni nodded. "I can pass it on to any person, or persons, I choose. I'm choosing you guys, and only you guys. If we split it up any more than that, we flirt with the risk of diluting it too much."

"How long will it last?" Two asked.

One rolled his eyes. "He already told you, dipshit. Forever."

"He said the magic'll last forever. Not us…dipshit."

"Good one."

Jinni moved on as if he hadn't heard their bickering. "It'll hinder the aging process. It'll sharpen your senses. It'll make you lighter on your feet. There will be occasions where it feels as though time itself slows down and allows you a moment to catch up or get ahead of a situation. It will allow you to do things you never dreamed possible. But it won't make you arrow proof. So don't assume you're no longer mortal."

"Will it be able to keep One and Two from arguing every thirty seconds?" Slightly asked.

"I don't know if it's that powerful," Jinni replied, never letting loose his smile. "But one day, a long time from now, you're going to feel your shell start to expire. And when you do, you'll have a choice to make. Then and only then will you be able to pass this on. So think about it. If this is a responsibility that you feel is too much to handle, go below deck now. But, if you're ready—here we go."

No one moved. It was mystical, surreal, and frightening all at the same time. Jinni closed his eyes and rubbed his palms together, creating an orb whose glow increased with intensity.

Chapter 29

He opened his hands to the sky, and a ball of shimmering silver light rose to the center of the circle.

"I don't even know what to say, Jinni," Peter said, mesmerized.

"Don't say anything," Jinni responded. "Just think lovely, wonderful thoughts. They'll help absorb the magic."

Peter and the Lost Boys looked up in awe as the orb sprinkled each of them with shimmering silver dust. Once the sprinkles disappeared, Jinni's skin dimmed ever so subtly, while Peter's and the Lost Boys' began to glow. Suddenly, they all felt different. Embraced by the shadows of the olive trees all around, they had just become part of something euphoric they never knew existed. Already bustling with youthful vigor, they were rejuvenated, reenergized, and ready to accomplish feats greater than any of their previous ambitions combined.

"What is that?" One asked.

The fluid orb circled as if trying to show off and settled on Jinni's shoulder. "A fairy. Born from some leftover magic I kept aside." Like a new pet cuddling its master, the orb glided up Jinni's arm and settled on his palm.

"She won't last forever. But she'll have a reserve in case you guys ever find yourselves in a pinch. Her small size will keep the magic amplified, and much more concentrated." He glanced over each of them, making stern but rapid eye contact.

"She'll be there to keep an eye on you, since I won't be able to do it forever."

Peter leaned forward with the same pensive look Tootles had shown just moments earlier. "What's gonna happen to you?"

"Not sure."

"And you don't have any magic in you anymore?" Slightly asked.

"Nope. You guys have it all. And her."

Two tilted his head curiously. "Can't she just sprinkle some on you?"

"Afraid not," Jinni said. "Once it's out, it's out. But don't worry about me. I may have been a slave most my life, but I've done great things. I've dined with kings and queens in some the finest castles ever constructed by hand. I've spent so much time in the battlefield that I've forgotten more about glory than most people will ever know. I've met merpeople, communicated with dolphins, rode on the backs of whales. And I've shared a bed with some of the finest women in the world. But in my entire life, I've never had more fun than I have with you guys… except for maybe the women," he said with a wink and smile. "No matter what happens, it's been good ridin' with ya. I don't care what *anyone* says about the Lost Boys," he concluded with another grin.

The Lost Boys, triggered by his smile, began to cackle as they were known to do. Moments later, the cackles turned to coyote calls as a newfound camaraderie took hold. They had never been closer than they were right then.

Chapter 30

Belowdecks on the *Elvira*, Otis, Jinni, and Peter hovered over a map of the area and several crude sketches of the castle's inner workings. Mac sat off to the side, admiring his father in the leadership role he'd always heard about.

"Mac," Otis said, waving his eager son into the conversation. "Now, this arms chest. What kind of locking mechanism does it have?"

"I'm not sure."

"Doesn't matter," Jinni said. "One and Two'll be able to crack it."

"About how many swords are in there at a given time?" Otis asked.

Mac pursed his lips and looked up to the ceiling. "Fifteen to twenty—maybe. More on Saturdays because the sharpener comes in."

"Out of how many total in the castle?" Otis asked.

"Thirty or so."

"That's perfect. We're only hiding half of them anyways."

"Why half?" Peter asked. "And not all of them?"

"Because when this thing starts, if all of them are unarmed, and all of us are, they'll be united against us. But if half of them are fighting the other half, that's less focus on us."

Peter nodded.

"When One and Two get back with the swords, we'll stash them here. Then Peter, Tootles, and Slightly will hightail it to the castle steps." Otis vigorously used his forefinger to pick and point at different spots on the map. "There, you'll await Jinni's signal. Then he'll wait for One and Two to get posted up at the clock tower for the next phase."

Suddenly, the orb burst into the room, bouncing around like a disoriented mosquito. Once it had its way with the room, it burst out just as quickly.

"What the hell was that?" Otis asked.

Before Jinni could explain, the orb bolted in again, repeated its dance, and left.

Up on deck, One and Two practiced an intense sword fight that went from best of three to best of twelve in a matter of two hours. They were just as evenly matched with swords as they were with fists. Both were drenched in sweat, and neither was willing to relent. The orb watched curiously, now like a puppy being forced to watch a game of fetch.

On the other side of the vessel, Tootles and Slightly practiced shooting bows and arrows. The orb joined, zigzagging between their bodies before knocking over the arrow barrel and leaving.

Tootles giggled. "She's got such a personality."

"Yeah," Slightly said, less amused as he picked up the barrel, replacing several arrows that had fallen out. "She's got a personality, all right. She hasn't let poor Cecil sleep since she's

Chapter 30

been here. If she's not messing with his tail, she's flying just out of his reach. And she's been tinkering with the dinner bell *every* night at three in the morning. I don't know how you slugs sleep through it."

"She likes to hide inside there," Tootles said. "And make it ring when she's hungry."

"Well, she's hungry a lot at three in the morning." Slightly reached down for a new arrow as the orb shot in and knocked it over again. "I don't know if you can hear me or understand what I'm saying, but if you knock that barrel over one more time, I'm going to smash you with a rock and feed you to the cat."

Slightly reset the barrel and walked away, waiting for the orb to pop out from hiding and knock it over again. But it didn't happen. "That's more like it," he said, pleased with the orb's evolving behavior.

Still mimicking an ornery puppy, the orb approached the barrel slowly and settled next to it. "Don't even think about it," Slightly said. He took a threatening step forward, prompting the orb to knock over the barrel and leap up into his chest. Despite its tiny size, the orb's impact forced Slightly to stumble backward until he fell overboard.

Otis, Jinni, Peter, and Mac rushed upstairs to see what was causing the uncontrollable laughter coming from Tootles, One, and Two.

"Yeah. Hilarious," Slightly said, submerged from the neck down.

No one heard him above the chorus of laughter.

"I hate that goddamn fairy," he said.

"How's the planning coming along?" Tootles asked.

"Good," Otis said. "How's it going up here?"

"I'll let you be the judge of that." Tootles proudly handed Otis a long, narrow object swaddled in burlap cloth.

Otis unwrapped the cloth to reveal a dull, blunt chunk of steel extending from a handle that was way too heavy and ornate to be part of the same design. "What the hell is this?"

"The sword you asked for," Tootles said. "It's the best one we could trade for."

"What—did you send your worst negotiator? This thing's a hunk of shit."

"It's all they had." Tootles couldn't have been more disappointed at the reaction. "What do you want me to do?"

Otis looked the sword over closely. "What *can* ya do? Just have to work with what we got," he said. "I'd use one of yours, but they aren't any nicer."

"Wait a minute," Peter said. "Doesn't the plan call for us to hide half the swords in the castle anyway?"

"Yeah, so?" Otis asked.

"Why don't we just steal them instead?" Peter asked. "You know how much we can get for those swords once all this is over?"

Otis scrunched his lips and raised his eyebrows.

"Otis?" Jinni asked.

"I don't see why not."

Later that night, after more intense rounds of training, the group sat around the mesmerizing dance of a bonfire. Physically drained and emotionally inflamed, they sat in silence deep within the space of their own thoughts. Eventually, Otis broke the silence. While they all hung onto his every word, by the time he'd finished, they were motivated enough to run through a wall of stone and confident enough to believe they could do it.

Chapter 30

While his words made their mark on all of them, the message only intensified in their minds as they replayed it.

The next morning, Mac did a series of push-ups, then pull-ups. The words echoed in his mind. "There are certain moments in life that are so huge, so monumental, that they have an impact in shaping every other moment in life."

At that very moment, even though the fight was still several days away, Tootles rubbed the red-mud-turned-war-paint over his face.

"Now I know I don't know you guys all that well, but I sailed with some Lost Boys from before your time. So I know who you are and what you stand for. And I know that the name recognition of the Lost Boys will always be bigger than any one individual Lost Boy. That's why when you hear of the accolades, no one's name is ever mentioned. That all changes today. From this day forward, whenever people think about or refer to Lost Boys in conversation, the memories and accolades they'll speak of will be described in only one of two ways: before this fight, and after it. It'll be the pinnacle moment of your entire existence. And they will remember your names when it's done."

Up on deck, One and Two sharpened all the swords and double-checked the security of the arrow tips. They heard Otis's words from the previous night as well.

"We have to stay sharp. We have to stay united. We have to take our time—the fastest. We have to have the most heart—but leave behind any fear of the ache that our loved ones will suffer should things go poorly and we don't make it."

Back on the stern, Peter gazed at a picture that Nibs hadn't finished painting and dropped it into the still water below.

"And we have to do whatever it takes to ensure that the side of right wins, and carries on, even if it means losing in the process."

Up on the bow, Jinni stared into the water's surface and his reflection looking back at him as it rubbed the wrinkles on its face.

Slightly was in the midst of a cold and intense swim. He moved fluidly with the motions of a rapid butterfly, revealing a variety of scars across his back every time he broke the air's surface. He was the only Lost Boy who wasn't aboard the *Elvira* that morning, but he, too, replayed Otis's words.

"There's not much I can say that you guys don't know already. You've probably been to a lot of the places I've been. You've probably seen a lot of the things I've seen. But we're about to be connected for eternity, as what we have waiting ahead will force us to encounter several—perhaps many—moments that will go on to define your lives. I know that no one here signed up for what we're about to embark on. So if you want to turn back, now's the time…but before you go, thank you for everything you've done. To those of you who stay, thank you—for everything you've done, and for everything you're about to."

Otis sat alone on the beach that morning, watching whitecaps turn pink in the sunrise as they washed ashore by his feet. He also thought back to his words, hoping they'd accomplished their purpose. "Now we're approaching what I like to call the seventy-two-hour rule. That means nothing bad goes into your body for the next seventy-two hours. No whiskey. No ale. No tobacco. None of that green shit I keep smelling on Tootles. Definitely no opium."

Chapter 30

Otis cracked a smile, recalling Peter's response to the seventy-two hour rule the night before.

"Are we at least allowed to put our body *in* something bad?" Peter asked.

"No," Otis said with a half smile. "I need you alert and fighting out there. Not itching and scratching your little noonies."

During the predawn hours, the castle was whisper quiet. It was also the only time the common area was empty, except a few who remained scattered about, having been too drunk or strung out on opium to make it up the stairs. Led by Otis, One and Two entered the castle, tailed by Jinni.

Once inside and posted up in private corners, Jinni and Otis stood lookout for One and Two while they worked on the arms-chest lock, visible to anyone who may have wandered out of their room.

"Looks like it's just a straight ward. Give me the pin betty," One whispered.

He extended his open palm toward Two, who placed a serrated notcher in his hand.

"The pin betty," One whispered a bit louder. "What—am I speaking another goddamn language?"

"That *is* the pin betty," Two whispered.

Jinni approached the two rapidly on tiptoes, in utter disbelief that he needed to quiet them now, of all times. "Will you two shut up? Shut the hell up, and get this thing open," he whispered. "We don't have time for this."

The suitors nearest them were dead to the world, but there was no telling who happened to be rustling behind closed doors. After some rather aggressive nonverbal communication, One and Two got the door open. They broke their pin betty in the process, but with all the income they stood to make from the swords and this mission, they could buy enough pin betties to corner the market.

Following some silent celebrations, One and Two watched in horror as the orb sprung from One's vest pocket and closed the door. The lock rattled shut inside, confirming their worst fears.

"Shit," Two said.

The orb dashed up the stairs and into the only open door before slamming it shut. In the tense moments that followed, a few of the men grumbled at the noise, but no one had been disturbed enough to wake.

Otis joined Jinni, One, and Two.

"Why on earth did you have that thing in your pocket?" Otis asked.

"I didn't put it there," One said defensively. "I'd *pay* to see someone catch that thing with his bare hands."

"Do you have another way to get in there?" Otis asked.

"No," One said. "Not unless—"

Suddenly, the thunderous ring of a large cathedral bell sounded in the castle.

"Please tell me that's not our fairy ringin' that bell," Two said.

"No," Otis said, curiously. "It went in a different room."

The repeated ringing was deafening and loud enough to wake even the deepest sleeper. The men in the common area began to wipe the sleep from their eyes and sit up while the rattle

Chapter 30

of bedroom doors opened to more groggy bodies. Everything happened too fast for Otis and his collaborators to leave without being noticed, so they did the best they could to blend in.

As all the men looked around at themselves, pondering the reason for their wake-up call, chatter began to erupt. It was a muffled mess of jumbled words, but somehow one conversation stood out in Otis's ears.

"What do you think this is about?" a random suitor asked.

"Maybe Mac's back. Or Otis," answered another. "Or maybe they're—" The man said no more as he ran his finger across his throat.

"What do you think, Eury?"

It was a name that Otis wasn't familiar with before his departure, but one that he'd heard twice since his return.

"That'd be nice," Eury said with a yawn. "But it's probably wishful thinking on our part to assume both of 'em are dead."

Otis cringed at the brazen comment and stared with veiled anger in Eury's direction. Suddenly, everyone went silent as Penelope emerged from her room and commanded attention from the banister.

"Good morning," she said with a playful smile. "I know there have been a lot of rumors swirling around about my son lately, and if there are any of you who don't know what I'm talking about—my son recently left Ithaca. He went to search for his father. I know the common belief around here is that Otis died many years ago. But truth be told, I've never believed that. And I've never let my son believe that.

"Nonetheless, Mac has returned. And before any more rumors get started, Mac has returned with no news of his father's whereabouts or any information on what happened to him. Just a tan, shaggy hair, and the stubble that shows up on a boy's face when he's becoming a man.

"Now, I know many of you consider Mac, and what he did, a threat. But I need you to know this before you think about bringing any harm to my son. Otis once told me that if he did not return before our son could grow hair on his face, I should move on and find happiness with another, if possible.

"As most of you also know, I've been knitting a shroud for Otis—in his honor. In the past, I've hinted that upon its completion, I would consider moving on and trying to find happiness. I feel it only fair to inform you that, as of this morning, I have finished the shroud. Due to the curious timing of these two events, it seems that the signs are clear, and the gods are speaking to my heart. It's time for me to move on."

The general mood of the place became noticeably enthusiastic as a new wave of chatter carried through the halls.

"For those of you interested in winning my heart, please bless me with your presence in the courtyard tomorrow at high noon. And remember, that's *presence*—not *presents*," she concluded with another playful smile.

"Huh?" a slovenly suitor asked.

Still mingling, unnoticed, Jinni approached Otis. "Is she serious? Or is she up to something?"

"I don't know," Otis said, erring toward the former and struggling to hide his devastation. "But this is definitely going to force a change in our plans."

Chapter 31

Otis sat on the beach not far from where he'd first landed, sinking in the sand with his face burrowing into his crossed arms. It was sad enough for Otis to know that she didn't even recognize him, but actually hearing her say aloud that she was ready to move on placed substantial weight on his psyche.

"Hey," Mac said gently. "How ya doin'?"

Otis raised his head but focused on the sea, actively avoiding eye contact to avoid the tears. "I suppose by now you heard."

"Yeah," Mac said. "It's bad timing, but that doesn't mean we can't go through with the plan. We can't give up now."

"Actually—I think that's exactly what it means."

"No," Mac said.

"I've been sitting here thinking. And…your mom…if this is what she wants, I don't know how good I feel about taking it away from her."

Mac swelled with raw emotion. "Taking it away from her? She's been waiting on you. All this time."

"She didn't even recognize me, Mac. You haven't the slightest idea how that feels."

"A shave and a haircut. That's all it is."

"No, it's not...what we have planned—it's gonna result in death. Carnage." Otis looked over the disappointed young face before him, needing it to understand. "It doesn't feel good to kill another man. It doesn't feel good to destroy another man's life. Even if you are the one in the right, even if there were... no other options, it never feels good.

"Once it happens and the dust settles, your mind races. You think about *their* ambitions, their hopes, their families. And you think about your own place in this world. Mortality. Morality. You spend enough time thinking, and you start to wonder if you were the good guy or the bad guy when it all went down. Your mom's current wishes can help us avoid that carnage."

"You're not the bad guy, Dad," Mac said. "Any one of those guys back at the castle would kill you in a heartbeat if given the chance. They're in your home—right now, as we speak. Indulging in what's rightfully yours, trying to steal your wife... and your fortune."

Otis's silence told Mac all he needed to know.

"So what then?" Mac asked. "Is that it? You're just gonna give up?"

"I've weighed the options. There's not much else I can do."

"If you leave now, everything I know about you—everything I've been told—was all bullshit."

Once again, Mac was met with silence.

"Go ahead, then!" Mac exclaimed. "I'll sleep just fine because at the end of the day, I did everything I could to get you back here—and you just gave up." His emotions sent several teardrops down his cheeks as he began to accept defeat.

"You can come with me if you want."

"No, thanks," Mac said, angrily.

Chapter 31

"It may not be safe for you here, at least not right away."

"It's not. That's why I'm going with the Lost Boys—start paying them back for all the work they've put in. You want to stay here and feel sorry for yourself, go right ahead. If you want to be a man and take back what's yours, you know where to find me."

Mac turned his back to Otis and began to storm off.

"Mac...for what it's worth, I'm sorry. I know that this decision puts the castle and fortune in jeopardy for you, but this is the way it has to be."

Mac stopped in his tracks and turned back around. "Dad, I don't give a shit about the castle or gold. I just want Mom to be happy. And I know she'll be the happiest with you." Mac wasn't confident that he'd changed Otis's mind, but he had no doubts that his words had left an impression. "Like I said, you know where to find me."

Otis sighed as his son walked away from him for the first, and potentially last, time. He didn't get much sleep that night.

Mac awoke the next morning before the red dawn began the day. Using a few smudges of mud and an oversized robe, Mac paid homage to his father's disguise and wandered into town alone. There were so many people there as a result of Penelope's announcement that he blended right in. Aside from the suitors, men and women came from all over out of curiosity. It was the social event of the year, and based on what Penelope had in store for the suitors, she saw no reason to deny the public access to this event.

Odyssey Tale

The cathedral bell rang out at high noon. By that time, anyone who was anyone in Ithaca had already claimed their spot within the courtyard. Once the bell had finished its song, Penelope stepped out on a handcrafted podium, immediately capturing the attention of everyone in attendance. She saw a lot of familiar faces out in the crowd but didn't notice Mac, concealed by his robe and tucked away within the ardent group.

She sent her voice out as far as it would carry as the silent crowd clung to her every word, the suitors with a bit more focus. "Good afternoon to all of you. Thank you for coming. To those of you in attendance who call yourselves suitors—I'm aware that a great many of you have been patient. But this process isn't going to end today. In fact, it's quite the contrary.

"This is only the beginning. I also know that I'm not as young as I was when Otis first left. But that doesn't mean I'm willing to compromise on standards. And to be frank, I can already say with confidence that many of you here lack the discipline and strength that I'm seeking in a husband. So this is what we're going to do."

Everyone watched curiously as two servants dragged a large sheet across the ground to reveal a mysterious display. It was Penelope's first test for the men. An exhibition of twelve axes stood upright, precisely placed in a straight line in holders specially designed for their handles. The glossy blades shimmered in the sunlight, as moderately sized circular holes within each of them created a tunnel that ran from the first ax all the way to the back ax.

"These axes placed before you were a gift to my husband, Otis, from the great archer, Robin Hood. Good marksmanship not only requires proper use of one's strength. It requires

Chapter 31

a sharp eye, keen senses, and the type of discipline that I was referring to before. Any of the men here today who want to earn my hand in marriage must first be willing to perform this task. Not only that, but he must also perform this task successfully."

It was at this point that the servants who had revealed the display rolled a cart roughly thirty paces from the first ax. On the cart was an unstrung bow and a barrel of arrows.

"First, you will need to string Otis's bow, adjusting the tension of its string to achieve maximum accuracy. Once you've accomplished this, you may move on to the next task—shooting an arrow through the circular openings of the axes. Any man who can make his arrow travel through all twelve will earn a private dinner with me, where we can discuss our potential future." Penelope paused to scan the courtyard before wishing them all the best of luck, and the contest began.

Much like any other sporting event, the crowd cheered the suitors as each took his turn. It didn't take long, however, for the crowd to lose enthusiasm and interest as the lackluster performances unraveled. Shooting an arrow with the precision required to accomplish this feat was challenging enough on its own. As each man came up to take his turn, the shot seemed to be the primary focus. After the first five suitors were unable to even muster enough strength to string the bow, the confidence of many was starting to diminish.

For most of them, the past thirteen years had been filled with gluttonous portions of meat, pastries, ale, and whiskey. Had she given more detail as to what they'd be doing, and time to train for it, their true effort would have been exaggerated, skewing the genuine performance that she was currently privy to. Their slothful ways had turned much of their muscle to mush.

Even the rare chiseled tone that remained among a few was a mere shell of its former strength and endurance.

Their eagerness to take their shots was quickly being overshadowed by their inept attempts to handle the bow and string. Some got closer than others, but no one had the strength or know-how to handle the tension with this particular string. Frustration mounted. Tension built. By the time half the suitors had given up on stringing the bow, half the crowd had become bored enough to leave. Penelope did notice, however, an older gentleman whom she didn't recognize accompanied by five or six young men in their late teens or early twenties, whom she also didn't recognize. From above, their presence was noticeable, but at ground level, they slithered in and joined the remaining spectators unnoticed.

As she turned her attention back to the contest, they spotted and approached Mac as he was still in disguise. "Hey," he said. "I thought you guys were scrubbing barnacle off the *Elvira*."

"Decided to come here for the wedding instead. Women love weddings."

"This isn't a wedding," Mac said, puzzled.

"Still—just the idea of marriage'll do it," Peter said, craning his neck, forcing eye contact with the nearest women looking his way.

"Do what?" Mac asked.

Peter thought Mac was joking. "*Do what?* I'll have to remember that one," Peter said.

"There is a lot of talent here," Slightly said, nudging Mac with his elbow.

Chapter 31

Otis hadn't left Ithaca yet. He'd claimed sanctuary on a barstool and sipped on a glass of whiskey, contemplating his future. It was bleak, to say the least. The saloon was empty when he arrived, but as more spectators grew bored with the suitors' lack of showmanship, a new herd of patrons entered every few minutes. Growing claustrophobic and uneasy about the swelling crowd, Otis decided that after his second glass of whiskey was gone, he would be too.

In the past, whiskey may have chipped away at his fear to stay and his desire to leave, but it wasn't happening now. And the harsh caramel liquid that hit his throat was actually doing just the opposite, confirming to himself that accepting defeat was the right thing to do.

Just as Otis slugged down his final swig, someone at the bar requested a bowl of olives to pair with her wine. When the bartender didn't answer her right away, her impatience took on a demanding tone. "I need some olives, you."

"You got it," the barkeep said, each word fighting through growing chatter. His rough and hairy arm gently placed the bowl on the bar before sliding it in her direction. "Best in the world," the barkeep concluded.

"They really are," the woman said, plac-ing that first olive between her ruby lips.

Suddenly, something within Otis began to shed the cloak of his defeatism. It echoed in his mind. *Olives you. Olives you. Olives you. Olives you.* "This is my home," he whispered. "This is *my* home."

Back at the courtyard, the few spectators who remained in attendance watched the final suitor take his turn. None of them had much confidence that this attempt would be any more fruitful than the previous attempts. Eury, however, approached the barrel with a swagger that gave promise to those who had waited all day, desperately hoping to see at least one shot attempted.

He rubbed some warmth into his hands and picked up the bow and string. There was little doubt that if anyone were going to have the strength to perform this task, Eury would be the man to do it. Suitors who hadn't been too embarrassed to leave looked among themselves as he started the process. His white knuckles gripped the string and pulled both ends with every fiber of his might.

He relaxed his shoulders and neck, took several deep breaths, and tried once more. Again, he just couldn't stretch the tight string far enough to make it reach both ends of the bow. Unable to accept his shortcomings, he began to question as to whether or not this was some sort of trick, getting it into his head that Penelope's deception was the root cause of his and everyone else's failure.

He gave himself one more chance to complete this task, feeling the heat on his neck, the sweat on his forehead, and the eyes all around. "Almost got it," he said, forcing the words out slowly. "There." He finally managed to secure the string.

Pleased, he held the bow in the air, rousing the cheers of the handful who were still in attendance. He reached down for an arrow and closed his eyes, visualizing a successful shot. He opened his eyes and took aim, forcing the string loose and causing it to snap off into his face.

Chapter 31

"Ow! God dammit," Eury cried out, grabbing the space between his cheek and right eye.

Everyone, including Penelope, burst into laughter. "Shut up," Eury said, feeling the world spin around him. "I said, shut up. I didn't see anyone else do better."

Penelope could feel his mood and the frightening impact it was about to have on the men nearest to him, so she stood and hushed the crowd. His nerves settled with their silence.

"Anyone else?" she asked. "Or will I have to choose another test, better suited to men of your skill level?"

Eury and the remaining suitors looked among themselves. Everyone was relieved to have a second chance, even though all remained embarrassed by their first.

"Let me shoot," a random voice called out.

Penelope looked down and scanned the crowd, only to realize that the man requesting to shoot was the beggar man who'd come to visit the castle several weeks earlier.

Eury rolled his eyes and grinned. "I don't think so," he scoffed. "You really think this lovely, elegant goddess of a woman wants to marry some smelly, senile old bum?"

The suitors turned their laughter from Eury to Otis.

"Let me shoot," Otis said, glaring at his developing nemesis.

"You shouldn't even be here. You're not welcome here. You were never welcome here." Eury, bow in hand, stepped forward and shoved Otis. "I said leave."

Before Otis could answer, Mac slid the hood of his robe off and stepped forward to reveal himself. "Let him shoot, Eury."

All the attention funneled toward Mac. Eury attempted to browbeat his young opponent with his eyes but didn't get the response he'd hoped for.

"Unless you're scared some bum is gonna come in here and show you up," Mac said. "And make you look like an asshole."

"Not at all," Eury said casually. "That's just fine with me, young'in. You want this stinkin'-ass vagabond to be your new pop-pop? I'll be happy to let him shoot." Eury shoved the bow and string into Otis's chest and stepped away.

Otis took both ends of the string and brought them inward, creating as much slack between his fists as possible. Next, he stretched the string, mysteriously extending its length before properly securing it to both ends of the bow. The suitors stood wide-eyed in disbelief as Otis plucked it with his fingers to play a little tune.

Eury was the most shocked. "What the hell?"

Otis looked over the bow and string and brought in a deep, emotional breath. "You know, ma'am. I recognize this bow. This was a gift—from Robin Hood. Not a lot of people know this, but way back, long before the war, Robin Hood taught Otis how to shoot a bow and arrow. And, as a result, Otis became one of the all-time greats. Otis taught you a thing or two, as well, if I'm not mistaken."

Otis readied his arrow. "Otis never got to be quite as good a shot as Robin Hood. I mean, let's face it. Robin Hood, before he lost his vision, was arguably the best archer of all time—a title that was well earned, and one that nobody will ever take from him." Otis took aim, filling the air with tension as he pulled back on the arrow. "But I will say this about your husband, ma'am. While he may not be the *best* shot of all time, he's in the top three."

Chapter 31

Otis released the arrow, and it cruised through the tunnel before piercing the wall in its path. The tension had been replaced with a powder keg of shock.

"Well," Otis said, holding the bow casually to his side. "Isn't anybody going to welcome me back?"

"Otis," Penelope said, hushed by the ensuing chaos.

"It's Otis!" a suitor shouted.

"That's Otis!" shouted another. "He's not dead."

"I'm here to take back my family and castle. And shame on you for how you've treated them both while I've been away."

The few remaining suitors began to scatter.

"It's really him!" one of them yelled, hightailing it away from the property.

"Those of you who leave now won't have it near as bad as those who choose to stay," Otis said.

More suitors hurried away at the threat, but not everyone was willing to give up their shot at the castle—and all that came with it—just yet.

Chapter 32

Otis let the robe slip down his back, revealing a chiseled chest, flat belly, and the shoulder span of a small gorilla. He rolled his shoulders back for a stretch, expanding his robust clavicle lines. He reached his left hand across his body and pulled the sword he had stashed on the right side of his belt.

"Is there anyone who feels like fighting me for what they've been taking all these years?"

"I'll fight you, Otis," one of the suitors said, stepping forward. "Not for what I've been taking—but for what I'm going to take in the years to come."

It was Antinous, a younger, braggadocios fellow, whom Eury had looked at as his only true threat before Otis's return.

Otis recognized Antinous right away as the little boy who used to scoop horse manure from the stables. Otis could have laughed him off, given his current memories, but a lot can happen to a boy who's constantly getting picked on over the course of sixteen years.

Antinous approached Otis with the confidence of a young man in his twenties and got off several potentially fatal sword swings and really showed off some pure speed with a few evasive maneuvers, but ultimately, experience clobbered youth. As soon as Otis sliced Antinous's right hand open, the young man realized that there was much more to life than castles and gold. He threw his hands up and lay on his back like a frightened puppy.

"Please," he said, with eyes that said he had given up, and a growing puddle that did the same.

Otis nodded him off. Antonius got up and ran away and would go on to live a happy, grateful life.

"Anyone else?" Otis said, still standing tall, broad, and ready.

The names of the next two suitors to step up and challenge Otis were the source of some debate, but he killed them both so quickly, it really doesn't matter all that much.

"Holy shit," Peter said, shocked and impressed.

"Right," Slightly replied.

With only a handful of suitors and spectators brave enough to have stayed this long, Otis looked around, saving his breath while waiting for the next challenger to approach. The Lost Boys looked among themselves, smiling and in disbelief at what they'd just watched Otis accomplish.

"That all?" Otis shouted. *No way it's gonna be this easy.*

Clunk. Clunk. The heavy thud of iron feet squaring up on the brick courtyard clapped like thunder behind Otis. He turned around as Eury stood before him, rotating a heavy sword and wrapped entirely in a suit of armor.

Eury was the only suitor who wasn't living in the area before the war, so the two of them had never officially met. Fear of the unknown was undoubtedly having an impact on Otis's nerves. If that wasn't enough, the armor looked brand new and sturdy, and lacked a penetrable point that Otis could sniff out.

"Can't fight me like a man?" Otis asked.

Chapter 32

"There's no honor in the afterlife," Eury said, closing his mask and wrapping both fists around his sword handle.

"I guess you'll find out soon enough," Otis said. Just as the two of them were about to approach each other, one of the spectators stepped forward, revealing himself as a ghost from Otis's past. The man quickly pulled a sword that he had previously concealed and pointed it at Otis's back.

"I'm afraid I'm going to have to stop you both right here."

Otis turned around. Much to his horror, he saw the face behind the voice that he'd hoped he'd misheard.

"Captain James," Otis said, standing still and increasingly rattled by his placement between the two foes.

"Nobe Ahhdie...*nobody*. I must admit, I felt quite stupid once I figured that one out."

"Sorry, old man," Eury said. "You're gonna have to wait your turn."

"You can have the castle, young fellow," Captain James said, looking past Otis's shoulder. "I just need *him*." He flicked his wrist and extended his arm, closing the distance between the point of his blade and Otis.

Mac watched only ten to twelve paces away but didn't want to be the first to make a move. Peter began to approach slowly, but while he took that first step toward Captain James, Mac rushed the captain like a rabid bull. One of Captain James's men almost called out to warn him, but it wasn't necessary. The captain saw his aggressor coming from far enough out that he paid little mind, taking a side step and drilling Mac with an elbow, knocking him to the ground.

Peter leaped at the captain with an eager fist. Once again, Captain James was ready for his attacker. He drilled Peter on the left side of his jaw, but Peter remained unrattled and sent his fist flying toward the captain once more. This time, Captain James took a shot, but something about it felt rejuvenating. He'd come here to fight Otis and collect the type of glory he always figured he'd have by now. Sure, Otis was about to be the property of the Sea Witch, but the battle and tale would belong to Captain James. But the power packed in behind this scrawny runt's fist was unlike anything he had felt in years, and the captain was hooked. He ran his thumb across his bloody lip and grinned at Peter. "All right then," the captain said. "A dance it shall be."

Suddenly, seven or eight of the captain's pirates revealed themselves, drew their swords, and charged at the fight. In response, Jinni, Slightly, One, Two, and Tootles rushed in, drawing their swords. Just like that, clangs of steel and explosions of sparks ensued. While the Lost Boys were outnumbered and lacked experience, there was a sharpness to the way they moved, a speed they achieved that seemed to be half again as fast as their opponents.

Meanwhile, amid the chaotic fights spreading about the courtyard, Eury and Otis remained still, neither taking his eyes off the other.

"You sure this is the hill you want to die on today, Eury?" Otis asked.

Eury, grinning in the shadow of his armored mask, charged without hesitation. He attempted to deliver several quick strikes from above, but Otis blocked every one. The heavy thunder of their clashing iron shook them both to the core.

Otis retrieved, trying to keep secret the fear beginning to run rampant. A cold chill slithered around his shoulders and wrapped his back, preventing him from taking a full breath.

Chapter 32

This went on for a moment while Otis continued to block Eury's persistent onslaught of downward strikes, eventually backtracking over his own feet and tripping over them. Anyone watching would have guessed that the fight was over, but something funny happens to people when they come that close to death. They realize, more than ever, they want to be alive.

Otis absorbed a surge of adrenaline and rolled away from Eury's sword before it chipped the brick where Otis's neck had just been. Otis popped back onto his feet and danced toward the armored brute, taking the offensive out of his possession. They continued to feel one another out, saving their most aggressive maneuvers and strikes until getting a better understanding of what they were up against.

If their focus wasn't so much on one another, they would have appreciated the gaggle of fights spreading about the courtyard and beyond. Jinni made short work of his opponent, slicing open the man's fighting arm and causing him to yield within seconds. Meanwhile, One and Two held their own while fighting off three of the pirates who had them pinned inside a triangle formation. Back to back, One and Two fought them off masterfully. After cutting one of the pirate's legs clear through to its bone, Two kicked the man in the chest, causing his head to thump off the stone surface of the courtyard. Once the triangle had turned into a duo, One and Two's opponents didn't stand much of a chance. The one thing that separated their fight from the others was how much physical contact there was between bodies.

One and Two were expert pugilists and mingled the use of their mighty fists with sharp, fast swords. Their first opponent got off easy compared to the remaining two pirates. Prior to

One cutting his opponent's throat, and Two driving his sword through the chest of the other, the unlucky pirates spit out at least nine teeth between the two of them. When the fight was over, One and Two remained back to back in silence, breathing heavily and reflecting on what they'd just done.

Neither had ever experienced such a sharp contrast in feeling. Once it was over, however, something weighed their hearts and drained so much strength that they would have passed out, had it not been for the magic coursing through their veins. They had the strangest, most dreamlike feeling. They felt as though they were leaves on a tree and had just cut three other leaves off the same tree.

Slightly matched well with his opponent but struggled to get his magic to conquer what seemed to be years of experience behind the blade. The shifty Lost Boy got and gave plenty of nicks and cuts. When he stacked the pain against that which he'd had to endure as a boy, the nicks and cuts of the present day were no more unpleasant than frosted cake. He and his opponent danced around the room, taking turns leading one another off the courtyard and onto the north stairwell.

The steep concrete steps worked in Slightly's favor. He wanted to throw his opponent down the stairs and watch him break apart like a cheap pocket watch, but the man refused to do so, despite being knocked off his feet. As he attempted to stand, Slightly stepped forward with quick and silent footsteps, grabbed the man by the ponytail, and slammed his face into one of the step's corners. Unlike One and Two, Slightly didn't feel emotional when it was over. He was too drained physically to feel anything aside from stairs pressing against his back and a warm pile of flesh resting under his arm.

Chapter 32

Of course, in true Tootles fashion, Tootles's fight took the longest. In all fairness, however, it was the fastest and most nimble Tootles had ever looked while on his own two feet. His graceful spins were the sugar to the spice of his aggressive thrusts. What's more impressive, he and his opponent had made it farther down the stairs than Slightly had without falling down any of them. Standing upright, Tootles arched his back, narrowly avoiding a potentially fatal swing to his belly, though it still managed to produce a flesh wound. Once the pain hit his skin, Tootles became a madman, ignoring all form and tact in favor of erratic swinging. Relentless, repetitive, and nonstop, Tootles came down like an angry woodsman trying to split firewood.

"Yield. Yield!" the terrified pirate cried out.

Tootles, dripping with sweat and struggling for breath, delivered a line he'd wanted to use since the first time a bully had used it on him. "That's what I thought," Tootles said, satisfied on a level he never knew possible. "That's what I thought."

Otis and Eury's match was still sitting at a stalemate. Eury was hoping Otis would tire himself out, and vice versa. Otis did what he could to poke and prod Eury's armor, looking for any sort of weakness. No matter what angle he took, or which spot he managed to connect with, however, Eury's hefty sanctuary was seemingly impenetrable.

"Getting tired yet, old man?" Eury asked.

"You quit while you're ahead, and I might let you live," Otis said, charging once more, only to be received by his ready opponent. One thing that was becoming certain for Otis was that his performance was starting to mimic that of his fighting days from yesteryear. He was getting stronger and hitting harder as the fight progressed. Eury could feel it too.

Unfortunately for Otis, his strike was too powerful for the weak and poorly crafted sword affixed to his fist. As he struck the right arm of Eury's suit, the sword's tip chipped and went flying out of sight. Eury rolled his arm over the sword, brought the blade to the ground, and stomped it with his hulking foot, splitting the blade in two at a spot just several fist lengths above the handle. As Otis watched in shock, a steel elbow met his nose and sent him to the ground.

Eury let out a vicious and condescending laugh. This was it. The great Otis Seehus was about to be undone by a broken sword and a suit of armor. "For what it's worth, you really did make this more difficult than I expected," Eury said, lifting his mask.

Otis lay on the ground, still trying to shake the dizzies from his head.

"Tell me something, Otis. Have you ever wondered *who* it was that caught you in that dolphin net—all those years ago?" Eury grinned.

Once again, Otis struggled to take in a full breath. He looked over and caught a glimpse of Mac, still unconscious from the hit he'd taken from Captain James. Otis needed something, anything, to give him the strength he needed to get up off his back and finish this thing.

"It wasn't until years later that I finally realized it was you," Eury said, seemingly amused by the coincidence. "That's when I came here. And to think—I almost got your castle without having to kill you. Funny how life turns out sometimes." Eury drew his shield back over his smug face and lifted his sword to deliver Otis a final blow to the afterlife.

Chapter 32

Within the blink of an eye, Otis flashed through his entire life, even having time to pause on a moment he hadn't recalled until just now.

It was several days after Mac had been born, and the outside light coming into the castle had a mystical, dreamlike feel. It was unlike anything either of them had ever seen. It was as though becoming parents to this beautiful baby boy had allowed them some unprecedented access to another dimension of love, time, and wonder that they never knew to be possible before that moment. Neither said anything. Otis just smiled at her, and she at him, knowing that they'd never come closer to joining their two hearts as one. It was beautiful and would later bring a tear of joy to his eye.

Otis's loop caught up to his present moment, just as Eury was about to drive his sword downward. Otis, taking advantage of his opponent's aggressive pursuit, rolled out of the way, kicked Eury's legs from under him, and brought the iron beast to his hands and knees. Otis retrieved his broken sword. Grabbing it by the remaining portion of the blade, and treating the handle like the blunt end of a hammer, Otis slammed the back of Eury's helmet.

After Otis delivered six towering strikes before anyone could count to three, Eury's head felt as though it was inside a cathedral bell. The violent vibrations shuddered from his skull, down his esophagus, and into his belly. Eury, barely able to open his eyes without a sharp and burning pain between them, pulled off his helmet and began to vomit. Several moments later, he went unconscious, landing facedown in a puddle of his own bile.

At that exact moment, Mac began to wake up slowly with an awful pain in his forehead. Otis attended to Mac to confirm he was OK, then looked up to Penelope with a familiar gaze that was visible through his unkempt beard. Jinni, One, and Two were making their way back to the courtyard, checking in on Mac and Otis.

"You guys OK?" Jinni asked.

"Yeah," Otis replied, grinning. "Great, actually." He stood up with that loving look and approached the foot of the stairwell leading up to the podium on which Penelope stood, stunned and speechless.

Somehow, as everyone calmed their nerves and checked themselves over for injuries, Eury woke up. Unnoticed, his arm extended slowly for a nearby arrow that had been left on the ground during the contest. As Otis approached Penelope with cautious and hesitant footsteps, Eury charged him from behind at full speed, holding the arrow like a spear with his eyes locked on the back of Otis's head.

"Dad!" Mac yelled.

Stunned by the quick turn of events, Otis turned around to see Eury closing in fast, only to be lassoed and pulled to his back by a rope thrown by Mac. It had been used to secure the sheets hiding the ax display, but Mac's quick thinking gave it much more use than it had been scheduled for that day. Desperate, Eury tried to throw the arrow at Otis, but Otis halted its weak trajectory, catching it with his nondominant hand.

Eury rolled over and began to crawl toward Mac, ready to wrap his cold, metallic hands around the throat of his newfound prey. Suddenly, Eury stopped crawling and opened his mouth in shock before falling face-first into the courtyard. Mac sat stunned, solely focused on the arrow now protruding from the back of Eury's lifeless skull. As Mac shifted focus from the

Chapter 32

foreground to the background, he became even more stunned as he realized that Penelope was holding Otis's bow.

"Should have chosen a different hill today," she said. "Asshole." Penelope never regretted taking that arrow from Otis's hand. Nor did she regret putting it in the back of Eury's head. Penelope was a mama bear, and Mac was her cub. Nonetheless, a jolt of nausea from the goddess of permanence caused her to vomit anyway as the weight of what she had done set in.

Otis looked at his wife with more shock than Mac and began to step forward to embrace her. But first, he walked to a nearby water fountain so he could clean his soiled and bloody hands. He didn't want to start their new life by staining her with remnants of the old one.

With a heavy sigh, Slightly approached the other Lost Boys from behind and was relieved to see that they had all made it out relatively OK—almost everyone. "Where's Pete?" he asked.

Chapter 33

Captain James was growing winded and frustrated by the baby-faced beanpole whose might surpassed what it should have. Initially, the captain had come to Ithaca for the fight of his life. It would be the marquee matchup he needed to send him off into the sunset, as all his mentors before him. *Captain James versus the great Otis Seehus* had such a nice ring to it. This *boy*, however, was dancing circles around the captain, toying with him the way a cat toys with a live mouse. What the captain didn't know about, and what frustrated him the most, was the magic that Peter was now hosting. Where Captain James saw youth, arrogance, and inexperience within his green opponent, Peter was being guided by forces beyond his control.

The two didn't have much to say to each other. As Peter pranced around, leading the captain into the castle and up the stairs, the captain's age and lack of stamina were starting to take a toll. As a result, it was becoming more difficult for the captain to separate his emotions from this fight.

Peter, seemingly retreating, led Captain James to the very top of the stairs, backing into Mac's bedroom and onto the concrete balcony extending from it.

"You can dance around all you want, ya dirty little bastard," Captain James said. "But sooner or later, I'm going to catch you. And when I do, the only reason anyone'll remember your name is because *I* took it from you."

Captain James stepped forward with a few aggressive swings of his sword, all of which were successfully blocked by Peter. The captain's right fist, however, came in unchecked. It cracked Peter in the bottom of his jaw, sending him down to the concrete.

The Captain brought his sword down for a final blow, but Peter kicked him in the knee and rolled away from the path of the incoming blade. He popped up to his feet, and the clanging of swords resumed.

"Sure you don't wanna break?" Peter asked, dancing from side to side. "You've been a little winded since we got up them stairs."

Peter attempted to fake the captain out with his next move, but James was ready, trapping Peter in a headlock and disarming him. Peter's sword slid across the balcony as Captain James lifted his young opponent to the sky and slammed him down on the concrete. Peter winced, rendered immobile as his neck and back broke his fall on the unforgiving concrete.

"Ahhhhh," the captain said, driving his sword deep in Peter's belly, releasing a heavy sigh of relief. "Any last words before I twist this and send you home?"

In throbbing pain and with fuzzy vision, Peter looked toward a nearby olive tree growing on the balcony and noticed the slightest twinkle. It was the orb, cloaked by leaves deep within the cluster of branches, calling to him.

"The name's Pan," Peter said, each word rendering more pain than the last.

Chapter 33

"What's that?" the captain asked, leaning in.

"The name's Pan," Peter said, his tone and volume unchanged.

"Huh?" The captain leaned in closer.

Suddenly, Peter's eyes sprang to life, and he raised his voice, proudly proclaiming, "The name is Peter Pan." Peter did a backward summersault, removing the captain's sword from his hands and pulling it out of his belly before stumbling toward the tree. Leaving thick gobs of blood behind, Peter climbed up into the branches, where he could hide with the shimmering orb.

Knowing his prey was fatally wounded, Captain James pulled a dagger from his belt. He wanted to finish the young man off with intimacy. This wasn't just any dagger, however. It had been dipped in an extremely concentrated dose of Sea Witch venom. As the captain looked at the tip and grinned at its potential, he followed the crimson puddles leading to the tree's base.

Inside the tree, Peter was just coming to the realization of how bad the wound really was. "Oh, shit," he said, noticing more of a gush than a dribble.

The orb flashed bright three times.

"I see that," Peter said. "I don't know. Not really sure." Peter swallowed a painful lump in his throat as the orb flashed three more times.

"You want me to *what?*" he asked through the pain and lightheadedness rapidly taking siege.

Down at the base of the tree, Captain James peeked his head up as a playful child would during a game of hide-and-seek. "Pan. Oh, Paaaaaan. Come out, come out, wherever you are."

Peter was moments away from losing enough blood to render him unconscious, but the orb wouldn't allow it, flashing three more times.

"If you say so," Peter said, his dull eyes growing impossibly heavy. Captain James finally spotted his foe behind the leaves and branches and cracked a smile. He carefully positioned his venom-tipped dagger within his gentle grip and threw it up in the tree. His line of sight was open enough to hit his wounded target, but the dagger's handle got snagged and ricocheted back toward the captain. It pierced clean through the front of his palm and out the back, bringing him to his knees.

"*Ahhhhhhhhhhhhh!*" The echoes of his screams could be heard throughout the castle and surrounding area.

Side by side with the orb, and guided by its communicative flashing, Peter took a leap of faith out of the tree and dropped like a stone over the balcony's edge. He and the orb fell at free-fall speed down the cliffside before altering trajectory and soaring over the coastline like a pair of playful eagles. Before Peter had noticed, the orb had healed the wound in his belly, leaving it unscarred, as if the incident hadn't even taken place.

Down in the courtyard, Otis raised his damp hands from the fountain and rubbed them over his face. When he opened his eyes and looked toward Penelope, she was already standing next to him.

"Hi there," he said, approaching her.

"Hi," she said. "Otis? Is it really you?"

Chapter 33

"Yes…yes, it's me, Penelope." Otis rubbed his face, hiding the shame and embarrassment. "I know I need a bath and a shave. But do you really not see that it's me under here? Or do I really just look that different? You're still every bit as breathtaking as the first time I ever laid eyes on you, Penelope…I'm not sure I can stand to live in a world where you don't recognize that it's me."

"I do recognize you, love. But…sometimes the eyes have a way of playing tricks, especially after this many years. I believe it's you. I want to believe it's you. And I'm sure we'll be able to confirm it eventually. But right now, I need some time. And I need some space. I've wanted for so long and prayed so many nights for this exact moment—right here. But now that I have it, it doesn't feel like it's supposed to. The air used to feel a certain way when we were in it together. I'm going to need a little more time to find that air."

Mac stepped forward. "Mom. How could you say that? Of course, it's him. Do you have any idea what he's been through to get back here? What he's done—for you?"

"Mac," Otis said. "It's OK. I understand, Penelope. Really, I do. And just knowing that you haven't moved on means… well, it means the world."

She paused, letting everyone catch up to their emotions. "I know you've been gone for a long time. And I can't even begin to imagine what you must have gone through to get back here. So if you'd like to sleep in our bed, I can arrange for it to be moved to another room. But right now, I think we should sleep in separate quarters."

"Penelope," Otis said. "You know that bed can't be moved."

He was right, passing the second of two tests with flying colors. Their bed was permanently affixed to an olive tree that the castle had been constructed around.

"There's another thing," Otis said, stepping forward, glancing at an area between her eyes and lips.

"What's that?" she asked.

"Olive you."

It was something they used to say to one another in the privacy of their bed—an inside joke that only he would know.

"Olive you," she replied, with a stream of tears carving brooks down both of her cheeks.

"More than all the olive oil bottles in the world," he said.

"And all the ones yet to be made," she added, jumping into the cocoon of his waiting arms. "Otis. It really is you."

Penelope went on to weep with joy as the happiest of smiles overtook her face. The setting sun before twilight shone behind them as their silhouettes shared the most dramatic hug and kiss—over a decade overdue.

"You have no idea how good it feels to be home," he said, adding his own tears to the collection she had started moments earlier. "I love you…Do you have any idea what he's been up to? To save me?" Otis asked, nodding toward Mac.

"I do now," she said, wiping a final tear from her eye.

"I'm proud of your boy," Otis said.

"I'm proud of *your* boy," she replied.

Confused and disoriented, Captain James lay still and silent on the mossy concrete, staring up at the sun and sky. He had

Chapter 33

long removed the dagger from his hand, but the damage was irreversible, and the shroud of purple skin was rapidly spreading toward his wrist. A slender silhouette joined him on the balcony, resting a sword on the captain's throat.

"Pan?"

"I think it's time for you to leave now. Captain." Mac said.

Later that evening, Mac and Jinni sat on the castle steps and took in the sun setting on the day's events. Tired, dirty, sweaty, and in some instances bloody, everyone involved with the fight reflected, decompressing in their own way.

"So," Mac said, breaking the lengthy silence, "what's next for you guys?"

"Not sure what they're doing. But I'm thinkin' a vacation for me." Mac grinned as Jinni stood up and brushed the dirt from his knees.

"If you ever make it back to Ithaca, don't be a stranger," Mac said.

"Oh, I ain't leavin' yet. Not till I get paid." Jinni spoke in a jokingly endearing tone. "But I won't. Take care of yourself, Mac." Jinni turned around and walked off into the sunset, never returning to collect his fee.

Neither Mac, Otis, nor Penelope ever saw or heard from Jinni again. In fact, no one really knows what happened to him. But none of them would ever forget the magic man named Jinni.

Peter Pan and the Lost Boys would go on to make use of Jinni's magic in more ways than he ever thought possible. Stories

Odyssey Tale

of their bravery would go on to shock the world, despite many of them being somewhat exaggerated.

It's uncertain what happened to every kindhearted individual who helped Otis and Mac along the way with their respective journeys, but a good many would go on to find fame telling their own life stories—most of which still hold their glory. Their tales continue to be retold and reimagined by every generation, adding more weight to the prestige of Otis's legend.

When it comes to the matters involving individuals who attempted to hinder Otis and Mac's progress, even less is known about what they went on to do, or where any of them ended up. However, in the words of Emperor Aladdin, there are rumors.

Back on Calypso Island, the aftermath of the queen's death eventually settled, and the war-torn Ogygia Village got back to some form of normalcy. As is the case any time there's a shift in power or royalty, certain details get lost in the shuffle, and since so few people knew about the queen's penchant for exotic pets, no one came to the innkeeper to claim them.

Late one night on a particularly hot and rainy evening, the innkeeper of the Ogygia Village Hotel listened to one of her prisoners play a fiddle as a group of dirty, stinking, sweaty pirates entered her establishment with an arrogance suggesting that they were in charge now.

Having just endured a one-sided battle with the humid, sticky jungle, a fatigued and moody Captain James led his pirates to the innkeeper's towering stone slab of a desk. She filed her elongated fingernails with purpose, as Captain James and

Chapter 33

his inferiors quickly lost patience with her lack of attention. He cleared his throat several times before she could be bothered to look up.

"What?" she asked, avoiding his eyes in favor of her next fingernail.

"Checking in. Please," he said, with an attitude that contradicted any pleasantries.

"Sorry," she said, setting her file down and leaning forward. "We don't allow bums here."

Captain James's left arm raised toward the ceiling before he slammed a glossy steel hook onto the surface of her countertop.

"Was that necessary?" she asked, squinting curiously. "Wait a minute. Are you the one they keep talking about—had a run-in with some Lost Boys in Ithaca?"

"I suppose that'd be one way to put it," he said.

"Tell me…is it true?" she asked, lowering her voice and glancing at his hook.

"Is *what* true?" he demanded.

"Did they feed your hand—to a crocodile?"

"What?" Captain James asked, appalled. "Oh, that's rich. By the time the story got to you, I suppose I was crying like a little girl and pissing down my leg."

"Well," she said, looking at the front of his pants. "Now that you mention it. Only in the story I heard, it wasn't piss running down your leg."

"Look. It's been a long day. Can we please just check in?"

"Of course. Do you have a reservation?"

"As a matter of fact, we don't. Is that going to be a problem? Does one need a reservation to stay in this shit box?"

"Not tonight," she said. "Just sign in here, and we'll get this ball rollin'."

Captain James stepped forward and signed the guest book, after which she promptly gave him a key.

"You'll pay upon checkout. I trust you're good for it," she said.

He glared at her as he snagged the key with his hook and headed toward the hall.

"Room thirteen," she said. "Last one on the left."

"You guys hear that?" Captain James asked his men, taking those initial steps toward room thirteen. "Sounds like the attitude just got adjusted in here."

The pirates laughed as their captain slipped farther into the hall. "Excuse me," the innkeeper said. "Captain? I need you to sign in here."

"I did!" he exclaimed.

"No. No. You see here? Where it says *Captain*? I need a name to go next to that. You know how many captains I've had travel through this place? How am I supposed to know who's who?"

"Lady, I don't give a good goddamn if you *only* allow ship captains to stay here. As long as I'm here and in my room, I'm *the* captain."

"Be that as it may, it is my hotel. And if you want to stay in it, I'm going to need a name. So. What's it going to be? Captain Crybaby? Captain Skid Marks?"

Captain James stepped back to her desk with heavy and hostile steps before slamming his hook down on her counter again.

"Ah," she said, smiling and pressing the ink to paper. "Captain Hook."

Chapter 33

Moments later, Captain James entered the darkness of room thirteen, only to be overcome with fright. Powered by its own weight, the concrete door slammed shut, forcing a breeze to move about the room, eliminating the flicker from five of the room's six candles.

"Hello...hello? Hey, lady. Let me outta here! Help!"

Captain James continued to waste his breath, screaming, yelling, and scratching at his door while the pirates on the other side failed to hear his desperate pleas. "Guys. It's a trap. Help!"

Once he'd managed to calm himself down after the hysterical display that kept him company for the first two hours of captivity, the captain tucked himself in a corner. "What's that? Who's there?" he asked, responding to a shuffle that sounded too real to be coming from his imagination. He inched forward, taking a couple of cowardly swings in the dark with his hook.

In the room's darkest corner, a thick yellow coil began to unravel and stand while a pair of glowing snake eyes opened at the top. Captain James screamed as he turned around and tripped over his feet. With terror saturating his senses, he drove the tip of his hook into the cold concrete floor. It screeched and scraped, excavating a violent line that divided one side of the room from the other.

His screams were said to be so loud that one could hear them beneath the surface of the coastal waters surrounding Ogygia Village. Of course, only a handful of fish and other wildlife would be able to confirm this, so it's hard to say where this information actually came from. Perhaps it was a mermaid. Or perhaps it was the Sea Witch, who heard his desperate cries for help and passed along the story of his unfortunate stay. No one really knows for certain.

Odyssey Tale

One thing that is for certain, however, is that the Sea Witch is still out there somewhere. Deep within the coldest parts of the dark abyss, her blond hair and fully extended tentacles wave with eerie grace as she looks up to the surface, waiting for her next meal and grinning at it with mossy teeth as it enters her field of vision.

A year or so following Otis's return home, he toyed with the notion of traveling abroad. Penelope lovingly told him he was out of his mind, but he insisted that she keep hers more open. "OK," she said reluctantly. "But traveling by ship is absolutely out of the question. If you want to take me anywhere overseas, it'll have to be on a magic carpet ride."

Odyssey Tale

Cody Schlegel

Made in the USA
Columbia, SC
19 September 2022